TEMPTING COUNTRY

RUTHLESS SINNERS MC

L. WILDER

Tempting Country

Ruthless Sinners MC Series- Book 6
Copyright 2021
L. Wilder- All rights reserved.

Book Cover Details:

Cover Design: Mayhem Cover Creations

Model: Alen Hasic

Editor: Lisa Cullinan

Proofreader: Marie Peyton

Personal Assistant: Natalie Weston

Catch up with the entire Satan's Fury MC Series today!

All books are FREE with Kindle Unlimited!

Ties That Bind (Ruthless Sinners #1)

Holding On (Ruthless Sinners #2)

Secrets We Keep (Ruthless Sinners #3)

Widow's Undoing (Ruthless Sinners #4)

Claiming Menace (Ruthless Sinners #5)

Summer Storm (Satan's Fury MC Novella)

Maverick (Satan's Fury MC #1)

Stitch (Satan's Fury MC #2)

Cotton (Satan's Fury MC #3)

Clutch (Satan's Fury MC #4)

Smokey (Satan's Fury MC #5)

Big (Satan's Fury #6)

Two Bit (Satan's Fury #7)

Diesel (Satan's Fury #8)

Falling for the President's Daughter (Satan's Fury #9)

My Temptation (The Happy Endings Collection #1)

Bring the Heat (The Happy Endings Collection #2)

His Promise (The Happy Endings Collection #3)

❄ Created with Vellum

Stay Connected with L. Wilder

Sign up for L. Wilder's Newsletter: https://
lwilderbooks.us18.list-manage.com/subscribe?u=
a2c4c211615b2d7b3dd46289a&id=7f8e916141

Social media Links:
Facebook: https://www.
facebook.com/AuthorLeslieWilder
Twitter: https://twitter.com/wilder_leslie
Instagram: http://instagram.com/LWilderbooks
Amazon: http://www.amazon.com/L-
Wilder/e/B00NDKCCMI/
Bookbub: https://www.bookbub.com/authors/l-wilder

PROLOGUE

Growing up, I was a bit of a chubster and not one of those cute, rosy-cheeked kids with a little extra meat on their bones. I was fat—at least in the eyes of all my friends at school, and we all knew how it went for the fat kid. They tended to be the butt of all the jokes, and some were brutal like "Hey, fatty-fatty, two by four. Can't fit through the kitchen door," or "You're so fat, you need a map to find your dick." One of my all-time favorites was "You're so fat I bet your nose doesn't even run."

The teasing and taunting were tough at times, and I couldn't deny that it got to me. As much as I tried not to let it, those words cut deep. I had a short fuse, and there were some days when I struggled to keep my rage under control. Those were the times when I'd go down to the basement and wail on my ol' man's punching bag. The older I'd gotten, the more time I'd spend down there. When my dad figured out what I was doing, he came downstairs and asked me, "You wanna tell me what's going on with you?"

"I'm just having a bad day, Dad."

"Any particular reason why?"

"I'm done with all the bullshit."

"What bullshit?"

"*You know*." I slammed my chubby fist into the punching bag. "I'm sick of everyone running their mouth about me."

"I see." He gave me one of his looks. "You can't let them get to you, Son."

"That's easy for you say. You aren't a fatass like me."

"But I was. I've been where you are, and I remember how tough it can be."

Looking at him now, it was hard to believe my father was ever overweight. Hell, I bet there wasn't an ounce of fat on the man, but I could tell by the sound of his voice he was being completely honest with me. Feeling completely defeated, I told him, "I'm just so tired of it. Why can't I just be like everyone else?"

"You are, Son. You're just carrying a little extra weight." He reached over and gave my shoulder a fatherly pat. "You'll grow out of it. As soon as your growth spurt comes along, you'll slim down and—"

"I've been waiting on this stupid 'growth spurt' forever."

"It'll come." I wanted to believe him, but at that moment, I felt like the whole world thought I was a fucking loser. I just needed a break—a moment to collect myself and forget all the crap people said about me, so I was relieved when my father said, "You know, everyone needs a day—a day to wallow and feel sorry for themselves, but only a day. After that, you gotta stand up and face the music."

I didn't respond. I just stood there and listened to my father. "The way I see it, you got two choices: you can continue to be the target of all the jokes, or you can be the one who cracks them first. In other words, you gotta beat everyone to the punch."

"I don't know."

"When I was your age, I went for the latter, and I got pretty damn good at it. I have no doubt you will, too."

"I'll try."

"That's all I'm asking."

After thinking about everything my father said, I decided to do like he'd done and be the first one to crack the jokes. It wasn't always easy. There were times when I wasn't sure I could do it, but in time, I got pretty good at poking fun at myself. Whenever someone would give me a disgusted look, I'd give them a wink and pat my belly. "It takes a body like this to contain me and all my fucking personality."

If I was at a party and trying to play it cool with the ladies, I'd say something like, "Yeah, I know I'm fuckin' sexy. Why don't you come over here and get you some?"

I poked fun at everything and anything, and little by little, the disapproving looks started to fade. The kids at school began to back off with the fat jokes. As time went on, I began to grow taller and taller, and like my father had assured me I would, I started to slim down.

After spending a summer working out at my grandparents' farm baling hay and cleaning out stalls, I developed a few muscles to boot. In a few months, I went from the round, dumpy kid to a tall, lean, fighting machine. My transformation didn't go unnoticed. It seemed everyone had something to say about it, but I never let it get to my head.

I might've lost the weight, but I was still me.

I still had my sense of humor.

I still had my short fuse, too.

Just like the blood running through my veins, they were a part of me.

Together, they made me the man I am today.

Country—*a Ruthless Sinner through and through.*

ONE
COUNTRY

AFTER A WEEK FROM HELL, I WENT OVER TO Dunkin's for a cold beer. It wasn't a place I went to that often. When I wanted a beer, I'd typically hit Stilettos or the clubhouse, but tonight, I wasn't just looking to have a drink or two, I wanted to get smashed. I hadn't let myself get down in the dumps for months. Thinking back, it had almost been a year. I had no reason to, considering things were going well, really well, but I needed a night—just one single night to blow off some steam.

I was having a pretty decent go of it when the front door opened, and every head turned, including mine, to watch a beautiful brunette saunter up to the counter. I didn't think I'd ever seen the chick before. Hell, I would've remembered a beauty like her. She was wearing a black top that fit snug around her breasts with a pair of loose-fit carpenter jeans and boots. Her long, wavy hair was down around her shoulders, and her neck and wrists were covered in jewelry, making her look like a gypsy or one of those hippie chicks on TV. She ordered a drink, and even though she had her choice of any seat in the house, she came over and sat down next to me.

Usually, when a beautiful woman approached me, I'd lay on the charm, toss out a few of my renowned "Country-isms", and do my best to get in her pants, but tonight, I wasn't in the right mindset—not even for a smoking-hot chick like her. I just wanted to kick back and sulk alone with my beer, but after a few brief moments, she leaned towards me and asked, "Tough day?"

I shrugged. "Yeah, you could say that."

"I'm sorry to hear that."

"It is what it is."

I continued to drink my beer while she sipped on her Blue Hawaiian. After ordering herself another, she looked over to me and asked, "Do you happen to know of a hotel or something nearby? I really need a place to stay tonight."

She could've easily asked the bartender, but she asked me. Had it been any other night, I would've taken that as a sign and told her she could stay with me, but instead, I simply replied, "There's a Hampton right around the corner."

"Okay, great. I'll give it a try." I could feel her eyes on me as I picked up my bottle and took another drink. I was slouched down with my elbows on the counter, picking at the label on my beer, giving out every sign that I wasn't interested in talking, but that didn't stop her from asking, "You from around here?"

"Yeah, you could say that." For the first time since she sat down, I turned to face her, and damn, something about the way she was looking at me had me reconsidering my earlier plan of ignoring her. I casually straightened my posture, then cleared my throat before asking, "You?"

"No, I'm just passing through on business." Before I could ask her what kind of business, she added, "But if things go well with my meeting tomorrow, I'll be coming here quite a bit. Do you have any suggestions on places I should visit while I'm here?"

"You could always check out my place," I replied with a playful wink. "It's actually not far from here."

"Oh, yeah?"

"Yep... just around the corner." I let my eyes slowly roam over her delicious curves. "You should definitely come by sometime. I guarantee you won't regret it."

"I'll be sure to keep that in mind." A sexy smirk

crossed her face as she looked down at my left hand. "I see you aren't married. What about a girlfriend?"

"Nope. No girlfriend. What about you? You got a fella?"

"No, I'm afraid not." She took another sip of her drink. "I don't have time for a relationship right now."

"I see." I studied her for a moment. "So, you're in town for business. You got no place to stay and no boyfriend. What about a name? You got one of those?"

"Let's not do that."

"Do what?"

"Let's not do the whole exchange names thing. Let's just keep it as two strangers who met in some random bar one night."

While I was a little surprised by her request, I was also equally intrigued by it. I knew nothing about the beautiful woman sitting beside me, and she knew nothing about me—not even that I was a member of an MC. Since I was planning on having a bender, I'd left my cut at home and wore a basic pair of jeans and a long sleeve t-shirt, so we were on an equal playing field. "Okay, suit yourself."

"I must say, you seem oddly familiar ... like I've seen you somewhere before."

"If we'd met, you would remember me. I can promise you that."

"I have a feeling you're right about that."

We continued to flirt back and forth for almost an hour, and no lie, I was really starting to like this chick and had a feeling she felt the same about me. She was facing me, and we were sitting close—extremely close while her legs intertwined with mine. I'd ordered us both another round of drinks, but we were so focused on each other that neither of us had touched them.

I also noticed that she couldn't keep her hands off me. First, she'd casually touch my arm and then my thigh. I was doing the same to her, making it clear that we had some major sexual tension building between us. She tucked a strand of hair behind her ear. "I have to say I'm kind of surprised you don't have a girlfriend."

"Oh? And why's that?"

"You're handsome. You're smart. Seem like a nice guy. I mean..." Her brows furrowed for a moment, and then her eyes widened as if she'd had some grand epiphany as she gasped. "Ooohhh."

"Oh, what?"

She sounded like she felt sorry for me. "You're not very good in bed, huh?"

"What?"

"It's okay. I'm sure you try and all that, but ..."

"Hold up!" I roared. "What the fuck makes you think I'm not good in the sack?"

She shrugged. "It's the only plausible explanation."

"The hell you say! I'm damn good in bed! Hell, I'd

fuck you up one side and down the other ..." I was about to get on a real tear when a mischievous grin crossed her face. "Ah hell, you're just fucking with me, aren't ya?"

"Yeah, maybe just a little," she answered with a flirty tone. "Thought I'd get a little rise out of ya."

"That's just wrong," I fussed. "Can't believe you'd do me like that."

"I'm sorry." She winked at me and inched a little closer. "I just couldn't help myself."

"Mm-hmm." It was at that moment I realized she was interested in more than just a little smalltalk. She was interested in a lot more, so I leaned in closer and whispered, "Well, just so we're clear ... I meant it when I said I'm good. *I'm damn good.* Hell, I'd fuck you right out of those boots and have you begging for more."

A spark of lust flashed through her eyes. "You sound pretty confident there."

"Only because I am."

"You going to back up those words or what?"

Without responding, I took her hand and led her to the back of the bar. As soon as we made our way down the dark hallway to the bathrooms, I stopped, pulled her over to me, and slammed my mouth against hers, drawing her in closer as I kissed her with everything I had. She didn't resist.

Instead, she wound her arms around my neck and

kissed me back. Need surged throughout me like a fucking wildfire as she eased her hips forward and started grinding against me. It was all I could do to keep from taking her right there in the hallway. Realizing I was on the brink of losing control, I stepped back and broke our embrace.

I looked back to the bar, noticing a few customers who were still lurking around. Not wanting to take any chances on us being seen, I pulled her into the women's restroom and locked the door. My eyes never left hers as she slipped her arms around my neck. "I've never fooled around in a public bathroom before."

"First time for everything, baby."

A wicked smile swept across her face as I drew her in closer and pressed my mouth to hers. This kiss was different. This kiss was filled with a hunger that matched my own. Her body melted into me as her tongue brushed against mine, and then it was over. I'd taken all I could. I dropped my hands to her waist and started to unbuckle her jeans. "You good with this?"

"Oh, yeah. I'm more than good." Her eyes flashed with desire when she added, "Let's see what you got, hot stuff."

The tip of her tongue slowly dragged across her bottom lip as she kicked off her boots, then lowered her jeans and panties to the floor. She stood there staring at me with a wanton look in her eyes as I grabbed a

condom from my wallet, then lowered my jeans and boxers down my hips. I took my aching cock in my hand and gave it a hard squeeze, trying to relieve some of the throbbing pressure. From the moment we'd first kissed, she'd had me all tangled up, so much so my cock pulsated against my fingers while I slipped on the condom.

Unable to resist a moment longer, I reached for her, pulling her close. Anticipation flashed through her eyes as my hands dropped to her hips and lifted her up, pressing her back against the wall. She bit her lip and wrapped her legs around me, making my cock grow even harder the second I felt her warm body against mine. My need for her was building, burning deep inside my gut. *Fuck.* I didn't know what it was about this woman, but she had me spiraling out of control.

With one hard thrust, I buried myself deep inside her. A rush of air hissed through her teeth as I withdrew and drove into her again and again. With her arms wound tightly around my neck, I growled into her shoulder and started thrusting harder and deeper, building up to a relentless pace. I'd been with many women in my time but never had a woman made me feel so on edge.

Needing more, I turned around and carried her over to the sink. Her legs widened, giving me better access as I lowered her onto the edge of the cold porce-

lain. She immediately leaned back and propped her hands on the sink's ledge. I was tempted to rip open her shirt and expose those full, round breasts, but since we were in a fucking restroom at a bar, I didn't have that luxury.

I lowered my mouth to her neck, kissing her like a hungry animal as I drove deeper, harder. Her head reared back with a sated groan. That was it. That was exactly what I wanted to fucking hear. Her nails dug into my lower back as her hips rocked against mine, meeting my every thrust with more intensity. I could feel the pressure building, forcing a growl from my chest.

"Fuck," I groaned as she tightened around me. She panted wildly, and her thighs clamped down around my hips when I tried to increase my pace. I knew she was close, unable to stop the inevitable torment of her building release. I lowered my hand between her thighs, raking my thumb across her clit, and that was all it took. The muscles in her body grew taut as her orgasm took hold. I continued to drive into her; the sounds of my body pounding against hers echoed throughout the room until I finally came inside her. With a ragged breath, I panted, "Holy shit, woman. That was fucking incredible."

"Yes, it was." She gave me a warm smile as she

glanced down at her boots. "You definitely lived up to your promise."

"If I'm anything, I'm a man of my word."

I slowly withdrew, then quickly tossed the condom in the trash. As I was pulling up my boxer briefs and jeans, she hopped down from the sink and started to get dressed. When she knelt down to slip on her boots, I asked, "Does that mean you'll give me your name and number?"

"Tonight was fun." She stood up and fastened the last button of her jeans. "Let's stick to the plan and not complicate it by doing the whole name-and-number thing."

"All right. If that's what you want."

"It's for the best." She stepped over to me and gave me a quick kiss on the cheek before heading toward the door. "Thanks for tonight. I really did have fun."

"So, that's it?"

"I've got a big meeting tomorrow. I need to get going."

I'd be lying if I said I didn't feel a little wounded that she was going to split on me, but I played it cool and followed her out of the bathroom. When we made it outside, she waved down a taxi. As she got inside, she gave me another wink and said, "I'll see ya around, hot stuff."

"Yeah... *See ya*."

With that, she closed the door, and I stood there watching as he pulled away from the curb and darted into traffic. Once she was gone, I hailed a cab of my own. As soon as I got inside, I regretted not riding my bike over to the bar, but I had no idea that I wouldn't end up plastered and needing a ride home. I gave the guy my address, then leaned back in the seat and started contemplating my life's choices. I'd just spent the most incredible fucking night with a chick and didn't even know her damn name. I was pissed that I hadn't pressed her to give it to me. Maybe then, I might've had some chance of finding her again. It was a thought that lingered in the back of my mind well after I'd gotten home.

I took a long, hot shower, grabbed something to eat, and watched a bit of TV. I thought I'd shaken all thoughts of her until I laid my head down on the pillow. It seemed strange to me. I'd rarely ever given one of my conquests a second thought, so I couldn't figure out what it was about this girl that had gotten under my skin.

After hours of tossing and turning, I finally convinced myself that I was making something out of nothing, and my odd draw to the beautiful stranger was just in my head. Eventually I fell asleep, and by the next morning, that heavy feeling in my gut was all but gone.

I had some free time before work, so I decided to run by the clubhouse and check in with the guys. When I walked into the bar, I found Viper, our club's president, standing over Menace, our computer hacker, as he messed around on his laptop, and neither of them looked happy. In fact, they were madder than two wet hens as they snarled at the screen.

Hoping to break some of the tension in the room, I glanced over Menace's shoulder and said, "Looks like somebody's been on the Porn Hub again. When are you gonna learn there are no hot singles in your area, brother? You gotta stop clicking the fucking link!"

"Fuck you, Country," Menace grumbled. "Don't got time for your bullshit."

I could tell by his tone that this whole thing was more serious than I thought. "What's going on?"

"That's what we're trying to figure out," Menace answered. "I just got an email on my private account. Someone is requesting a meet at one of the cafés on Second at four this afternoon, but we got no idea who it's from."

"What the fuck?" I grumbled. "Any idea what they wanna meet about?"

"Apparently to discuss some kind of business opportunity." Viper sounded completely outraged. "But they didn't give us any other information."

"I don't like the sound of that."

"I don't either. I also don't like that they got the address to my private account." Menace was scanning through lines and lines of code, trying to get a lead, but he clearly wasn't having any luck. "This is fucking insane. It's one firewall after the next with these assholes."

"So, what are we gonna do?"

"The only thing we can do." Viper crossed his arms with a huff. "We're gonna take the meet."

TWO

KIERSTEN

I'D ALWAYS HEARD THAT LOSING A MOTHER IS ONE of the deepest sorrows a heart could ever know. It certainly was for mine. I couldn't begin to describe how distraught I was when I lost my mother. It was so unexpected. A reaction to medication took her from me. I was just thirteen at the time, and I found it nearly impossible to cope with the loss.

I struggled with the fact that I would never see my mother's smile again, that I'd never hear her voice or feel her arms around me. It was a tough pill to swallow, and not only for me. It was tough on my father, too. He loved and adored her and didn't want to face the world without her by his side. Unfortunately, neither of us had a choice in the matter.

Days after my mother's death, he quit his job in forensics and spent the next year focusing on me. No one was surprised by his decision. He was a good man and an even better dad. We'd always been close—maybe even more so than my mother and I had been. He was always there for me, even when I didn't know I needed him, and after my mother's death, I needed him more than ever. With his support, I was able to get up and face the day. Each day got a little easier, and I eventually accepted the fact the world hadn't stopped turning just because my mother died.

———

"YOU ALL SET?" Braylon asked, trying to sound upbeat.

"Yes, Bray." It was the third time he'd called, and every time he sounded more anxious than the last. "I've got everything I need to knock the socks right off these guys."

"You sound oddly confident. What gives?"

"Not sure what you mean?"

"Last night, you were on the brink of hysteria, and now, you're all ready to face the world. What's the deal?"

"Well, I might've taken your advice and hit a bar last night."

"Seriously?" he gasped. "Does that mean you got you a little tension relief?"

A smile swept across my face as my mind drifted to last night's encounter with the mysterious stranger in the bar's bathroom. I'd never tried the whole one-night-stand thing or had sex with a total stranger, but honestly, I'd never experienced anything so unbelievably hot in my entire life. Not only because of the random sex, but this man was gorgeous with a touch that set me on fire.

As much as I wanted to exchange names and numbers, I knew it wasn't a good idea. I was trying to get a business deal off the ground, and the last thing I needed was to be distracted by a hot guy in tight jeans. I cleared my throat before answering, "I might've, but you know I'm not one to kiss and tell."

"You little slut," he snickered.

"Sorry, I just couldn't help myself."

"Well, I'm glad you got a little action, but I don't want it to derail your focus."

"Don't worry. I'm focused," I assured him. "I'm ready for this."

"Are you sure? I mean, *really sure*?" I could hear the skepticism in his voice. "'Cause if you aren't, we can forget this whole thing. You can get in your car and come straight back—"

"I'm not backing out." Braylon had been with me from the beginning, and I adored him for being concerned about me, but I'd worked too hard to chicken out now. "It's going to be fine."

"I don't know." His voice sounded strained as he reminded me, "I have a bad feeling about all this."

"We've been through this a thousand times, Bray." I recalled the days when I first started my small business. Back then, I was terrified that I'd never get it off the ground, but after busting my ass for the past three years, it was doing better than I ever imagined—which was why I'd arranged this meeting with a local group in the same line of business. "I know it's a little scary to think about branching out, but this could take us to another playing field."

"But we're doing great where we are."

"I know, but we could do better," I insisted. "You're going to have to trust me on this, Bray."

"Okay." He inhaled a deep breath, then let it out slowly. "You promise to be careful?"

"Yes, I promise."

"And you'll call me the second you're done with the meeting."

"You know I will."

"How much longer before you have to leave?"

"Not long at all." I glanced over at the standard hotel alarm clock sitting on the nightstand and said, "I better get going."

"Okay, good luck."

"Thanks. Hopefully, I won't need it."

I hung up the phone, then rushed over to the mirror and quickly gave myself one last check. I figured it was best to dress casually, so I wore a pair of my favorite black jeans and a flowing white sweater with my ankle boots. My hair was pulled up in a fishtail braid, and I was sporting my favorite bangle bracelets. This was one of my favorite outfits—one that I'd worn many times before, but as I stood there looking in the mirror, I didn't even recognize myself. I certainly wasn't the same girl I used to be—no longer trusting and naïve. That part of me was stolen the night I discovered my father wasn't the man I thought he was.

AFTER MY MOTHER DIED, my father could see that I needed him more than ever, so not long after my fourteenth birthday, he started renovating our basement into an office. The remodel was quite extensive, but I didn't ask questions, just happy he'd be home more, so I left it alone. I kept quiet even as I became curious about all the time he spent locked away in his office and the late-night phone calls.

At first, I figured it was his way of coping with the guilt he felt over Mom's death, but then he started reno-vating the basement again and also bought a white van that he never drove—at least not with me, which I found strange and wondered why he'd purchased it in the first place. Soon after, the late-night outings began. I still didn't ask questions since he seemed happy with whatever he was doing, so I just left things alone.

It wasn't until years later that I discovered my loving, doting father had a secret—one that would change everything.

I'd gotten up in the night to get myself a glass of water when I heard strange sounds coming from the basement. Curiosity got the best of me, so I crept down the stairs to see what was going on. There was no sign of him, and everything looked exactly like it always had. I assumed it was my imagination and started back upstairs, but something just didn't feel right.

I stood there for a moment, trying to figure out what was different about my father's office, and after several seconds, I finally realized it was his bookcase. It was no longer flush to the wall, and a strange light shone from beneath it. I inched closer to get a better look and was surprised to find a secret passage hidden behind it.

The hairs on the back of my neck prickled against my skin as I gave it a slight push, making just enough room for me to slip through. I noticed a second door that had a key-coded lock pad, but on this particular night, it was open. An uneasy feeling fell over me as I silently padded down the concrete hallway and had only taken a few steps when I heard men's voices coming from inside one of the mysterious rooms. I inched closer and closer until I could see inside the room.

Complete horror consumed me when I saw my father, along with two other men, piling bloody dead bodies in the middle of the floor. He was barking orders about cleaning out the van as he and another man lifted one of the bodies and shoved it into a flaming inciner-ator—an incinerator that was in our house, under our roof, and I never had a clue it was there. The whole thing seemed so surreal—like being stuck in a terrible nightmare.

I was in complete shock as I crept down the hall and back upstairs to my room, then spent the remainder of the night silently crying in bed while unsuccessfully trying to make sense of what I'd seen. I'd always thought my father hung the moon and never dreamed he could do something so horrific. It killed me to think he had this dark side that I never knew about, one that he'd hidden from me for years.

The next morning, he acted as if he'd done nothing remotely out of the norm and behaved like the man I'd always known. I, on the other hand, felt completely different. I still loved my father; he was always good to me and took care of me but seeing him do such a horrific thing and then pretend as if it never happened changed something in me. My innocence had been stolen, and that was something I would never get back.

Over the next year, I lost count of how many times I heard my father in the basement with those men. I didn't have to go rushing downstairs to see what was going on. I already knew. My hurt eventually turned into anger, and that's when I became determined to figure out why by doing a little investigating.

I matched the newspaper headlines of gang shootings and unexplainable disappearances of cartel members with the dates he'd be locked away in the basement, and eventually started to piece everything together. I knew he hadn't killed the men I read about in those articles, so there was only one explanation that made sense.

My father had used his expertise in forensics to become a cleaner for some of the most notorious men in the South—men like the Ruthless Sinners MC.

I MADE sure to get to our meeting spot early so I could mentally prepare for my presentation. It was impossible not to have doubts about whether I was doing the right thing by meeting with these men, but I'd done my research. I knew everything there was about our prospective partners. Now, I just had to convince them that it was in their best interest to go into business together.

I was pleased to see the place I'd chosen wasn't

crowded. In fact, there were only two customers, and they were far enough away that I didn't have to worry about them overhearing anything that was said. At the same time, their presence offered a level of safety I wouldn't have if I'd chosen a more remote location.

I hadn't been waiting long when my guests walked through the front door, and my stomach did an immediate nosedive. These men were even more intimidating than I expected, and it was all I could do to keep myself from rushing out the door. My knees started shaking, and my heart began racing as I suddenly wondered what I'd gotten myself into. I watched silently as they scanned the room, searching for the person who'd invited them here, and it wasn't long before their attention was drawn to me.

I didn't move. I simply waited as one of them started walking in my direction. As he got closer, I quickly realized I knew him. I still didn't move or speak. I sat there until he made his way over to my table. He stood there for a moment, studying me with an odd expression as he tried to place my face. His eyes widened as he gasped, "Kiersten?"

"Hey, Menace. It's nice to see you again."

I wouldn't have had a clue who he was if it hadn't been for my father and his eccentric line of work. I'd met him and his girlfriend, Parker, a few months earlier when they'd come to see Dad. While I didn't know all the details, I had a feeling it had something to do with Parker; otherwise, she would've never been at the house. If my father was anything, he was careful and discreet.

Having her there ended up being a blessing for me. Menace was slightly distracted and left his computer out on the table, which gave me the opportunity to swipe a copy of his hard drive—something I'd done with my father's computer. It's amazing what could be found on anyone's computer, especially when they thought no one had the means to hack into it.

I was doing my best to keep a calm composure as Menace looked down at me with utter confusion and asked, "What are you doing here?"

"I'm waiting on you and your brothers."

"You're the one who requested the meet?"

I tried to hide the anxiety building in my stomach and answered, "I am."

"Does this have something to do with Billy?"

"No. He has no idea I'm even here." I motioned my head towards the front of the coffee shop. "It's getting late. Why don't you ask Viper to come on over, and we'll get started?"

"Kiersten, this isn't some game you're playing here," Menace warned. "You've called a fucking meet with the Ruthless Sinners. You don't do that shit without a good reason."

"I have a good reason, and as soon as you get Viper to join us, I'll tell you what it is."

Menace studied me for a minute, then turned and walked over to the group of men. They spoke for a moment, then all eyes were on me as Viper and Menace made their way over to my table. As soon as they sat down, Viper gave me a quick once over, then asked, "You're Billy's daughter?"

"I am."

"Does this have something to do with him?"

"No, sir. This has nothing to do with him or the work he does for you."

"Then, what the fuck is this all about?"

"I have a business opportunity for you."

MY HURT, anger, and overall resentment over what my father had done stuck with me as I left home and headed off to college. I tried to put it all behind me, but no matter how hard I tried, my father and all his secrets were always lurking in the back of my mind.

I was in my second year of studying botany, learning all there was to know about plant life when the topic of marijuana came up in class. Our professor was discussing how, when used correctly, the drug could be beneficial for cancer patients and people experiencing chronic pain. This was a thought that struck me deeply because of my mother. The more he talked about the benefits of marijuana, the more intrigued I became. I began doing my own research and discovered even more advantages of the notorious drug.

I also learned that some states considered it legal, but Tennessee and four other southern states did not. In fact, they considered it just as illegal as any other illicit drug. That alone should've put an end to my thoughts of marijuana altogether, but it didn't. Instead, it made me even more eager to develop a method to grow a stronger, purer form of cannabis—one that could make me a great deal of money and possibly help a few people along the way.

I knew it was a crazy idea. I wasn't the kind of person who would venture into something illegal like growing and selling weed, but if my father could pretend he was someone he wasn't, so could I.

If I was going to pull off this little charade of mine and create a new method of growing a purer form of cannabis, I would need money and lots of it. Thankfully, my mother and my grandparents were both very wealthy and had left me with a hefty trust fund. I used it to buy a large piece of property half an hour from my college campus.

It was an abandoned religious commune that included several small homes, a large barn, and a school with a gymnasium. The place was in rough shape, but it didn't matter. I planned to renovate the entire property —just like my father had done with our basement. It took some time, but once I was done, I had a state-of-the-art set up, and I got to work. After six months of busting my ass, I had my first harvest.

I gave a few samples to some friends at school, and it wasn't long before they got the word out about the mind-blowing pot. My plan worked. In a matter of days, I started selling to students all over campus, and it wasn't long before I was able to add another old classroom to the mix and even hired a couple of extra hands— including Braylon.

With their help, I was able to expand my small business into something bigger than I'd expected. Using the connections my father had made, I gained a huge buyer in Memphis, and with their monthly purchase, we were averaging just over fifty grand a month. There was just one problem. We had enough supply for three to four times over our distribution and lots of product was going to waste.

I NEEDED HELP MOVING IT, which was why I reached out to the Ruthless Sinners. Unfortunately, they weren't exactly pleased with my method of contact.

I'd seen Viper on the Sinners' security camera

footage on many occurrences and knew he was a man who demanded attention, but the Sinners' president was even more intimidating than I had ever expected. He looked like he wanted to wring my neck as he growled, "Billy's daughter or not, you have a lot of fucking nerve messaging us on Menace's private account."

"I understand that you're upset with the way I handled this meet, but I needed to get your attention. Clearly, I succeeded." I inhaled a quick breath, then quickly got to the point. "I think when you hear my offer, you'll see that it was worth the unsettling nature of my email to Menace's account."

Viper was absolutely fuming as he barked, "What makes you think the Ruthless Sinners would ever be interested in going into business with you? You're just a fucking kid."

"Because I can make you and your club a great deal of money—much more than you make at your strip clubs or by selling coke."

"How the fuck do you know about that?" he roared.

"It's my job to know everything there is about the people I do business with." I could see by the expression on his face that Viper was both angered and confused that I knew about his club's business dealings, so I looked over to Menace. "You really should be more careful with your laptop. It's not safe to leave it sitting around."

"Holy shit," Menace grumbled. "I knew something wasn't right."

"What the fuck is she talking about?"

"I left it on the table. Right there in the wide open. *Goddamn it.*"

"Not following, brother."

Menace raked his fingers through his hair as he told Viper, "It was back when Parker and I were at Billy's... Fuck! I just wasn't thinking."

"Damn." Viper turned his attention back to me. After letting out a disgruntled breath, he said, "Enough of the bullshit. Just tell me why you're here."

He sat back and listened silently as I told him about my business endeavor, and he seemed intrigued when I told him about how well I'd done and how I'd managed to pick up a big buyer out of Memphis. "Honestly, I hadn't expected to ever make it to this point, but I have, and now, I need your help."

"Help with what?"

"Our distribution." I could see the wheels turning in his head. "My product was in such high demand, I expanded my manufacturing. I overcompensated a little, and now I've come to the point where I have more product than I can move on my own. I was hoping you and your club could be the answer to my quandary."

"So, what you're saying is that you want us to help move your product for you?" Before I could respond, he grumbled, "I hate to break it to ya, doll, but we've got bigger fish to fry than this bullshit."

"Bigger fish than two to three hundred grand a month, 'cause that's what I'm offering."

"By selling fucking pot?"

"This isn't just any pot, sir," I argued. "Like I mentioned, this is the cleanest, purest cannabis on the market. I guarantee it."

"Okay, it's good stuff." Viper shrugged. "Who gives a shit? It's only a matter of time before they legalize it, and what then?"

"If they do, it still isn't going to be easily accessible. They'll make sure of that. Plus, I have other options. I can either sell off everything or continue to grow and become a legal distributor. Until that times come, we stand to make a great deal of money."

"So, even if I consider doing this, how would it work? You supply the goods, and you want us to move it?"

"Exactly." Feeling like I was finally getting somewhere, I smiled and said, "With a seventy-thirty partnership, we both—"

"Seventy-thirty?" he scoffed. "I don't think so, little girl."

"I'm sure we can come to an agreement on the percentages."

"I don't know. Why wouldn't I just become another buyer? I could buy it outright and sell it on my own. Get rid of the need for any kind of cut."

"I'll tell you what. Why don't you come and see for yourself what I'm offering? You can get an idea of how I run things, and if you like what you see, we can go from there."

Viper thought for a moment, then looked over to Menace. "What do you think?"

"I figure we owe it to Billy to check it out."

"No," I interjected. "My father has nothing to do with this. If you decide to come, keep him out of it."

"You know he has ties to us. Hell, we wouldn't be here if you didn't. So, he's a part of it whether you want him to be or not." Before I could counter, he asked, "When do you want us to come by?"

"The sooner, the better."

THREE

COUNTRY

As ordered, Rafe, Lynch, and I remained outside the coffee shop to keep an eye on things while Viper, Menace, Axel, and Hawk went inside for the meet. It had been almost an hour since they'd gone in, and I was growing concerned. We all were but remained in our positions until we noticed Viper and the others walking out. Their faces were void of expression, making it difficult to get a read on how things had played out. When they approached the SUV, Lynch got out. Before he could speak, Viper shook his head and growled, "Not here."

Without saying a word, he got back inside the truck and waited as Viper and the others followed suit. As soon as the last door closed, Viper turned to Menace and growled, "How much do you think she knows?"

"No way to know for sure, but you heard her. *She knows enough.*"

"But I don't get it. How would she get that kind of information from your fucking laptop?"

"It would depend on how well she knows her way around a computer's hard drive," Menace answered. "If I had to guess, I'd say it was the club's security cameras. I was checking them while I was at Billy's. I'm pretty sure they were still pulled up when she got access to my laptop."

"Damn, I don't need this shit right now."

Even though I was curious as to what the hell they were talking about, I knew better than to ask. It was clear Viper was pissed and needed some time to cool off, so I kept my mouth shut. Once back at the clubhouse, we all followed him into the conference room and took a seat, then Viper grumbled a line of curses under his breath. "The meet was with Billy's daughter. She's been growing some kind of 'power-house' marijuana and wants us to go into business with her."

"Hold up... You're telling me Billy the Butcher has a daughter?"

"Yeah, I told you about her. Parker and I met her when we went out to Billy's place."

"Nah, brother. You didn't tell me shit." Billy was the club's cleaner, and he was incredible at his job, but the guy had always given me the creeps. Knowing the kind of mess he was about to encounter, he'd show up at the end of some big rival shootout in a pair of fucking khakis and a dress shirt.

Then, before getting to work, he'd put on an orange hazmat suit like the kind from some apocalyptic movie. Billy was so methodical and efficient about it, too. Just thinking about it had me rambling off, "So if Billy has a daughter, that means Billy had sex with someone. *Ugghh.* What kind of crazy-assed hooker would fuck the Butcher?"

"Oh, come on, brother. Billy's not that bad," Menace replied, trying to defend him.

"He's a little off, and you know it."

"Maybe, but Billy and who he screwed around with isn't important right now," Menace grumbled.

"The hell it's not. We need to know the kind of crazy we're dealing with here. A little crazy, kinda crazy, or *batshit crazy*. We gotta know that kind of stuff."

"She's not crazy." Menace thought for a brief moment, then added, "At least, I don't think she is."

"Well, she hacked into Menace's fucking computer and used what she found to request a meet. She's either got a little crazy in her or she has balls of fucking steel."

"He's got a point there," Hawk snickered. "Pretty ballsy move, if you ask me."

"Yes, it was." Viper shook his head, "Fuck, if she was anyone other than Billy's daughter, I'd—"

Before he could finish his sentence, Axel leaned forward and interrupted him, "Well, she is, so like it or not, we can't touch her. Might as well get that thought out of your head and decide what the hell we're gonna do about all this."

"Easier said than done." Viper raked his hand over his goatee and gave it a hard tug. "We need to find out everything there is about this girl, and I mean everything."

"I'll see what I can come up with."

Hawk was the Sinners' sergeant-at-arms. It was his job to make sure things ran smoothly for the club, so I wasn't surprised when he offered, "I could go to her place and check it out. See if this business of hers is legit, then we can decide our next move from there."

"Yeah, we need to check it out, but I'm not sending you out there alone."

"I'll go with him," I volunteered.

"Me too," Rafe told him.

"Whatever you need, Prez," Menace added. "Just say the word."

"If we do this, I don't want y'all fucking around. I need to know everything, from how she got this business off the ground to who she's got on her payroll. I want you to see for yourselves how she moves her product and who's moving it. Leave no stone left unturned."

"Understood."

"All right then, pack your bags, boys. I want you on the road first thing in the morning."

With that, our brief meeting was adjourned. I still had a million questions but hoped I'd get all my answers the following morning when we met up with Billy's daughter. I said my goodbyes, then left the conference room and started out to the parking lot. I'd just made it through the back door when Rafe came rushing up beside me. "Hey, man. What do you think about all this with Billy's daughter?"

"Not sure what the hell to think." I shook my head as I got on my bike. "Could be a good opportunity for us to branch out, or it could be something that might bite us in the ass. Won't know until we see what's really going on."

"Yeah, I was thinking the same." He got on his Harley as he asked, "Where ya headed?"

"Figured I'd go on home." My mind drifted to the night before, and I shook my head as I grumbled, "I had a late night last night. Think I'll just crash early, and then I'll be ready to roll out in the morning."

"Sounds good." Before starting his engine, he glanced over at me and smiled. "You know, one of these days, those late nights are gonna catch up with you."

"I think you might be right."

Rafe chuckled, then without saying anything more, whipped out of the club's parking lot. I took that as my cue to head out myself, and it wasn't long before I was on the highway out to my house. As much as I liked Nashville, I preferred living out in the country more, so I'd bought a barn-style home on the outskirts of the city. In comparison to my brother's homes, it was a little out of the way, but every time I pulled up to that long drive next to my thirty acres of land, the extra miles were all but forgotten. When I got to the house, I took a minute to give things a once over, making sure all would be good while I was gone, then headed inside to grab a quick bite to eat.

After finishing off some leftovers, I packed a bag, took a much-needed shower, and called it a night. By the next morning, I'd gotten caught up on my sleep and was feeling like a new man. I grabbed a quick cup of coffee and then, I was on my way. When I arrived at the clubhouse, I wasn't surprised to find Hawk and Menace already there and waiting with Rafe. I'd barely pulled into the parking lot when Hawk asked, "You all set?"

"I reckon," I answered. "You know where we're headed?"

"Yeah, we're good." Hawk gave me a quick nod. "I got the address yesterday at the meet."

He motioned for us to follow, and moments later, we were on our way. I hadn't been there to listen in on the meet, so I had no clue where we were headed when Menace took Route 70 towards Murfreesboro. Again, I didn't ask questions. I figured it wouldn't be long before I knew everything there was about Billy's daughter and her little business proposition.

We'd been riding for about forty-five minutes when Menace led us off the highway towards a small town between Nashville and Murfreesboro. There were a few houses here and there, but for the most part, it was one winter wheat field after the next until we came upon a town. With its country square, old-fashioned light posts, and dated stores, the place reminded me of fucking Mayberry. The only thing missing was a Ford Galaxy 500 cop car with Andy Griffith behind the wheel.

We continued riding through the small town and out of its limits. Soon after, Hawk took a turn down what looked to be an abandoned road. After ten or so more miles, we came up to a metal gate and searched around for some semblance of a guard, but there was none to be found. Having no other choice, Hawk got off his bike and pushed it open.

Once Hawk was back on his Harley, we continued down the road, winding up in the middle of what looked to be a religious community. A large church stood in the center with several small houses surrounding it, as well as a mid-sized school with a gymnasium and a barn in the back.

Hawk pulled up to the large parking lot in front of the school and turned off his engine. As soon as we got off our bikes, I looked around at the odd-shaped houses and the hundred or so acres of land that surrounded us. "What the hell is this place?"

"The sign back at the gate said it's the Langford Nature Preserve."

"Well, I'm not feeling the whole nature preserve vibe." I nodded my head towards the old church house. "I mean, look at this fucking place. I'm just waiting for David Koresh to show up with his 'Army of God'."

The words had barely left my mouth when two guys came out of the old school to greet us. There was nothing all that menacing about either of them. They were just two regular guys dressed in camo cargo pants and t-shirts. The older of the two with the military-style haircut walked straight up to Hawk and extended his hand as he said, "Hey, you guys must be the Ruthless Sinners."

"We are."

"Great. Welcome to Langford Manor." He shook Hawk's hand. "I'm Braylon."

"Good to meet ya, Braylon. I'm Hawk, and these are my brothers, Menace, Country, and Rafe." Hawk sounded displeased as he said, "We were expecting to meet with Kiersten."

"Of course. She's waiting for you inside."

Hawk nodded, and as we followed the two men towards the schoolhouse, I kept expecting to see armed guards or, at the very least, some high-tech security system but found neither as we approached the front door. I followed Hawk, Rafe, and Menace inside and was surprised that the place looked nothing like a school.

The floor had been redone with marbled concrete, and the walls were drywalled and freshly painted. There was an oversized sectional sofa with end tables and lamps and a colorful rug positioned in the center of the room, making it look more like an office or a home than an old school building.

Once the door closed behind us, Braylon turned to Hawk and said, "I'll let Kiersten know you're waiting."

Before any of us could respond, he vanished through two large wooden doors. I took a quick glance around, making sure we were alone before leaning over to Hawk and Menace and whispering, "Is it just me, or is this some crazy shit?"

"It's different. That's for sure."

"Maybe we should just get the fuck out of here and be done with this shit."

"As tempting as that might be, we can't." A look of

distress crossed Menace's face as he reminded us, "She's kind of got us by the balls with—"

Before Menace could finish his sentence, the wooden doors swept open, and I felt like I'd been knocked on my ass when I saw the beautiful brunette from the bar sauntering towards us. She was wearing a long-sleeved, vintage AC/DC t-shirt with jeans and black boots, and she looked fucking incredible. Unable to hide my surprise, I grumbled, "Fuck."

"What?" Rafe asked.

"I might've fucked up." I prayed that it wasn't the same chick, but as she got closer and smiled, I had no doubt it was her. "Nope, I *definitely* fucked up. I fucked up big."

"What the hell are you talking about?"

Before I could answer, she walked up to Hawk and said, "Hey there. I'm glad you guys could make it."

"Appreciate you having us." Hawk motioned his hand. "You've already met Menace. These are my other brothers Country and Rafe."

"Hi, I'm Kier...Oh, umm..." Her voice trailed off the second she noticed who I was, and the blood drained from her face as her eyes widened. We both stood there, silently reliving the events of the other night in our minds. I felt like the fucking wind had been knocked out of me, and by the expression on her face, Kiersten felt the same fucking way. Thankfully, she recovered quickly and went straight back to business. "I'm Kiersten. I think it's best if we start the tour here in the school."

"Just lead the way."

I was hoping no one noticed her odd reaction to seeing me, but no such luck. As soon as we started down the hall, Rafe gave me a hard nudge with his elbow and whispered, "What the hell was that?"

"That was my fuckup."

Rafe looked over to her and then back to me. His head fell back as he groaned. "Oh, damn. You didn't."

"I did."

"What the hell were you thinking, man?"

"It's not my fault. Seriously—"

Before I could finish, Hawk glanced back at us and gave us both a scolding look, putting an immediate end to our conversation. He then turned his attention back to Kiersten. "Gotta say, it's an interesting place you got here."

"You haven't seen anything yet," she replied proudly.

Kiersten opened one of the wooden doors and motioned us through.

As I walked past her, she did everything in her power to avoid eye contact with me, making it painfully clear she wasn't happy about me being there. I couldn't exactly blame her. I felt the same fucking way, but neither of us was going to let it interfere with the tour.

When we continued down a long, dark hall, she stepped in front of the group. "If you haven't noticed, we've completely renovated the entire property. Every room has been updated to fit our needs."

She opened one of the doors, revealing row after row of cannabis plants. As she waited for us to gather inside, she said, "We've created a state-of-the-art greenhouse using the best lighting on the market, a filtration system above all others, and we've developed the perfect blend of nitrogen, potassium, and phosphorus for optimal growth of our plants."

"Damn, seems like a lot of trouble for fucking weed," Rafe grumbled.

"It is, but it's worth it. You'll see."

I had to give it to her. Kiersten had certainly outdone herself. Damn, the chick wasn't only beautiful, she was intelligent and driven, too. I was impressed—so much so, I couldn't seem to take my eyes off her. She had my full attention as she continued, "This is just one of our many start-up rooms. We use this and a hydroponics room to start the process. Once the plants are thriving, we move them to the gymnasium. Come with me, and I'll show you."

Hawk nodded, then followed her out of the room. I

was about to do the same when Rafe reached for my arm and tugged me back. "What are you going to do?"

"About what?"

"*Kiersten.*" He shook his head. "I'm watching the way you're looking at her. Damn, brother. You got a thing for this girl?"

"No, it was nothing. I'm good."

"Then what's your plan here?"

I knew he was concerned, and he had every right to be. Viper already had his misgivings about Kiersten. Not only was she Billy's daughter, but she'd also breached Menace's computer. If he'd known that she and I had gone at it in the bathroom, I had no doubt he'd lose his shit, and for good reason. I had to tell him what happened, but I didn't know how or when. We were in the middle of the fucking tour, so I told Rafe, "Fuck if I know."

"Well, you best be figuring it out."

"Okay, Judge Judy. Court is adjourned," I grumbled, then turned and walked out. Rafe followed after me, and we quickly caught up with Menace and Kiersten. As soon as he saw that we were back, Hawk gave us both another reprimanding look.

Kiersten was either ignoring it or hadn't noticed our odd behavior and simply continued on with her tour.

When we walked into the gymnasium, I was blown

away by the number of fucking marijuana plants lining the floor. "Each of our startup rooms offers a different harvest time, so we have to use a variety of methods to ensure we'll have the right amount of product we need." She waited a moment, then said, "If there aren't any other questions, I'll take you over to the barn where we dry and cure the plants."

Kiersten was about to lead us out of the gym, when Hawk said, "I think we've seen enough."

"Oh? Okay, well we can go to one of the meeting rooms, so we can—"

"That won't be necessary," Hawk cut her off.

"But—"

"Look, Kiersten. I appreciate you taking us around to see everything. It's clear you've put a lot of time and money into this place, but the Sinners won't be partnering up with you." Menace's voice never wavered. "Not like this."

FOUR
KIERSTEN

I'd lost them and had no idea how to fix it. I thought the Sinners would be blown away by what I had to offer, but clearly, that wasn't the case. I needed to act fast, to propose something that would convince them to stay, but nothing was coming to mind. It didn't help matters that the hot guy, *Country*, from the bar was staring at me again. With every step, I could literally feel the heat of his gaze on my skin, and knowing he was watching my every move made it impossible to think straight.

I had no one to blame but myself. I should've known better than to pick up some guy at a bar. It was just another one of those things that was entirely out of character for me, and it had come to bite me in the ass. And to make matters worse, I knew in my gut something wasn't right—that there was something familiar about him, and I was stepping into trouble, but I let my overactive hormones get in the way.

In my defense, I never would've dreamed he was one of the men I'd seen on the Ruthless Sinners' surveillance footage, but there he stood. Holy cow, the man was even hotter than I remembered, which was hard to believe since I'd been so incredibly attracted to him that night, and apparently, that didn't change. I couldn't even look at him without remembering how amazing his hands had felt on me.

Yep. There was no doubt about it. The man was a distraction—a big, whopping distraction, and that was the last thing I needed, especially now when there were millions of dollars at stake.

I knew the Sinners had doubts about going into business with me, but I wasn't ready to throw in the towel. "Is there something in particular that you're concerned about?"

"Oh, I'm more than just concerned."

"About?"

"Everything." Hawk inhaled a deep breath, clearly trying to collect himself. "You got people living here, and they come and go as they please. That shit alone is enough to make us walk, but the fact that you're out here in the wide-open is pure insanity. You're a sitting duck."

"Just so we're clear, the people who live here work

for me. This is their livelihood. I trust them, and they trust me. It's no different than you and your club." There was so much I wanted to say, but I couldn't. I'd given my word to keep certain aspects of my work under wraps. "And we have security. More than you might think."

"Not the kind you need with all this high-dollar equipment and hundreds of thousands of dollars' worth of drugs."

I wasn't exactly surprised by his skepticism. I had a feeling from the minute he walked through the door, Hawk was going to be my biggest challenge, and I was right. I was trying to think of a way to ease his agitation when I felt my phone vibrate in my back pocket. I quickly pulled it out, and relief washed over me the second I looked down at the screen. I read the message, then looked back to Hawk and said, "Riggs wants me to tell you not to worry. We have a state-of-the-art security system."

"Riggs?"

"Yes, I think you might know him. He's a member of Satan's Fury."

"You gotta be shittin' me."

"Satan's Fury is the buyer from Memphis that I mentioned yesterday. I wouldn't have revealed his name or his club's just now if he hadn't given me the okay to do so."

"And they're good with the security here?"

"Riggs installed the system himself. Even hooked up a large generator to make sure it stays up and running when the power goes out. He's thought of everything."

"Clearly."

I pointed to one of the hidden cameras and waved. "He knows how important today is to me and has been watching since you arrived."

"I gotta say, I'm surprised."

"I thought you might be." I walked over and grabbed one of the hidden remotes. "Riggs added some special features to our security system to help us out in case anything was to happen. I think you will be impressed by it."

I pushed the red button, and the hidden compartments above the windows opened. Seconds later, the light in the gymnasium started to dim as the bulletproof panes lowered and covered each of the windows, sealing us in. I couldn't help but think of the movie *I am Legend* when I saw those thick metal panels come down from the ceiling. It felt so surreal, and I wasn't the only one who was impressed. It was clear from their expressions, all four Ruthless Sinners were equally blown away by Riggs' special set up. Menace walked over to get a better look at one of the window coverings and said, "Damn, I gotta admit, this is pretty fucking cool."

"Yeah, until they come down and lock the wrong person inside." Hawk turned his attention to me. "What are you going to do when that shit happens? You gonna give them some of your miracle pot?"

"I'll take care of it," Braylon answered as he stepped through the side door. "Along with Timms and Duggar. We're all ex-military and have no issue handling whatever comes our way."

"What about the cops?" Hawk pushed. "How are you gonna handle them?"

"The police here aren't an issue," I answered.

"The cops are always an issue."

"Well, we live on a nature preserve, so they have no reason to disturb us." I could tell by his expression, Hawk wasn't convinced, so I added, "Besides, the deputies here are under a great deal of stress and need a way to unwind."

"Hold up." Hawk's brows furrowed. "You're selling to the fucking cops."

"I didn't say that." I shrugged as I repeated, "I said they were under a great deal of stress."

"Unbelievable."

I took a step towards Hawk. "Look, I get that you and your brothers have your concerns, and I'm sure many of them are justified. But you've come here to see how we run our business, so please, stay and see the entire process. I believe that in the end, you'll be glad you did."

When he didn't immediately answer, Menace gave him a pat on the shoulder. "What do you think, brother?"

"I think we'll be wasting our time, but we came prepared to stay, so we might as well stay."

"Great." I tried my best to hide my excitement as I said, "I'll show you to the guest quarters, and we can meet back up after you've gotten settled in."

"Sounds good." Hawk looked up at one of the security cameras as he told me, "Tell Riggs I'll be in touch."

"Of course."

I pressed the button on the remote to disengage the security brigade, then showed the men back to the front parking lot. After they grabbed their things, I took them across the grounds to the guest house. It was a little bigger than the other houses on the property with a large kitchen and living room and four bedrooms. After I'd given them a brief tour, the men dispersed to their chosen rooms. Each of the doors closed behind them—all except one. Country was standing in his doorway, glaring at me like I was public enemy number one. "Did you know?"

"I didn't."

"Well, I didn't have a clue." I felt even worse about

the whole situation as I admitted, "I would've never... *you know*, had I known you were a Sinner. I'm actually surprised you thought I did."

"Why wouldn't I? I mean, come on. You were laying it on pretty thick that night."

"What?"

"You asked about places to stay or sights you needed to see. It was all a crock of shit." Country's face was void of expression, which made it difficult to tell if he was being serious when he said, "You live thirty minutes away."

"I was making small talk, Country. That's what people do. They talk. They flirt. Blah, blah, blah."

"*Flirt?* Oh, I see. Guess that explains why you were all over me."

"What!" I gasped. "I was not all over you!"

"Yeah, you were, and you know it, but I don't blame ya." A mischievous smirk crossed his face as he arched his back and ran his hands over his muscular chest. "I'm quite the catch."

It took all I had to keep from laughing—not that what he said wasn't true because it was, but the playful way he was poking at me helped to ease the tension I'd been carrying around all afternoon. "You're an ass."

"Yeah, I'm that, too, but don't hold it against me."

"I'll try my best." We stood there for a moment,

just looking at one another, until I finally said, "Well, I guess I'll let you get settled."

I gave him an awkward wave, then rushed out of the house and back over to the main office to find Braylon. I wanted to take a minute to fill him in on everything that had transpired with the Sinners—including my conversation with Country. When I walked in, he was sitting at the desk going over our numbers for the day but put them aside the second he saw me enter the room. "Well, how do you think it's going?"

"Couldn't be going much worse." I walked over and sat down in the chair beside his desk. "I think I've handled this whole thing the wrong way."

"What do you mean?"

"I should've never done the whole cryptic email thing."

"I tried to tell you that."

"I know, and you were right. They don't trust me or anything I'm doing here." I dropped my head into my hands. "I should've just gone to their clubhouse and met with them face to face. I certainly shouldn't have had sex with one of them."

"Hold up... You had sex with one of them?" He gasped.

"Afraid so." I lifted my head from my hands just long enough to say, "Remember me telling you that I met someone at a bar?"

"Oh, damn."

"Yeahhh, I screwed up." I lowered my head back into my hands. "I should've known I couldn't do something like that without it coming back to haunt me."

"There's no way you could've known the guy was a Sinner."

"That's just it!" I looked back up at him. "I should've known! I've been watching that security footage for weeks now. He'd crossed that screen a hundred times, but it never entered my mind that he would be sitting at that bar."

"Did he know?"

"There's no way he could've known." I dropped my hands to my lap and sighed. "I've made such a mess of things. I don't know what I'm going to do."

"Nothing. You're going to do nothing."

"But..."

"You didn't know who the guy was. You just wanted to let off a little steam, and that's what you did. Leave it at that."

"I wish it was that easy." I leaned closer to Braylon as I whispered, "The sex with him was unbelievable, like really, really unbelievable, and I can't even look at him without thinking about it."

"Unbelievable? Hmm..." My heart literally stopped beating in my chest at the sound of Country's voice. "Glad to know you enjoyed it. Maybe we should try again sometime."

I whipped around in my seat, and just as I feared, Country was standing in the doorway, smiling like the Cheshire cat. I was completely mortified and wanted to crawl into a hole and die, but sadly, there was literally nowhere for me to hide. I couldn't let him think that I was talking about him to one of my employees, so I was left with only one choice. I had to lie. "I hate to burst your bubble, but I wasn't talking about you."

"*Yeah* ... If you say so." His smirk faded as he said, "The guys wanted me to let you know that we're heading out for a bit."

"Oh, okay. Any idea when you'll be back?"

"Can't say for sure."

"But you'll be back, right?"

"Yeah." Country's tone was soft and reassuring. "We'll be back."

"Okay, I'll see ya when you get back."

He gave me a quick nod, then turned and disappeared down the hallway. I leaned back, making sure he was gone before turning my attention back to Braylon. "How much do you think he heard?"

"Enough."

"Damn." I let out a groan. "I just can't win."

"Well, he's clearly interested in hooking up again." Braylon shrugged. "So, it isn't all bad."

"You aren't helping."

He chuckled. "I had to try."

"Yeah, thanks." I rolled my eyes, then stood. "Wonder where they ran off to."

"I don't know. If it was me, I'd be checking out the surrounding area, but it's hard to tell with those guys."

"You're right about that." I shook my head as I started for the door. "I have a feeling they're going to give me a run for my money over the next couple of days."

"I certainly hope so, or they aren't the men we thought they were."

"Very true." As I headed down the hall, I shouted, "Let's hope Riggs was right about them!"

I left the office and went to start getting dinner prepped for the night. Since the weather was nice and not too cold, I decided to use the picnic area out by the old church to grill burgers. I asked Lumley, one of our workers, to gather some wood for a fire and place it by the pit. Thinking it would be a good place for us to talk, I moved some chairs over and got a cooler of beer, then placed them around the fire pit.

Even though I had no idea how long they'd be gone, I decided to start on the burgers while Braylon and Lumley got the fire going. As I hoped, the guys returned not long after I'd finished grilling the burgers. They all gathered around and made themselves a plate, then carried them over to the picnic tables. We sat down to eat, and I expected them to start talking, but no one said a word—not to me or each other.

I wasn't sure what was wrong. It was a perfect night. It wasn't too warm. It wasn't too cold, and the food was really good—even if it was just burgers. I thought maybe one of them would eventually say something, but no such luck. The silence was getting to me, so I tried to open the line of communication. "I was thinking we could use this time to talk a little."

None of them said a word. They simply gave each other an odd look, then continued eating. Hoping to get at least one of them to open up, I asked, "So, none of you have any questions about Langford Manor or the products we have to offer?"

"It's too soon for questions," Hawk answered. "We still have a lot to see."

"Yes, you definitely do. I was just wondering if there was anything you saw today that ..." None of them seemed to be paying me any attention, so I decided to rip off the bandage and discuss the elephant in the room. "I know the cards are stacked against me here, and I have no one but myself to blame for that. I used my father's connection to your club to gain access to Menace's computer, and then I used what I found on the hard drive to lure you into a meet. I'm sure that makes you think I'm not trustworthy, that I broke some unspoken code, but I had my reasons for doing what I did."

"Those reasons cost you our trust, and if you don't have trust, you don't have anything."

"I understand, but I didn't do anything you wouldn't have done if you were in my position." I reached into my pocket and pulled out the flash drive I'd used to access Menace's hard drive. I put it on the table and slid it over to Hawk as I said, "That being said, here is everything I got from Menace's laptop ... It's the only copy."

"And you think giving me this makes things right?" Hawk shook his head. "'Cause it doesn't."

"No, I didn't think it would, but I'm hoping it'll be a start in making things right."

Hawk lifted the flash drive as he asked, "What exactly were you able to find on Menace's laptop?"

"Enough."

"That's not an answer."

"I get that you're concerned I might have something to use against you, but that's not why I did what I did. I was only looking for things that would help me determine whether or not your club would be the right fit for my business." Sensing that it wouldn't help my case, I didn't want to go into lengthy detail, so I simply told him, "I did that by watching your security footage. I know you have your girls selling coke in your clubs ...

I know you're careful, really careful, and that's why you've done so well with it. I also know you have a secure holding place at a storage lot that's run by a woman named Ada May. I did a little digging and discovered that you have several other Ruthless Sinners chapters throughout the country—including Idaho, Kansas, Nebraska, and North and South Carolina— states where marijuana is entirely illegal. Still, you also have chapters where the legal status is mixed. In other words, you have plenty of options for distribution."

"Looks like you've done your homework."

"Again—I only did what you and your brothers would've done if you were in my position." I took a moment to catch my breath, then added, "Look, I know right now I don't have your trust, but if you give me a chance, I'll do whatever it takes to earn it."

Hawk nodded, but he didn't verbally respond. None of them did. They simply sat there in complete and utter silence, making me question whether or not I'd ever be able to regain their trust. We all went back to eating, and just as everyone was about to finish up, Country looked over to me and said, "I have a question."

The other brothers looked at him like he'd lost his mind, but he didn't seem to care. Relieved to have one of them open up a little, I quickly replied, "You can ask me anything."

"I'm just curious... You say your stuff is good, but exactly how good is it?"

"It's the best around. Seriously, you should try it." I leaned forward and smiled. "All of you should."

Country looked over to Hawk, Rafe, and Menace. When they gave him a nod, he turned back to me and said, "Bring it on."

And just like that, our night took a totally different turn.

FIVE

COUNTRY

When Kiersten said her stuff was the best around, she wasn't kidding. I hadn't smoked pot in years, but when I did, I smoked the hell out of it. I acquired the habit when my grandfather got cancer. He'd shared a bit of his medical marijuana with me from time to time, and I liked the feeling. I actually liked it a little too much, so I knew firsthand Kiersten's shit was the real deal, and it had me thinking I might pick up the habit again. I'd never felt so mellow—like I was dreaming but I was wide awake.

Everything had stilled, and for the first time in months, I could sit and breathe without feeling the weight of the world on my shoulders. It was a good feeling—a really good feeling. I looked down at the fire and watched as the flames danced and flickered about, and before I realized what I was doing, I started mumbling the words to the song "Ring of Fire" by Johnny Cash. After a few lines, I looked over to my brothers who were also feeling the effects of Kiersten's powerful weed. They were all leaning back in their chairs, silently studying the fire like they didn't have a care in the world.

I, on the other hand, had a hundred thoughts running through my head which led me to ask, "Y'all ever wonder why Viper doesn't have an ol' lady?"

Each of them shrugged and grumbled, but none gave a real answer. Unable to just let it go, I took another drag, then said, "I mean, I'm no expert, but I wouldn't think a man like him would have any trouble snagging himself a woman."

Still nothing from the guys, so I just kept at it. "Maybe it's the whole running the club stuff. It's gotta be tough dealing with all the bullshit, and we don't make it any easier on the guy."

"You seem awfully concerned about Prez and his fucking love life," Hawk grumbled.

"Only 'cause I care." I shrugged. "I mean, come on, Pappa Bear needs love, too."

"Don't gotta worry about Prez, brother." Menace sounded sure of himself. "If he wanted an ol' lady, he'd have one."

"No doubt," Hawk mumbled. "Chicks are all over him at the club."

Rafe looked down at his joint and studied it for a moment. "I gotta say, this is some pretty good shit right here."

"It's one of our most popular hybrid blends," Kiersten replied proudly.

"Hybrid?"

"You've got three types of cannabis... *sativa, indica,* and hybrid, and they each have a different effect."

Rafe looked down at his joint with confusion. "Different how?"

"Sativa is like the Hulk Hogan of pot. It gives you the umph you need to work out and shit, while indica is more chill and mellow like Cheech and Chong," I explained. "Mix a little Hogan with some Cheech, and you've got yourself a hybrid."

"This shit must be better than I thought." Hawk shook his head and laughed. "Country actually sounded like he knows what he's talking about."

"Fuck you, brother."

The guys snickered and made their side comments, but Kiersten didn't join in. Instead, she waited until they grew quiet, then smiled and said, "I'm impressed. Most people don't know about the different types of weed. Most just want to feel the high and move on."

"I learned a thing or two from my grandfather."

Maybe it was just the pot talking, but there was something about the way she smiled at me that got me right in the gut. I held her gaze for a moment, soaking her in as long as I could without the others noticing, then quickly turned my attention back to the fire. Damn, it'd been a long time since a woman had gotten to me like she did, and I had no fucking clue what I was going to do about it. For now, I just had to bide my time and pray the feeling would fade.

I didn't know how long I was staring at the fire when Rafe, who was feeling all kinds of good, said, "I'm gonna learn to play the guitar. Been wanting to since I was a kid but just kept putting it off. Yep, I'm gonna get me a guitar, and I'm gonna start learning to play."

"Hope that doesn't mean you're gonna start singing, too," Hawk grumbled. "Don't think my ears could take it."

"Nah, I'll leave the singing to Country."

"Awe, that outta be good." Hawk snickered. "You two will drive us to drinking for sure."

I nudged him with my elbow. "Isn't that the point?"

"You two already drive us all to drinking. Don't need you adding guitar playing and singing to the mix."

"You gotta be kidding me." Rafe threw up his

hands. "We could be the next Willie Nelson and Waylon Jennings or Brooks and Dunn."

"Nope. Never gonna happen."

"Still gonna get me a guitar," Rafe argued. "I'm gonna learn to play, and then I'm taking Delilah down to Mexico. We'll sit on the beach and have a few drinks while I play my gee-tar."

"Poor girl doesn't stand a chance."

Like he hadn't heard Hawk's last comment, Rafe smiled and started chuckling under his breath. He was clearly hitting that ultimate high when he eased back in his chair and asked, "Hey, what do you call a potato that smokes weed?"

"No idea."

"*A baked potato.*" Rafe coughed, clearing his throat, then asked, "How do you get a one-armed stoner out of a tree?" Without giving us a chance to answer, Rafe started chuckling and said, "You wave."

I immediately thought about that crazy GIF of Tom Hanks on that fishing boat waving like there was no tomorrow. Unable to resist the temptation to join in, Hawk grinned, then said, "You know scientists say marijuana lowers your body temperature, so it's true. Smoking pot really does make you cool."

We all groaned at the cheesiness of the joke, and each gave Hawk a teasing jab. He threw his hands up in the air as he said, "You can't say I didn't try."

"Wait, wait. I've got another one. Weed really isn't a drug. It's a plant." Rafe snickered as he said, "So, Kiersten really isn't a drug dealer. She's a florist."

"A florist? Really?" Hawk shook his head as he told him, "That one might be the worst yet."

"Okay, how about this one? What do stoners do when they get lost?" Rafe giggled under his breath, then answered himself, "They turn down the music so they can see better."

"Nope." Hawk groaned. "Not any better."

"I've got one." I looked over to Hawk as I said, "Your mom is like marijuana—everyone does her, but no one admits it."

"That's just wrong."

"I'm out on that one." Menace stood and tossed his empty beer bottle into the trash as he continued, "I'm gonna call it a night."

"Seriously?" I fussed. "It's not even ten o'clock."

"I need to call Parker."

"Ah, yeah," Rafe chuckled. "He's still in that puppy-love stage where he's gotta check in with his ol' lady every five minutes."

"Might do you good to do the same."

"Don't worry about me, old man. Me and my woman are just fine."

"Don't be too hard on him, brother." I smiled as I watched the exchange between Rafe and Menace.

A smirk crossed his face as Rafe poked, "Our boy here is just getting too old to hang with us like he used to."

"Not too old, smartass. Just gotta limit my time with you people to small doses." Menace gave us both a look and said, "It's the only way I can keep my sanity."

"Yeah, yeah. Whatever you say, boss."

"Keep running that mouth, brother, and see what it gets ya," Menace warned as he turned and started back to the guest quarters.

"After all that, I think I'm gonna call it a night, too," Hawk announced as he stood up. "And don't give me any mouth about it either."

"Who? Us?"

"You two need some help." Hawk shook his head. "Be ready to roll first thing in the morning."

"Will do."

Before he was out of earshot, Hawk shouted over his shoulder, "Thanks for dinner, Kiersten."

"Welcome!" she shouted in return. "Sleep well!"

Once they both went into the house, Rafe looked over to Kiersten and then to me. I was worried he was going to say something about us hooking up, but instead, he simply stood and said, "I'm starving. Are there any leftovers from dinner?"

"There are tons." Kiersten pointed to the church's kitchen back door. "It's all in the fridge."

"Awesome."

Moments later, Rafe disappeared into the kitchen, leaving Kiersten and me alone by the fire. I was still feeling the effects of the marijuana when I glanced over to her and said, "You know, you did good tonight."

"Oh? And how's that?"

"By coming clean with the guys." Even high, I knew better than to say too much. "I think it was a step in the right direction."

"I hope so." She studied me for a moment, then asked, "Was I right when I said I didn't do anything you and your brothers wouldn't have done if you were in my shoes?"

"Can't say for sure, but it's not out of the realm of possibility."

"I thought so." She shrugged. "I just hope I didn't go to all that trouble for nothing."

"Only time will tell." Seeing the worried look in her eyes made me ask, "So what makes a girl like you decide to start up a marijuana farm?"

"A girl like me?"

"You're beautiful and smart with a good head on your shoulders." Her gorgeous eyes were locked on mine as I continued, "I know your father does well, so it's not like you're doing it for the money."

"Money has nothing to do with it." She turned her focus to the fire, and the flames illuminated her face with an angelic glow. Once again, I was mesmerized by how beautiful she was. The tone in her voice changed from light-hearted and free to strained and full of anguish. "I hadn't planned on doing this. I went to college thinking I would study botany or biochemistry, and I'd make some amazing discovery that would change the world, but I lost interest in saving the world when I discovered what my father was doing."

"So, you know?"

"Not everything, but *I know enough*." She brushed her hair out of her face and looked at me. "I'd always thought he was this great man who could do no wrong. I always thought he'd love me and protect me from the evil in the world. Instead, he brought it into our home."

The girl who seemed to be so strong and had it all together wasn't as tough as she tried to make us think. I knew it might've just been the effects of the pot, but I liked the fact that she'd given me a glimpse of her vulnerable side. Hoping she might open up a little more, I asked, "How did you find out?"

"I heard a noise, I went to check it out, and I saw things I never should've seen—which would've never happened if Dad hadn't forgotten to shut a door. If he just kept it closed, I would've never known he wasn't the man I thought he was." She shrugged. "Don't get me wrong. I love my father, I really do, but I grew up thinking he was someone who wouldn't hurt a fly. *I was wrong*. He thinks I'm just a college student studying to be a biochemist. Turns out, he's wrong. too."

"So, you decided to grow pot as a way of getting back at your father."

"No, I..." She let out a breath, then shrugged again. "Maybe a little. I really did want to find a way to grow it to help people. Like Braylon, for example. He spent years suffering from chronic pain, and marijuana was the only thing that seemed to help him, but he couldn't get it living here. Now he can, and I've seen for myself how much it's helped him, but there's still this piece of me that likes that my father doesn't know what I'm doing. So, yeah. I guess, in some small way, I did do all this as a way to get back at him."

"I get It. I really do. It had to have been tough to see what you did, especially as a kid, but you gotta know that what a man does for a living isn't the be-all and end-all of his existence, Kiersten. *It's just a job.*"

"Yeah, but what he's doing is more than just some job, Country," she argued.

"He's still your father. He's still the man who did whatever he had to do to give you the life he thought you deserved."

"I know, and I appreciate that, but I would've rather he stayed the man I always thought he was."

"I'm sure he'd say the same about you."

She cut her eyes towards the dark sky. "I'm sure he would."

"So, Billy really doesn't have a clue about your operation here? He thinks you're just off at college doing your thing?"

"Yep."

"Damn." I shook my head. "He's gonna blow a fucking gasket when he finds out."

"I have no intention of him ever finding out." Before I could tell her that she was crazy if she thought a man like Billy wouldn't figure out what she was up to, Kiersten stood and brushed off her pants. "Mind if we change the subject?"

"No, I'm good with that." I watched as she walked over and started tossing the empty cans and bottles into the trash. I had the feeling she was a little bothered by our conversation and hoped that a change of subject might ease her mind. "What about Satan's Fury? How'd you tie up with them?"

I got up and went over to help her with the trash as she said, "That was all Braylon. He and Shadow were in the military together, so he reached out to him, and the rest is history."

"They're good guys. You did good getting them on board."

"Yeah, well, it wasn't easy. Gus is a lot like Viper. They're both pretty intimidating."

"Only because they have to be."

"I guess." After she tossed the last bottle in the trash, she turned to me and said, "It's late, and we have a big day tomorrow. I better call it a night."

"Okay." I smiled as I stepped over to her. "I'll walk you back to your place."

"You don't have to do that."

"I want to."

A warm smile crossed her face as she gave me a nod. Neither of us spoke as we made our way across the dark, grassy field and up to her doorstep. Kiersten looked up at me with those beautiful doe eyes and asked, "You want to come in?"

"Yes, but it's not a good idea."

"Oh, yeah. You're probably right." A look of disappointment flashed through her eyes as she said, "Maybe some other time."

"Maybe."

Those doe eyes remained locked on mine—tempting me, drawing me in like a fucking moth to a flame. I knew what she wanted. Hell, I wanted the same fucking thing, and the temptation was only growing more intense as we stood there staring back at one another. Unfortunately, it didn't matter how much I wanted to kiss her. I couldn't do a damn thing until I'd discussed the situation with Viper. Unable to force myself to leave, I motioned my head towards the door and said, "Go inside, Kiersten."

"Is that what you really want?"

"Don't ask me that."

"It's a legitimate question, Country."

"It's not a question I can answer."

Not willing to give it up, she crossed her arms and asked, "Why not?"

"Because it doesn't matter what I want." I motioned my hand between us. "This can't happen."

"I didn't ask if it could or couldn't happen. I asked what you wanted."

"Say goodnight, Kiersten."

She studied me for a moment, then opened her door and stepped inside. She turned back to me with one last soul-searching stare, then whispered, "Goodnight, Country."

As soon as she closed the door, I stepped down from her porch and walked back over to the sitting area to look for Rafe. Every step I took was harder than the last. I didn't want to leave Kiersten. I wanted to grab her up, carry her back into the house, and spend the entire night tangled in her arms. My only consolation was the fact that I'd be seeing her again later that night. I'd have those soft, warm lips on mine once again—even if it was only in my dreams.

By the time I made it back over to the picnic area,

Rafe was done pillaging the fridge and ready to call it a night. We both went back to our guest quarters and crashed. The following day, Kiersten treated us all to one hell of a breakfast, then finished her tour of the grounds.

Once we were done, she led us back into her conference room to share the files she created for each of her employees. As I sat there listening to her talk about the background checks she'd done on each of them, I couldn't take my eyes off her—not just because she looked amazing in her jeans and boots, but because of the way she spoke about her work. Kiersten was passionate and determined, and she was incredibly smart—more so than I'd realized.

She'd done a great job piecing this place together, and she knew it. Even when Hawk or Menace would question her on her methods, she didn't let it get to her but instead stuck to her guns and forged ahead—just like she did when Menace pointed to the files she'd made on her employees and asked, "You mind if I take a look at those?"

"Okay." Kiersten slid the stack across the table. "But you have nothing to worry about when it comes to the people who work for me. I've been very meticulous in that regard."

"I'm sure you have. We just need to be sure, Kiersten." Hawk leaned back in his chair and asked, "So, who's actually moving the goods?"

"We all are. Regan, Mia, and I cover the college scene. We try to limit our days to Mondays, Wednesdays, and Fridays, but we never miss sporting events and frat parties. They're both big moneymakers for us. Braylon, Timms, and Duggar take care of deliveries with our larger buyers."

"Like Fury?"

"Exactly."

"And Braylon, Timms, and Duggar handle security?"

"They do."

"And you feel certain they can handle any trouble that might come their way?"

"Braylon told you himself that he's ex-military, but what he didn't tell you was that he was steps away from becoming a Navy SEAL. He would've made it if he hadn't been injured during his qualification training and lost his leg."

"Damn, that's tough."

"It was very tough, especially since he was hurt helping one of the other men he was in training with. They made the mistake, but Bray was the one who paid the price for it." Her tone turned serious as she said, "That being said, I have full faith that Braylon can handle whatever he needs to."

"That's a lot for one man to take on."

"It's not just one man. He has Timms and Duggar to help out, and they're equally qualified."

"Not sure I agree."

"I need you to understand something. When I decided to do this, I knew what I was getting into." She cleared her throat, before continuing, "I knew what would happen if I got greedy or tangled up with the wrong people. I'd either end up in jail or six feet under —that was something I learned from my father. I'm not going to let that happen. I've been careful from the start, and I'm going to continue to be careful. And that goes for every aspect of this business—from how I grow my product to who I get to protect it."

"You've clearly put a lot into this place, and it's doing well. Certainly better than I expected, but I'm still concerned about the level of security you have here." Hawk glanced up at one of the cameras in the corner of the room. "Even with everything Riggs has done and with Braylon's expertise, I'm not sure you have the means to protect yourself if things go south."

"Well, if I do my job right, that won't happen."

"Things happen, Kiersten. No matter how well you plan. No matter how careful you are. There's always someone who will come along and try to fuck it all up."

"So, what are you saying?"

"If we were to join forces, you would have to make some changes."

"What kind of changes?"

"For one, you need to stop selling at the college. You would have to leave the distribution up to us."

"But I make good money there."

"Maybe, but it's too close. It leaves you too exposed. It's only a matter of time before those sales lead someone here, and that can't happen."

"And what about Fury?"

"We'll take care of them."

"So, you'll just take things over?"

Hawk shook his head. "No, just the sales and distribution. That way you can focus on things here."

"Is that the only option?"

"I can't say for sure. I'll have to run this all by Viper, but yeah. If we were to go into business with you, it would be the only way we'd do it."

"I'm going to need to talk it over with the others before I make a decision."

"Take your time." Hawk stood, then said, "We're going to head back. Once we've had a chance to discuss things with the rest of the club, we'll be in touch."

"Okay, sounds good."

I could feel Kiersten's eyes on me as I stood and followed the others towards the door. I wanted to look at her, take her in one last time, but I knew it would only make it that much harder to leave—which was already something I didn't want to do. I wanted more time with her, but there was only one way that was going to happen.

I had to talk to Viper.

SIX

KIERSTEN

"It sounds like a sweet deal to me."

"Yeah, but we'd be giving up all control," I argued.

"And all the hassle that comes with it." Braylon had always been my voice of reason. He was older and somewhat wiser, and I trusted him—something that didn't come easy to me. I valued his opinion, so I tried to keep an open mind when he said, "I think this could be the answer you've been looking for."

"I just don't know. We've worked so hard to get here, and I'm not sure I'm ready to just hand it over to someone else."

"You won't be. You'll still have the say, and you can get back to working in the lab. That's where you've always wanted to be."

"I know, but—"

"You need to remember why you started this whole thing."

"To get back at my father?" I scoffed.

"Yeah, well, there's that," he chuckled. "But I remember you telling me you wanted to create something that was better. Something that could end up helping people who are suffering. Maybe this is your chance to start focusing on that again."

"Maybe."

"So, if this deal with the Sinners comes through, what are you going to do about your boy toy?"

"My boy toy? Really?"

"Call him whatever you want to. I'm just asking what you're going to do about him."

"Well, his name is Country." It seemed strange to say that out loud, so I added, "At least, that's what his brothers call him, and honestly, I don't know what I'm going to do. I guess there's not really anything I can do."

"Do you like the guy?"

"Yeah, I do." Just thinking about him brought a smile to my face. "He seems pretty great, but I've been wrong about men before."

"Gah, you really need to get past these daddy issues of yours."

"Easier said than done."

"I know, but it's just been a while since I've seen that spark in your eyes. I just don't want you to let the past interfere with your future."

"It was one night in a bar." My smile faded as I continued, "Besides, he's a biker, and we might be going into business with his club. I doubt I'll be seeing him again, much less have a future with him."

"You never know. Stranger things have happened."

"I never knew you were such the romantic." I stood and started to the door. "I'm going to check in on things at the lab. I'll let you know if I hear anything from the guys."

"I'll be waiting."

I left the office and headed down the hall to my lab. I hoped it would help take my mind off of things, and it did for a little while. Unfortunately, experimenting with a new fertilizer wasn't enough of a distraction from the phone call I was expecting from the Sinners. I started to worry that something might've been wrong with my phone and that I hadn't heard it ring, so I pulled it out of my pocket and checked the screen. That's when I noticed the date. It was my father's birthday. With everything that had been going on, I'd totally forgotten all about it.

I immediately dropped everything and rushed over to my house for my keys and purse. After sending

Braylon a message about where I was going, I got in my car and drove over to my dad's. On the way, I stopped to pick up a small cake and a generic card, but I didn't bother with a gift. The man already had everything he could possibly want and more. The only thing he didn't have was a real relationship with me, and no matter how hard he tried, that was something he would never have—not after years of trying to deceive me.

When I got to the house, the front door was wide open and coffee was brewing, but there was no sign of Dad. I placed the cake and card down on the table, then opened the basement door. "Dad?"

No answer.

I stepped over to the back door and opened it before shouting, "Dad!"

Again, no answer.

Worried something might be wrong, I rushed to the front to make sure I hadn't missed him, and that's when I spotted him out on the pier. I hated myself for it, but my heart ached seeing him out there all alone. It was his birthday. He should've been with family or friends, but he'd spent the last ten years living like a recluse and had neither. I didn't want to feel sorry for him. I knew his work was why he'd chosen to distance himself from the world, but that didn't stop the sorrow dwelling in the pit of my stomach. I inhaled a deep breath and feigned a happy smile as I walked over to join him at the pier.

He was just about to cast out his line when I said, "Happy birthday, Daddy."

"Kiersten!" He dropped his fishing pole and opened his arms wide, then stepped over to me and hugged me tightly. "I didn't know you were coming today."

"I couldn't miss your birthday."

"I'm so glad you came!" He released me from his embrace, then looked down at me with a warm smile. "You look good, kiddo."

"You do, too." My father was in his mid-fifties, but he was a bit of a health nut and appeared much younger. Even now, as he stood there in his loose-fit t-shirt and old-man jeans, he looked in better shape than most twenty-year-olds—which wasn't always the case when he was in his dress pants and button-downs. I glanced over at his fishing pole. "Are you catching anything?"

"Not a thing, but I wasn't really trying. Just wanted an excuse to get outside for a bit." He grabbed his pole, then motioned me towards the house. "Let's head up to the house, and I'll fix us both something to eat."

I nodded, then followed him up the pier and to the house. Once we were inside, Dad went over to the counter, and an excited smile swept across his face when he spotted his surprise. "You got me a cake?"

"You can't have a birthday without birthday cake."

"You didn't have to do that." He picked up my card and quickly scanned it, then smiled like I'd given him the moon. "Thank you. I don't deserve you."

"It's just a cake and a card, Dad."

"But it's from you, and that makes it even more special."

It was times like these that were the hardest. Dad actually sounded sincere when he said those words to me, and maybe he truly meant them. I just couldn't get past the demons in my head to believe him. Don't get me wrong. I knew it wasn't fair to judge him so harshly. Like Country said, his job was just a job, and it didn't define him. I also knew he had his reasons for becoming a cleaner, and they probably had something to do with me, but the pretending unnerved me. True or not, it made me feel as if everything that came out of his mouth was a lie.

I didn't have a response for him, so I walked over and grabbed a couple of paper plates from the cabinet. When I started cutting each of us a slice of cake, he asked, "You want a cup of coffee or a soda?"

"Soda will be fine."

"You got it." He opened the fridge and got each of

us a can of soda. Once I had our plates ready, I asked, "Do you want to carry this out to the porch?"

"That would be perfect." I followed him outside and over to the swing. Once we were both seated, he asked, "So, fill me in on things. How's school? How are your friends? Are you seeing anyone?"

"Whoa, slow down." I giggled. "One thing at a time."

A wave of guilt washed over me when he said, "Sorry, I've just missed you. It feels like we haven't had a chance to catch up in months."

"Because we haven't. *Not really*. You've been busy with work, and I've been busy with my school projects, but there's not much either of us can do about that."

"No, but we have some time now. I'd really like to hear how things are going for you."

"Okay, well... my classes are fine. Even though some of them are tough, I'm enjoying them, and as far as I know, my friends are doing well, too." My mind suddenly drifted to Country. Fate played a dirty hand when she threw us together... And now I was left wanting something I couldn't have. It shouldn't have mattered. My focus needed to be on my deal with the Sinners, but he seemed to be all I could think about. As much as I'd enjoyed our night at the bar, I relished talking to him by the fire even more. I'd never felt so comfortable having a conversation with a man I barely knew. I'd also never been so attracted to a man before, and the whole thing was completely frustrating. I liked to be in control of things, but this is one situation where I had none.

I considered telling my father I'd met someone, but I worried he might ask questions that I wasn't ready to answer, so I simply said, "I'm not seeing anyone—at least nothing steady."

"But you have met someone?"

"Yeah, but I'm not sure if anything will come of it." I shrugged. "It's kind of complicated."

"Don't worry. You have plenty of time to figure things out. You know, I was almost thirty before I met your mother." His expression softened. "I can still remember the day I saw her walk into that coffee shop. She was the most beautiful thing I'd ever seen. She was simply breathtaking. I'm pretty sure I fell in love with her right there on the spot."

"Yeah, Mom was incredible."

"She was definitely that. I still miss her every day." Anguish filled his voice when he continued, "I'd give anything to have her here with me. If I had only known then, maybe—"

"There was nothing you could've done, Dad."

"I could've reminded her not to mix her migraine medication." He shook his head. "*She knew* ... I'd told her a hundred times, but when she was hurting like that, she was desperate to make them stop."

I'd remembered him telling her to be careful. I also remembered how horrible those stupid migraines were. She would be so happy, so full of life, but as soon as they hit, she'd be out of commission for days. It was as though those damn headaches stole the life right out of her.

Mom would lock herself away in her room and close all the blinds, sealing herself off in darkness, and she'd stay there until they finally went away. It was the only thing she could do. I hated seeing her in so much pain, and I had no doubt my father felt the same. I placed my hand on his arm and said, "You know it wasn't your fault. There's nothing you could've done to change what happened."

"I wish I could believe that." He glanced down at his uneaten cake, then inhaled a quick breath. "I'm sorry. You came all this way to celebrate my birthday, and here I am messing the whole thing up."

"You didn't mess up anything. I know you miss her. I miss her, too. I think about her all the time." I wasn't exaggerating. I did think about her all the time. We had such a good life, and while there were still some good times, it just wasn't the same without her. In fact, everything changed. I had to fight back my tears as I said, "I often wondered what our lives would be like if she was still here."

"I don't have to wonder. I know my life would've been better with her in it, and I have no doubt yours would've been, too." A soft smile crossed his face as he said, "But we have each other, and we're doing okay, right?"

I was tempted to tell him that he was wrong, that we weren't doing as well as he might've thought, but I couldn't form the words. I wasn't ready to tell him about what I'd seen so many years ago. I wasn't sure I would ever be ready, so I simply nodded and said, "Yeah, we're okay."

"Good." He turned his attention back to his cake, and in a matter of minutes, he'd eaten every bite. "Why don't you tell me a little about this guy you're seeing and why it's so complicated?"

"I'm not exactly seeing him."

Before I could say anything more, my cell phone started ringing. I grabbed it out of my pocket, and when I saw that it was Braylon calling, I turned to Dad and said, "I'm sorry, but I have to take this."

I slipped inside the house and closed the door before answering, "Hey, what's up?"

"I hate to bother you while you're at your dad's, but a guy came by here looking for you. Said he knew you from school. I believe he said his name was Drake Coburn."

"Damn." Drake was in my agronomy and crop science class. He was a nice guy and not bad-looking, but I found it creepy the way he was always staring at me. Even though I'd tried to make it clear that I wasn't interested in him, he was always trying to strike up a conversation and used every excuse in the book for us to meet up outside of class. "I have no idea how he found out where I lived."

"I was afraid of that."

"Did he say what he wanted?"

"Nope." I didn't like the sound of Braylon's voice when he said, "I gotta tell ya. I don't have a good feeling about this guy. I think he's up to something."

"What makes you say that?"

"Just the way he was snooping around. I caught him looking down the hall, but he played it off and said he was just searching for you."

"Damn, he had no business coming there like that."

"What do you want me to do?"

"Look through the security feed and find out exactly what he saw. Maybe ask Riggs to check them out, too—just to be sure we don't miss anything."

"You got it."

"Thanks, Bray." Before I hung up, I told him, "I'm on my way."

I was just returning my phone to my back pocket when I heard my father ask, "Is everything okay?"

"Yes," I lied as I turned around to face him. I had no idea how much he'd heard, so I tried to choose my words carefully. "My partner and I have run into a little snag with our project, so I need to be heading back."

"So soon?"

"Afraid so." There was no missing the disappointment in his eyes when I said, "I really need to get back and take care of this before a real problem arises."

"I understand." He stepped over to me and wrapped his arms around me, hugging me tightly. "I can't tell you how much it meant to have you here with me today. I enjoyed it so much."

"I enjoyed it, too." I gave him a quick squeeze back, then said, "I'll try to get back soon."

"I really hope you will."

He walked me outside to my car, then waited as I got inside. I was looking at him as I started my car, and for a brief moment, I didn't see the man who made dead bodies disappear. I simply saw my father—and only my father, and that was something I hadn't seen in years. It felt good to see him like that, which made it difficult to leave. Sadly, I didn't have a choice. I had to get back to Langford Manor and figure out what the hell was going on with Drake Coburn.

By the time I finally returned to the office, Braylon, Timms, and Duggar were done looking through the security feed. I hoped that meant they'd figured out what Drake was up to, so I asked, "Find anything?"

"Hard to say." Braylon pulled up the surveillance footage, then pointed at Drake's red pickup truck. "Looks like he walked around to the gym. Never looked inside but seemed to just casually walk around. Then, he made his way into the school. He wandered down one hall and had just made his way to the other when I found him."

"Did he look inside any of the rooms?"

"Nope. Just stuck his head through the door like he was searching for you."

"This makes no sense." I'd always been very careful not to mention where I lived. I certainly wouldn't have told Drake. "I don't even know how he found his way here. I never told him where I lived."

"He must've followed you home." Timms' brows furrowed as he asked, "Who is this guy anyway?"

"That's just it. He's nobody. Just a guy from one of my classes. He's been trying to get me to go out with him for months, but I've made it clear that I'm not interested."

"Apparently, he didn't take the hint."

"Obviously not." I let out a deep breath. "This is bad."

"It certainly isn't good."

"So, what are we going to do?"

"Riggs is looking into him. He'll be able to tell us if there's anything we need to be concerned about. Hopefully, he's just a fucking nutjob who doesn't know how to take no for an answer."

SEVEN

COUNTRY

"I talked to Gus this morning." Viper sat down next to me and Hawk at the kitchen table. "He seemed to agree with you about Kiersten's pot. Said it was the best he'd ever come across."

"Told ya," Hawk replied. "The shit we tried the other night was pretty damn good. Best I've ever had. This girl really seems to know her stuff."

"She damn well better." Viper leaned back in his chair as he said, "We'll be putting a lot on the line if we go into business with her, especially if we bring both the Carolina chapters into it."

"I think they'll be impressed with what she has to offer. They shouldn't have any problem moving it." The intense expression on Viper's face started to fade when Hawk said, "Hell, I'd be surprised if they didn't want more than the twenty pounds they agreed to."

Viper had good reason to be relieved. A pound of marijuana typically brought anywhere between two and three grand, but Kiersten had the potential of making even more—which meant we, along with our North and South Carolina chapters, stood to make anywhere between fifty and sixty grand a month. That, along with what we pulled from the two strip clubs and our nightly coke sales meant we would be eating high on the hog. Viper almost smiled as he said, "Guess we'll see about that."

"So, we're doing this?" I asked.

"It's definitely looking that way." Viper stood, then let out a deep breath. "Axel and I need to get with Menace, crunch some bottom-line numbers, and then we'll need to take a vote on it. I'll call church as soon as we get everything sorted."

"Sounds good."

"I best get to it. You boys try and stay out of trouble."

"We'll do our best," Hawk answered.

When Viper walked out of the kitchen, I quickly got up and followed him out into the hall. "Hey, Prez ... You got a minute?"

"Yeah, what's on your mind?"

"Need to talk to you about something."

"All right." He opened the door to his office and said, "Come on in and tell me what's going on."

Dread washed over me as I followed him inside and over to his desk. Once we were both seated, I said, "I should've come to you days ago, but with everything that's been happening—"

"What's this about, brother?"

"Kiersten."

"Kiersten as in Billy's daughter, Kiersten?"

"Yes, sir, that's exactly who I'm talking about."

"I'm not going to like this, am I?"

"Probably not, but it's something you need to hear."

I sat back and told him about the night at the bar. I made it clear that neither of us knew about our unlikely connection until we met again at Langford Manor. Viper's brows furrowed as he asked, "You're sure she had no idea who you were?"

"I'm positive. It was just a crazy coincidence."

"You can say that again." Viper ran his hand over his goatee. "Well, it is what it is. Don't see why this should cause any issues with our partnership with Kiersten. You two are both grown adults, and things happen. It's over now, so we—"

"That's just it, Prez. I'm not so sure it's over."

"Come again."

"I like her, Prez. I like her a lot." It felt strange to say it out loud. I'd never really done the whole relationship thing. It wasn't that I didn't want to. It just wasn't me. I never had the desire to truly pursue a woman—at least not after we'd hooked up. We'd both get what we were after and move on, but for reasons I couldn't explain, I hadn't been able to move on from Kiersten. I had no idea how to explain that to Viper, so I simply said, "I'm not sure I want it to be over with her."

"Oh hell, Country," Viper groaned. "You sure it's not just your dick talking?"

"Don't get me wrong, Prez, he's got plenty to say when it comes to her, but it's more than that. There's something about her..."

"You know, it would be nice if just one of y'all... *just one,* would find a girl without some kind of fucked-up strings attached. I mean, damn, we've had it all—a father in the cartel, issues with dirty cops, a crazy ex-husband, a brother who caused the club problems, and even had one on the run. Now, we've got you and Kiersten."

"Well, you did end up letting Danny prospect, and he's a Sinner now, so I'm not so sure that one should even count."

"This is not the time, Country."

"I know. And I get that Kiersten isn't exactly an easy choice, I really do, but that doesn't change anything. It certainly doesn't change how I feel, but at the same time, you gotta know I'd never do anything to cause problems for the club."

"Yeah, I've heard that before." Viper's tone changed. "You know, it's not just the club you gotta be worried about here. If this thing goes south with you and Kiersten, you might just find Billy on your ass, and God help you if that happens."

I'd been so concerned about Viper and the club, I hadn't even considered Billy. We all knew the kind of shit he could do, even more so after all he'd done to help us with Parker. When the mafia was after her, he'd managed to make it look like she'd committed suicide and got them off her back, and no one was ever the wiser. I couldn't deny that just thinking about it was a little unsettling. Clearly amused by my state, Viper chuckled as he said, "Guess you hadn't thought about ol' Billy, huh?"

"No, can't say that I have."

"This girl worth it?"

"Yes, sir. I believe she is, but I won't know if I don't see this thing through."

"Well, do whatever it is you gotta do. Just make sure it's not something stupid that'll cause any issues with this upcoming partnership."

"I'll do my best." I stood up and added, "Thanks, Prez. I'll see ya at church."

I left Viper's office and went to the bar to join the others. I didn't mention my conversation with Viper. I just sat back and listened to Locke and Lynch as they went on and on about some brawl that had broken out at Stilettos the night before. Locke motioned his hand towards our brother as he told Shotgun, "Before we had a chance to do anything, Lynch just plowed right through them. Sent 'em flying one by one. You should've seen it."

"Just did what needed to be done." Lynch took a pull from his beer. "Glad we got those assholes out of there before they made a mess of the place."

"Yeah, no doubt about that." Clearly ready to change the subject, Lynch turned to me and asked, "Anyone heard anything from Jagger lately?"

Jagger was one of our brothers who'd found himself in a tight spot with his sister. She'd run into some trouble with her piece-of-shit boyfriend and called Jagger to come help. When he showed up at her place, Jagger discovered that the boyfriend had done a real number on her. He started laying into the asshole, and after a hard blow, the guy fell back and hit his head on the coffee table, killing him instantly. Jagger was put away for involuntary manslaughter, and there wasn't a damn thing we could do to stop it. It was hard on all of us to see our brother behind bars, but Menace took it especially hard.

The two were always close, and Menace felt an undeserved sense of guilt for not being able to do more to help him, so I wasn't surprised when Rafe replied,

"Yeah, Menace was out there a couple of days ago. He and the lawyer got him hooked up with some anger management counselor."

"What's up with that?"

"They're hoping that by talking to this chick it'll help him get an earlier parole."

"A chick, huh? Is she hot?" Lynch snickered.

"Never met her, but don't figure it matters. Jagger is pissed about the whole fucking thing." Rafe shook his head. "Doesn't think he needs anger management, and neither do I. It's just something that needs to be done to get him the hell out of there."

"I hope it fucking works. It's time for him to get his ass back home."

"No doubt." I turned to Rafe and said, "I need to get down to see him soon. Maybe we can head out there when we get all this shit settled with Kiersten and the deal."

Lynch sounded intrigued as he said, "Heard Billy's daughter has some pretty impressive weed on her hands."

"She does."

"And she grows it herself?"

"She has some help, but the process is hers, and the product is pretty fucking impressive."

Rafe was quick to add, "Definitely the best shit I've ever had."

Rafe went on to tell them about his venture into the kitchen and how he'd cleaned out the fridge, which led Locke into telling about an experience he'd had in high school. One story led into the next, and the guys would've probably stayed there all night sharing stories if Viper hadn't called us all into church.

Prez gave everyone the rundown of Kiersten's business proposal, and how we would be joining forces with our North and South Carolina chapters along with Satan's Fury to create a pipeline of sorts. Each chapter would be responsible for moving twenty pounds a month with the possibility of more if the need arose. We took a vote, and as expected, all the brothers agreed that we should move forward, and the vote went through unanimously.

I left church and went straight out to my bike. Moments later, I was on the road and driving towards Langford Manor. I had no idea what I was going to do or say when I got there. I just knew I needed to see Kiersten. I had to know if this pull I felt towards her was just in my fucking head or if it was something more. The second I knocked on the door and Kiersten opened it, I had my answer. Hell, the mere sight of her in nothing but a fucking t-shirt nearly knocked me on my ass.

"Country?" Kiersten opened the door a little wider, and it was all I could do to keep myself from taking her into my arms right then and there. "What are you doing here?"

"I came to see you."

She looked behind me, checking for any sign of my brothers before she asked, "You're alone?"

"I am."

"Is something wrong?" Before I could answer, panic filled her eyes. "Oh, are you here about the deal? Have you decided not to go through with it?"

"Not here about that." I took a step closer. "I'm here about you and only you."

I was taking a chance, but it had to be done. I stepped closer, narrowing the gap between us, and looked down at Kiersten. I carefully brushed a strand of hair from her face before lowering my mouth to hers. I feared she might pull away, but instead, she wrapped her arms around my neck and kissed me back with the mother of all kisses.

My hand fell to the nape of her neck, and I gently pulled her closer. A shudder ran through Kiersten's body as she parted her lips, giving me full access to delve deeper. Our tongues tangled, and I knew this one kiss would never be enough. Just as things were starting to get heated, Kiersten placed her hands on my chest, pulled back, and inhaled a deep breath. As she slowly exhaled, she muttered, "Come inside and close the door."

As soon as the door was closed, Kiersten looked up at me and asked, "You said you came here about me. What does that mean?"

"I think you know." I brought my hand up to her face and gently ran my thumb across her bottom lip. "The question is... did I make the right choice in coming here?"

"I'm not sure what you mean."

"I don't do the whole relationship thing, Kiersten. Don't even know if I'm capable, but since that night in the bar, I haven't been able to get you out of my head."

Her eyes were fixed on mine as she whispered, "I can't seem to stop thinking about you either."

"So, what are we going to do about that?"

"I guess there's only one thing we can do."

The words had barely left her mouth when she was back in my arms, and we were kissing once again. Damn, she felt fucking incredible. I'd watched my brothers fall for their ol' ladies and the way they'd moved mountains to claim them. At the time, I didn't get it. I thought they were crazy to get tied down to just one woman, but now, I finally understood why. Everything about Kiersten, from her sheer will and determination to her dark brown eyes and warm smile had me spiraling in ways I never had before.

She'd cast some kind of spell on me, and I'd let myself get drawn in. Now, the time had come for me to decide what I'd do about it. I could take a chance with her or walk away before things got even more complicated. The decision might've been easier if she didn't feel so fucking good in my arms again. I pulled back from our embrace and said, "I'm gonna fuck this up."

"Maybe. Maybe not. There's only one way to find out."

"You need to be sure about this. You've got a lot on the line here, and I—"

Before I could finish, she whispered, "Country, stop. I'm sure. I want this just as much as you do."

"No, *Country* is for my brothers. When it's just you and me, call me Grayson."

"Grayson," she whispered.

Unable to wait any longer, I slipped my arm around Kiersten's waist and drew her closer as I lowered my mouth to hers. I couldn't believe how good she felt—like her body was meant to be next to mine. When she inched her way closer, I was done. I delved deeper, tasting and teasing her, driving us both crazy with need. I felt a smile creep along her lips as her hands slowly drifted over my chest. She knew she was getting to me, and she liked it. "You're an evil, evil woman."

"What can I say?" she purred. "You bring it out in me."

"Is that right? Well, let's see what else you've got."

I lowered my hands to her hips and lifted her. The second I took a step forward, her legs instinctively made their way around my waist. My breath caught when she grazed her center against my throbbing erection. Knowing there was just a tiny piece of fabric between us was driving me crazy and hearing all her little moans and whimpers sent my desire for this woman rushing through me like a fucking wildfire. When we finally made it up to Kiersten's room, I carried her over to the foot of the bed and slowly lowered her feet to the floor.

Those beautiful wanton eyes met mine once again, and I warned her, "This isn't going to be like it was in the bar. I'm going to take my time with you. I'm going to fuck you long and hard, and when I'm done, I'm going to fuck you again."

As soon as the words left my mouth, she pulled the t-shirt over her head and stood before me with her perfect, bare breasts and black lace panties, waiting for me to make my move. Damn, I'd never seen a more incredible sight. From head to toe, the woman was positively flawless. Just looking at her made it difficult to keep it together, and seeing that spark of eagerness only made it even more so as I kicked off my boots and removed my shirt.

I dropped my hands to her waist and slowly lowered her sexy little body onto the bed. Impatient for more, her hands quickly dropped to her hips as she slowly slid her panties, inch by inch, down her long legs. Kiersten's eyes never left mine as she kicked them off the bed. She lay there, her naked body sprawled across the quilt as she waited for me to come to her. "Do you have any idea how beautiful you are?"

"Show me."

"Oh, I am. You can fucking count on it."

With that, the dam broke, and all my resistance was washed away. I had to have her. My eyes drifted down her body, her delicious curves calling me as I lowered myself onto the bed next to her. Goosebumps rose along her skin as I began tracing the slope of her breast with my fingertips. She was stunning, every damn inch of her. My mouth moved to her neck, kissing and nipping gently at her soft skin before traveling to her collarbone and then her breast. I rolled my tongue around her nipple and watched with satisfaction as her back arched off the bed, silently pleading for more. I trailed kisses along her stomach ever so slowly, teasing her before settling myself between her legs. I hovered over her, teasing her sensitive flesh with the heat of my breath. She arched her back and shifted her hips as she pleaded, "Grayson, please."

"You want my mouth?"

She nodded.

"Say the words, Kiersten."

"Yes, Grayson," she rasped.

Without waiting a second longer, I lowered my head between her legs and ran my tongue slightly across her center, teasing her, tormenting her as she squirmed beneath me. Damn, everything about her had me burning for more. I never dreamed I could want anyone like I wanted her.

Kiersten gasped and her back arched off the bed as I pressed the flat of my tongue against her clit. I loved seeing her come apart, knowing that I was in complete control as I watched her body respond to my touch. I wanted to make her come undone, to hear all of her little gasps and whimpers again and again as I pushed her to the edge of her release.

"G-Grayson," she stammered and threaded her fingers into my hair, guiding me as her knees widened. With the sounds of her moans echoing through the room, I eased my fingers deep inside her and searched for the spot that would drive her wild. When I found it, I covered her with my mouth, teasing her until her body started to tremble beneath me. Kiersten's hands dropped to her sides and clutched at the sheets, tugging them tightly as her orgasm surged through her body like a bolt of lightning. Gasping for air, I could hear her mumble, "Yes, God, yes."

She was still lost in the haze of her release when I stood up and removed my jeans and boxers. I quickly pulled on a condom, then lowered my body on top of hers. Eager for more, she spread her thighs and wrapped both legs around my waist, pulling me close and grinding her hips against mine. I raked my throbbing erection against her, and as soon as I felt the warmth of her center, I whispered, "Are you ready for me, beautiful?"

"Yes," was the only word she could muster.

I knew right then that I'd never get tired of hearing that breathy, desirous tone in her voice. She pressed her lips to mine in a possessive, demanding kiss, and using her legs to pull me forward, I felt her tremble beneath me as I slid deep inside her, giving her every aching inch of my cock. Fuck, she was so tight, so warm and wet, engulfing me in pure splendor. After pausing for several breaths, I started moving, slowly rocking against her.

I watched as Kiersten writhed beneath me, her neck and chest flushed pink with desire, and her eyes clenched shut while lost in all the sensations. The mere sight of her called to me, making me want to claim her, and as much as that thought rattled me, nothing was going to stop me.

I lowered my mouth to hers, kissing her deep and rough before I started to increase my pace. I thrust against her, hard and demanding, and she moaned with pleasure when I hit the spot that drove her wild. With the same fever-pitched rhythm, our hips rolled and slammed into each other. Kiersten didn't hold back, but instead met my every move, letting me know without words exactly what she wanted. Her nails dug into my lower back as she lifted her hips, trying to force me deeper, and when she started to tighten around me, there was no question that she was getting close. I could feel the pressure building, forcing a growl from my chest, and began pounding harder as her head reared back, and she cried, "Don't stop!"

I couldn't wait to see her orgasm take hold once again, to hear those little sounds she made over and over. "That's right, baby girl. Come for me."

Unable to stop the inevitable torment of her impending climax, the muscles in her body grew taut as her thighs clamped around my hips. She held her breath for several moments until her body began to quiver, and a rush of air escaped from her lungs.

I could feel my release quickly approaching and tried to resist it, hoping to prolong the moment, but it was a losing battle. The sound of my skin pounding against hers echoed throughout the room as I drove into her a few more times, and with one last deep-seated thrust, I buried my cock inside her, and my orgasm finally took hold.

After several deep breaths, I lowered myself down on her chest. I rested there for a brief moment, then rolled onto my back, slid off the condom, and tossed it in the wastebasket next to her night table. When I pulled her over to me, she placed her head on my shoulder, the palm of her hand on my chest, and a satisfied smile on her face. "You are really something."

"Right back at ya, babe."

"I'm really glad you came here tonight."

"Me, too."

She eased up on her elbow and studied me as her teeth toyed with her bottom lip. "You got something on your mind?"

"I was just wondering how this"—she motioned her hand between us—"is going to work if my deal goes through with the club or if it doesn't."

"Either way, we'll figure it out." I could tell she was anxious and as much as I wanted to ease her mind about the deal, it wasn't my place. Besides, I knew it wouldn't be long before Viper would be reaching out to her. I leaned over and kissed her on the forehead. "'Cause after tonight, there's no way in hell I can just walk away."

A soft smile crossed Kiersten's face as she whispered, "That's good because I kind of like having you here."

"I hope you mean that."

"I definitely do."

After a short recovery time, I was pleased to see

that she was more than willing to have another go and then another. By morning, we were both completely spent and sleeping soundly when Kiersten's phone started to ring. She grabbed it from the side table, and her eyes widened when she saw that it was Viper calling. I already knew what he was going to say, so I simply gave her a nod and waited as she answered the call. The second she started smiling, I knew he'd confirmed the deal. I also knew it was going to be a while before we got out of bed, and there was no place I'd rather be.

EIGHT

KIERSTEN

I couldn't believe it. I'd gotten the guy and the deal—something I never dreamed was possible. I should've felt like I was walking on cloud nine, but instead, I was freaking out in a way I never had before. I didn't know if it was the fact that I was on the back of a motorcycle for the first time or that Grayson was taking me to the Ruthless Sinners' clubhouse for a meet with Viper, but I was struggling to keep it together. When I tightened my grip around his waist, Grayson glanced back over his shoulder and shouted, "You okay back there?"

"I'm trying to be."

Without any warning, he immediately slowed and turned onto an old road on the backside of town. As soon as he was parked, he got off and removed his helmet. "What's going on in that head of yours?"

"Nothing... I mean, I don't know." I brought my hands up to my face, shielding myself from Grayson's skeptical eyes as I muttered, "*Everything.*"

"Sorry, babe, but you're gonna have to give me more than that."

I looked up at him as I admitted, "I've never been to a clubhouse before."

"It's just a clubhouse. It's no different than Langford Manor."

"Easy for you to say." I rolled my eyes. "It's *your* clubhouse."

"What exactly are you worried about here?"

"I don't know. I'm just nervous, I guess."

I thought back to the night before and how wonderful it had been. We were still getting to know one another, but I liked the way I felt safe when I was with Grayson. Considering my issues with trust, it wasn't something that came easily for me. But he made it so easy. Just like now—when most men would've just tossed back some reassuring words, Grayson actually took the time to stop and talk to me. I could see the concern in his eyes when he asked, "What do you have to be nervous about? You got the deal with the club. It's easy sailing from here."

"It's far from easy sailing, Grayson. This is the Ruthless Sinners you're talking about."

"Yeah, and?"

"And they're pretty freaking terrifying. You don't know how close I came to bolting when Viper walked into that coffee shop."

My heart started racing at the thought, and I feared I might have a panic attack right there on the side of the road. Grayson, on the other hand, found the whole thing amusing. He chuckled as he said, "Let me get this straight. The girl who had the balls to hack into Menace's laptop, then use what she'd found to set up a meet with the Sinners, and not only met with them but also had them come out to her place to work out a business deal is now having second thoughts?"

"I'm not having second thoughts. I'm just nervous about being on their turf instead of mine. What if something goes wrong?" With my helmet still on, I dropped my head on his shoulder and sighed. "I don't know why I thought I could do this. I just got caught up in this whole charade of mine, and now I'm terrified that I might not be able to pull it off."

"You've come too far to start thinking like that." He reached over and placed his hand under my chin, forcing my head up so I'd look at him. "You've got this. I know you do."

"Okay, you're right." I inhaled a deep breath. "I just need to pull it together."

Grayson smiled warmly at me. "You good to get back on the road?"

"Yes, I think so." While he put on his helmet, I said, "Thank you. I don't think I would've made it this far if it hadn't been for you."

"Nah, something tells me you would've done just fine."

He gave me a wink, then got back on and started the engine. He had no idea how much our little chat had helped me. While I was still nervous, I wasn't completely freaking out. I just had to make it through the next twenty-four hours, and then maybe I could breathe easy again. Grayson eased back onto the road, and it wasn't long before we were in the Nashville city limits. I'd been there hundreds of times but seeing it now on Grayson's bike made it seem like a whole new world. The sounds, the smells, and even the colors were more pronounced. With the wind whipping around us, I finally understood why he loved riding his motorcycle so much.

After a few quick turns, we pulled up to a ware-house with a ten-foot fence around the perimeter and a gate with two Sinners standing guard. As soon as they motioned us through, my nerves returned, and my stomach twisted into a knot. Grayson pulled up to the front and parked, then extended his hand to help me off the back before throwing his leg over the bike. Once we'd removed our helmets, he asked, "You good?"

"I've been better, but I'm okay."

"It'll be fine. You'll see."

I was glad he was with me as we headed inside. We'd barely made it through the door when I heard a familiar voice say, "It's about time you two got here. We were beginning to think you got lost or something."

"What's wrong, sunshine?" Grayson chuckled as he looked over to Rafe. "You miss me?"

"You know better than that shit."

"Mm-hmm. Whatever you say, boss." Grayson's smile faded as he asked, "Prez around?"

"Yeah, he and Axel are in his office waiting for you." Rafe was sitting at the bar with Hawk and two men I'd never met before. Rafe looked over to me and smiled. "Good to see you again, Kiersten."

"Good to see you, too, Rafe."

"We better get going." Grayson nodded for me to follow. "We don't want to keep Viper waiting."

"Okay." I gave Rafe a quick wave and said, "Hope to see ya later."

"I'm sure you will."

Grayson led me out of the bar and down a long, dark hallway lined with various doors. I was so busy taking in my surroundings that I'd almost forgotten I was about to meet with Viper, but the realization hit me the second Grayson stopped at the end of the hall. I was expecting my heart to start racing again or my throat to close up, but neither happened. Instead, I remained perfectly calm as Grayson tapped on the door and stuck his head inside. After a few brief words, he motioned me inside. "Good luck."

"Wait... You aren't coming with me?"

"No, babe. This is all you."

"Seriously?" I inhaled a deep breath, then let it out slowly. "Okay, I've got this."

"I know you do." He leaned down and kissed me on the forehead. "I'll be waiting in the bar when you're done."

I nodded, then stepped into the office. Viper was sitting behind a large desk, and there was a man sitting in front of him. The man stood and extended his hand as he said, "You must be Kiersten."

"Yes, sir. I am."

"Good to meet ya. I'm Axel. The club's VP." He was older, maybe in his late forties, but like Viper, he was tall, muscular, and clearly able to handle himself. He pulled out the chair next to him and said, "Make yourself comfortable."

"Thank you."

Once I was seated, Viper looked over to me. "I appreciate you coming down to meet with us. I know you're busy, but I didn't want any distractions while we discussed the final details of our agreement."

"I understand, and I was more than happy to come." I shifted in my seat, trying to make myself a little more comfortable. "I'm eager to hear your thoughts on how this should play out."

"Hawk has already discussed some of the ground rules. Before we continue, I want to be sure that you understand our expectations." He leaned forward and clasped his hands on his desk. "Your safety is a priority to us. We don't want to put *you* or our partnership in danger. In order to do that, we must limit your exposure. Your sales to the college have to stop, and we will become your primary source of distribution."

"I understand." While I wasn't exactly thrilled about losing the college sales, I knew Viper was right. I was putting my entire operation in danger every time I sold on that campus, and I was more than happy to take that risk out of the equation. Besides, with them taking over distribution, I could put all my focus into my production—where I'd always wanted it to be. Maybe then, I could do more to help those in need. "I just have one request... actually two requests."

"Okay, let's hear them."

"I don't want my father involved in any of this. I want to keep it between us—at least for now."

"I respect Billy and appreciate what he's done for our club. I don't want any grievances to arise because you've chosen not to discuss your work with him. You should consider talking to him."

"He never talked to me about the work he was

doing with you, and I'm fairly certain you wouldn't want him to either."

Axel raised his eyebrow as he looked over to Viper and said, "She's got a point there, Prez."

"That she does." Viper's brows furrowed as he asked, "So, what's your other request?"

"I had my reasons for going into this line of business, and it wasn't just to make money. While that's been great, and I hope it continues, I started this whole process in hopes of helping people. That's very important to me." I swallowed hard, praying that Viper wouldn't shoot me down. "I have a few people I donate my product to. Most are suffering from cancer, while others have issues with chronic pain from injuries or crippling migraines like my mother had."

"And you want to continue supplying to these people?"

"Yes, it's extremely important to me and to them." He didn't immediately respond, so I added, "You can look into each and every one of them. You will see that they genuinely need the help and—"

"I don't see any problem with you continuing to supply these folks. In fact, I might have a few more to add to that list."

"That would be great." Feeling an overwhelming sense of relief, I rested back in my chair and asked, "Okay, so I guess it's time for us to discuss numbers."

"Yes, it is." Viper eased back and crossed his arms, taking on a look of authority. "We've examined the expense reports you sent us and understand there's a great deal of cost that goes into your production. With that in mind, we will strictly focus on the profits. We're willing to go sixty-forty after all expenses have been paid."

"Sixty-forty?" I sat up straight and gasped. "You've got to be kidding me? I'm the one supplying the goods."

"And we're the ones who are taking all the risks in moving the product." His tone remained firm as he continued, "We're not trying to take advantage here, Kiersten. You'll still bring home a great deal of money, and with us running the distribution, you can put your focus into your work."

"And all expenses will be handled first, including what I pay my people?"

"Absolutely."

"Okay, I can agree on that."

"Good. I plan on coming out to your place this week to take a look at your operation for myself. And when I do, I'll be bringing two of the brothers along with me, who'll be staying there to help out with security. They'll rotate out each week and—"

"Wait! That's not necessary. I have Braylon, and Riggs has—"

"I know all about the security system Riggs set up

for you, and while it's impressive, he and I both agree that you need more than three men to watch over everything."

"You spoke to Riggs?"

"Of course, I did. I owe it to you and to Fury to be fully informed about Langford Manor, including what kind of security you have and who's in charge of it. And frankly, Braylon and the other two just aren't enough."

"Okay, if you think they need to be there, then that's what we'll do."

"I'm glad you agree."

"So, that covers everything, right?"

"I believe it does." Viper stood and extended his hand. "We look forward to doing business with you."

I shook his hand and then Axel's as I replied, "And I look forward to working with you as well."

"I hope you'll hang around for a while." Axel smiled as he said, "The boys have a little celebration planned for later tonight."

Grayson and I were planning on heading back tonight, but after that night by the fire, I was intrigued by the idea of a party with him and his brothers. "Sure, I'd love to."

"I'll let them know that you'll be there."

I nodded, then headed out of the office and started back down the hall. I was tempted to open one of the many doors, just to see what was inside the different rooms, but decided against it when I noticed one of the brothers walking in my direction. He was around my age, extremely handsome with dirty blond hair, and a friendly smile. When he approached, he gave me a quick once over and said, "You must be Kiersten."

"I am." I was feeling pretty good after my meeting with Viper, so I smiled and asked, "And you are?"

"The guys call me Locke."

"It's nice to meet ya, Locke."

"You coming to the party tonight?"

Before I could answer, Grayson stepped into the hallway and growled, "Time to move on, Locke."

"What?" He turned and gave Country an innocent smile. "I was just asking the pretty lady if she'd be at the party tonight."

"I know exactly what you were doing, and I'm telling ya it's time to move on," Grayson barked.

Locke threw his hands up in surrender as he stepped back and said, "Okay, brother. Point taken."

Without another word, Locke turned and disappeared down the hall. Once he was gone, I stepped over to Grayson and asked, "What was that all about?"

"You know exactly what it was about."

"He was just being nice."

"He was trying to get in your fucking pants."

"I doubt that, but even if he was, there's only one

Sinner that's gettin' in these pants."

Grayson cocked his eyebrow. "Is that an invitation?"

"Absolutely." I smiled as I slipped my arms around his waist. "But it'll have to wait until later 'cause we've got some celebrating to do."

"Oh yeah?"

"Mm-hmm. My meeting with Viper went even better than I expected."

"That's what I'm talking about." He leaned down and gave me a kiss. "I knew you had nothing to worry about."

"Well, I wasn't so sure, but I really think this could be a great deal for all of us."

"I'm sure it will be." He slipped his arm around my back, inching me closer as he teased. "Now, what about that invitation?"

"I'm ready when you are." The words had barely left my mouth when I was lifted into the air and tossed over Grayson's shoulder. "Grayson! I thought we were going to wait until later!"

Ignoring me, he continued down the hall, then suddenly stopped and opened a door, revealing a small bedroom that reminded me of a hotel room. I didn't have time to notice much more before Grayson lowered me to my feet and pinned me against the wall. He didn't speak but simply planted his lips on mine and began devouring my mouth with a kiss that made my knees tremble. He dropped his hands to the button of my jeans and quickly lowered the zipper. Seconds later, his hand was between my legs, and he was raking his fingers across my center. "I'm glad you're ready for me, baby, because we don't have time for all the bells and whistles. We gotta be quick. The guys will be waiting for us."

"I'm good with quick."

I kicked off my boots and made fast work of my jeans and panties. When I turned back to Grayson, he was standing in front of me with his jeans lowered to his hips and rolling on a condom. I barely had time to blink before he picked me up and again had my back pinned against the wall as I wrapped my legs around him. He slammed into me with one hard thrust, filling me entirely. I clung to him as he continued in an urgent pace. It wasn't long before I felt that familiar churn in my abdomen. My orgasm was coming hard and fast just like Grayson's rhythm. I cried out as my release crashed over me, and Grayson soon followed as we continued to cling to one another.

After a minute or so, I looked up at him and smiled. "That might've been quick, but I'm pretty sure I heard some bells and a whistle."

"Well, if you thought you heard them now, just wait until later tonight."

NINE

COUNTRY

I never thought a woman would be able to wrap me around her finger, but Kiersten had done it. And she'd done it without even trying. Hell, I couldn't take my eyes off her as she sat at one of the back tables talking with Parker and the other ol' ladies. They were all laughing and carrying on as they tossed back a few beers, and I was pleased to see that she fit right in. I knew she would. Kiersten had this undeniable charm that drew everyone in and had them coming back for more. I watched as she glanced over her shoulder, searching for me in the crowd. As soon as our eyes met, a warm smile crossed her face, and it got me right in the gut.

"Damn, boy. You got it bad."

"What are you talking about?

"You know damn well what I'm talking about." Rafe

motioned his head towards Kiersten as he said, "I've known you a long damn time, and never once have I seen you look at a chick the way you were looking at her."

"I was just making sure she was all right. You know how vicious the ol' ladies can be."

"Yeah, they're a regular pack of wolves." Rafe took a pull from his beer. "I don't think you have anything to worry about. She seems to be holding her own."

I glanced back over at Kiersten, and I couldn't help but smile when I caught her laughing at something one of the girls had said. "Yeah, she does."

"You planning on heading back with her tomorrow?"

"Yeah, Viper and Lynch are coming, too. After he gives everything a good once over, Viper will head back, and Lynch and I will stay for the remainder of the week."

"You thought about how this thing is gonna work with you two?"

"Well, Lynch isn't exactly my type, so it shouldn't be an issue."

Rafe's tone turned serious. "I'm not fucking around, Country."

"I don't know what to tell ya. I guess we'll just take things day by day and see how it plays out."

"That's fine, but don't fuck it up." Rafe motioned

his head at the back table. "Or that pack of wolves over there will have your ass."

Rafe gave me one of his looks, then turned and headed over to the back table to check on Marlowe. I finished off my beer, then turned and motioned to Caitlyn, one of the club's hang-arounds, signaling I needed another. She nodded, then reached into the cooler to grab me a cold one. Caitlyn was a cute blonde with a killer figure, and she always made a point to show it off by wearing low-cut tops and skin-tight miniskirts. Everyone knew she had a bit of a thing for me, so I wasn't surprised when she sauntered over with a seductive smile. She placed my beer down on the counter, then leaned forward, making sure I saw every inch of her cleavage as she purred. "Here ya go, handsome."

"Thanks, Caitlyn."

"You having a good night?"

"Yeah, I can't complain."

"Well, if you're looking to make it better, I'm free later tonight." She inched a little closer. "I'll show ya a real good time."

"I'm sure you would, but—"

"He's got other plans," Kiersten interrupted. "He's got some bells and whistles to tend to."

"Excuse me?" Caitlyn glanced back over to me

with confusion. "Bells and whistles? What the hell is she talking about?"

I didn't answer. Instead, I slipped my arm around Kiersten's waist and pulled her closer. "I thought you were still with the girls."

"I was." Her eyes skirted over to Caitlyn as she said, "I just came over to get another beer."

"Mm-hmm. Okay." I looked over to Caitlyn. "You heard the woman. She needs a beer."

Caitlyn rolled her eyes and huffed as she whipped around and headed over to the cooler. Kiersten was glaring at her as she asked me, "Who is that anyway?"

"That would be Caitlyn. She's one of the club's hang-arounds who helps out at the bar from time to time." Remembering our earlier conversation about Locke, I decided to use her words against her and said, "You've got nothing to worry about, babe. She was just being nice."

Realizing what I was doing, she cocked her eyebrow and sassed, "Really? That's how you're gonna play this?"

"You know," I lowered my mouth to her ear and whispered, "You're beautiful when you're jealous."

"I'm not jealous, Grayson. I was just asking who she was."

"Whatever you say, boss." I grabbed the beer

Caitlyn had left for her on the counter and handed it to her. "You having fun with the girls?"

"I'm having a great time with them." She glanced over her shoulder, making sure no one could hear then lowered her voice and said, "They're nothing like I expected. I mean, I met Parker when she and Menace were at Dad's, and she seemed super nice, but even she's different than I thought she'd be."

"Not sure what you mean."

"It's hard to explain. I spent weeks watching them on your security feed." My back immediately stiffened, causing her to wince. "I know that's a touchy subject, and I'm sorry about that, but it's not something I can take back."

"Just finish what you were saying."

"Okay, well, I saw them on the surveillance footage. They were all so beautiful and seemed so self-assured. When they got together, they looked like they'd been best friends forever. I guess I just thought they wouldn't be quite as welcoming as they've been."

"They're cool girls. You've got nothing to worry about there." Hearing how she'd watched our security feed spurred a thought—one I'd failed to consider until that very moment. "So, did you see me on that security footage?"

"Well, yeah... Many times."

Kiersten answered like it was no big deal, but to

me, it was huge. *The deal of all deals*. I immediately became enraged—not just at her but at myself. I couldn't believe I'd been so fucking stupid. I'd known all along that she'd hacked into Menace's computer and had gained access to our security footage. I should've put two and two together and realized that she'd seen me on it, but for whatever reason, it just hadn't sunk in —more than likely because I didn't want it to. I wanted to believe Kiersten was telling the truth when she said she didn't know who I was the night we met at that bar, and it hit hard to discover that she hadn't been honest with me.

A million thoughts raced through my head, but I was too angry to speak. I needed a minute to collect my thoughts and get the hell out of there before something came out of my mouth that I would regret. So, I removed my hand from her waist and stormed out the back exit of the bar. The door slammed behind me but not before I heard Kiersten call out my name. I paced back and forth, grumbling curses as I chastised myself for being such a fucking idiot. I didn't know how long I'd been out there when I heard Shotgun. "Something wrong, brother?"

"You could say that."

I turned and found him leaning against the exterior wall smoking a cigarette, so I walked over and joined him. He pulled out his pack of smokes from the inside of his cut and offered me one. "What seems to be the trouble?"

"You know how Kiersten got access to our surveillance footage?"

"Oh, yeah. I know all about it." The end of Shotgun's cigarette glowed when he took another drag. "I still can't believe she managed to pull that shit off."

"Yeah, me neither, but she did. And she saw me on it."

"Sorry, brother. I don't see the issue here."

"Never mind." I shook my head and grumbled, "It's not important."

"This got something to do with the fact you two got a thing going?"

"You know about that, huh?"

"It's my job to know." I wasn't surprised by his response. Shotgun was the club's enforcer, and it was his job to protect the brothers. To do that, he made it his business to know everything that went on with us, inside the club and out. "Okay, she saw you on the surveillance footage. I figure she saw all of us, so what's the problem?"

"She said she didn't know I was a Sinner when we met at the bar."

"Well, she ever given you reason not to believe her?"

"No, but you gotta admit the whole thing's a bit of

a stretch. I mean, damn, look at the lengths she went to just to meet with us."

"Yeah, but she came clean about what she'd found on Menace's laptop and why she'd done it. So, what reason would she have to lie about knowing who you were in that bar? It's not like fucking a brother was gonna get her foot in the door. If nothing else, it'd hurt her more than it would help."

Shotgun was right. Kiersten didn't gain any leverage that night. She never asked me anything about the club or my being a Sinner, and I certainly didn't bring it up. I wasn't even wearing my cut. "Damn, you're right."

"I usually am."

"I'm just not good at this shit." I felt like a complete asshole. I should've stopped for two fucking seconds and thought the whole thing through before storming out of the bar like a fucking two-year-old. I ran my hand down my face and groaned. "I knew I'd fuck it up."

"Don't be too hard on yourself. We all make mistakes. I certainly made my fair share with Remington." He tossed his cigarette and ground it into the dirt with his boot. "Just talk to her. I'm sure you two can sort it out."

"I showed my ass, brother. Doubt she's gonna wanna talk to me."

"Give her some time. She'll come around."

"Maybe." I wasn't quite ready to admit my mistake, so I lifted what was left of my cigarette and asked, "Mind if I have another?"

When I tossed the butt on the ground, Shotgun handed me another, and I immediately lit it. After taking in a long drag, I leaned my head back against the brick wall and exhaled slowly, letting the smoke billow above us. Shotgun didn't say a word. He simply stood there with me while I collected my thoughts. Once I was done with my smoke, I tossed the finished cigarette to the ground, then we both started for the back door.

I'd like to say I was feeling better about things as we headed inside, but I wasn't. Things were going pretty fucking good with Kiersten, better than I could've ever anticipated, and I hated that I might've screwed it all up by assuming the worst. I expected to walk in the bar and find her mad as an old wet hen, but that wasn't the case—*far from it.* Instead, I found her back over at the table with the girls, and she looked like she was having herself a grand ol' time. They were all laughing and carrying on even more than they were before and were tossing back what looked to be their third round of tequila shots. I was standing there watching them all wince and groan from the burn of the liquor when Lynch came up behind me and asked, "Where'd you run off to?"

"Just went to get some air."

"Well, your girl was looking for ya." Lynch snickered as he glanced over at the back table. "And she was pretty pissed you disappeared on her. Was even talking about leaving, but Parker and Marlowe managed to convince her to stay."

Even though Kiersten had ridden here with me, I had no doubt she would've found a way home if she really wanted to. With that in mind, I replied, "I'll talk to her."

"You better, 'cause I don't wanna spend the next two weeks up there at her place with you two fussin' and shit."

"We aren't fussin'. Just a misunderstanding."

He cocked his eyebrow. "That's where the fussin' starts."

"Yeah, well, *I'm gonna fix it before the fussin' ever starts.*"

"Mm-hmm." He reached over the counter and grabbed us both a cold one from the cooler. As he offered one to me, he suggested, "I'd give those shots a little time to soak in before you try and *fix it.*"

"Not a bad idea."

I sat down next to him and took a slug of my beer as I glanced back over at Kiersten. She and Parker were leaned in close and whispering to one another. Kiersten's smile faded, and she started shaking her head. I assumed they were talking about me, but when Kiersten glanced over her shoulder and glared at me, I was certain of it. She held my gaze for several moments, then turned her attention back to Parker. After seeing our little exchange, Lynch leaned over to me and chuckled. "I think she's gonna need another shot or two."

"I think you might be right."

I called over to Caitlyn and sent her over to the girls' table with another round of shots—which they all took without complaint. In fact, they ordered one more round, and it wasn't long before they all started feeling the effects of the added alcohol. Their laughter became borderline obnoxious and their words even more slurred, but sadly, that fiery look in Kiersten's eyes remained. The girls were getting a little out of hand, so it was no surprise when the brothers started gathering their women and headed home. Kiersten was still talking with Parker when I walked over to them. "You about ready to call it a night?"

"Nooo, act-ually, *I'm not.*" She motioned her hand over to Parker as she said, "We-ee were just about to have an-nother drink."

"I think you two have had enough."

"Well, nooo-body asked you, *sooo ...*"

"He's right." Parker slurred as she reached over and placed her hand on Kiersten's arm. "I'm gonna lose my stomach if I have another shot. Besides, you guys have things to talk about."

Parker stood, then immediately started to sway. I quickly reached over and took a hold of her arm, keeping her steady as I quickly scanned the bar for Menace. When I didn't spot him, I motioned over to Lynch and told him, "Get Menace and let him know I'm taking Parker down to his room."

"Sure, man."

"You don't have to take me," Parker mumbled as she tried to keep her balance. "I can get there on my own."

"Yeah, I'm sure you can, but I'm gonna take ya just the same." I glanced down at Kiersten and ordered, "Stay put until I get back."

With a roll of her eyes and a grumble, she replied, "Whatever you say, boss."

I shook my head and let out a deep breath as I led Parker out of the bar and down the hall. We hadn't gotten far when she slurred, "She's *reeal-ly* mad at you."

"I know."

"You hurt her feelings."

"I know."

"You gotta fix it."

"Gonna try."

"You better." Parker glanced up at me with a scornful look. "We like her."

"I like her, too." I opened Menace's door and helped her over to the bed. Once she was seated, I asked, "You good?"

"Mm-hmm." She leaned over and dropped her head down on the pillow. "Thank you, Country."

"No problem."

When I started for the door, Parker mumbled, "Country?"

"Yeah?"

"You're a really good guy. She'd be lucky to have ya." She rolled over and curled into the blankets. "Make sure she knows that."

I didn't respond. I simply closed the door and headed back to the bar to find Kiersten. When I walked in, I was surprised to find that she was no longer sitting at the back table. In fact, she wasn't in the bar at all. Most of the place was already cleared out, so I stepped over to Caitlyn and asked, "You seen Kiersten?"

"Who?" I gave her a fierce look, and she immediately pointed to the back door. "Oh... I'm pretty sure she went outside."

As soon as the words left her mouth, I charged over to the back door and stormed outside. I took a quick look around, but I didn't see her. Worried something might've happened to her, I shouted, *"Kiersten!"*

"Stop yelling." I whipped around and found her sitting on the ground with her back against the brick wall. "I'm right here."

"I thought I told you to wait for me inside."

"You did." She looked up at me with determination in her eyes. "But I didn't listen."

"Clearly." I walked over and sat down next to her. "I need to apologize for earlier."

"For which part? The not giving me a chance to explain or for storming off and leaving me?"

"Both."

"Hmmm." Still suffering from the effects of the alcohol, she leaned her head back on the brick wall and closed her eyes. "I didn't lie about not knowing who you were at that bar, Country."

I knew she'd used my road name on purpose. She was trying to make a point, and she did. It was loud and clear. "I fucked up, but in my defense, I told you I would."

"Yeah, you did, but I didn't think it would be so soon." She slowly turned her head in my direction and squinted at me as she mumbled, "Maybe this isn't a good idea."

"What do you mean?"

"Us." She closed her eyes and turned away from

me as she said, "It was just supposed to be a one-time thing. Maybe we should've left it at that."

"Maybe so."

It could've been my pride or the ever-growing knot in my stomach, but I didn't say anything more. I simply stood, then reached down and lifted Kiersten into my arms. She rested her head on my shoulder as I carried her back inside and down to my room. I placed her down on the bed, then took off her boots and covered her up. As much as I wanted to crawl in next to her, I didn't. Kiersten needed time to sober up and figure out what she really wanted. I wasn't going to make the decision harder than it already was, so I walked out of my room and left her there sleeping, hoping by morning, she'd see things differently.

I'd soon realize that was a mistake.

TEN

KIERSTEN

THERE WERE MANY REASONS WHY I RARELY DRANK, but mainly it was because of the morning after—the throbbing headache, the queasy stomach, and the foggy haze that took hours to get over. But the absolute worst was remembering all the stupid things I did or said while I was partaking in *said drinking* and the regret that came with it. Sadly, I wasn't thinking about that while I was partying with the girls last night. I also wasn't thinking when I got upset with Grayson and drank even more—*much, much more*. I hadn't even opened my eyes the following morning when dread washed over me. My head was pounding, my mouth felt like it was full of cotton, and I thought I would be sick. I cracked my eyes open, just enough to see that it was daylight, and that's when I realized I was alone in Grayson's bed.

I eased up from the bed with a groan, then wiped the sleep from my eyes and groaned even louder. I felt like absolute death and seeing there was no sign of Grayson didn't make me feel any better. I tossed the covers back and was about to get out of bed when I noticed a bottle of water and two Tylenol sitting on the bedside table. I reached for them both and, after swallowing the pain relievers, forced myself out of bed. In desperate need of a shower, I shuffled into the bathroom, turned on the faucet, and slowly removed my clothes; after checking the temperature, I stepped under the hot spray.

With my head dipped forward, the warmth cascaded down over my body as I rehashed the night before. I was having such a good time with Grayson, his brothers, and their ol' ladies. I couldn't remember enjoying myself more with a group of strangers. They treated me as if I belonged there—like I was one of them. That was why it hurt so much when Grayson thought I'd lied to him and stormed off without giving me a chance to explain. It also stung that he never even tried to convince me I was wrong when I said we'd made a mistake by not ending things after that night in the bar. I knew it was a stupid thing to say. I didn't really mean it. I was just drunk and being dramatic, but clearly, he found some truth in what I'd said. Otherwise, he wouldn't have left me in the bed alone—

which made me wonder where he'd ended up sleeping last night.

My mind immediately went to the scantily dressed bartender who was basically throwing herself at him at the party. The thought of him ending up in her bed had my heart hammering in my chest. I quickly finished my shower and got out to dry off. Since I hadn't packed a bag, I had no choice but to put on my dirty clothes, which didn't exactly help my state of mind. I towel dried my hair and swished around some mouthwash I found sitting on the countertop and spit it in the sink. Then, I charged out of the bathroom to hunt down Grayson, only to find him standing in the middle of the room with his arms crossed and a scowl on his face. "How ya feeling this morning?"

"I've been better. You?"

"The same."

"Hmmm." I placed my hand on my hip and glared back at him. "So, ah ... where did you end up last night?"

"You mean after you told me that seeing each other was a mistake?"

"Oh, so you're going to play it like that?"

"I'm not playing anything. I'm not the one who said it."

"Just tell me where you were."

"Where do you think I was?"

"I have no idea." I was acting like a complete ass, but I couldn't seem to stop myself. "Maybe you were with that hoochie-mama who was hitting on you last night."

"Would it bother you if I was?"

"*No*," I lied.

He cocked his eyebrow. "You sure about that?"

"Okay, fine!" I threw my hands up in the air. "Yes, it would bother me. I don't like the idea of you being with someone else."

"And why's that?"

"Because I want you to be with me, Grayson. Is that what you want to hear?"

"Yeah, as a matter of fact, it is."

"So, were you with her last night or not?"

"No, Kiersten. I slept on the couch in the family room *alone*." He stepped over to me and slipped his arms around my waist, pulling me close. "I have no desire to be with her or anyone else. I only got eyes for one girl, and she's standing right in front of me."

Hearing those words from him hit me hard. Up until that moment, I hadn't realized just how much he really meant to me. I buried my face in his chest and fought back the tears as my words came out muffled, "I want you, too. More than I realized."

"Does that mean you're done with your little tantrum?"

"I wasn't having a tantrum."

"Mm-hmm." Grayson slipped his hand under my chin, forcing me to look up at him. "I fucked up last night. I jumped to conclusions and didn't hear you out. I won't make that mistake again."

"And I won't get drunk and say things I don't mean."

"Fair enough." Mischief danced in his eyes as he teased me. "You really are cute when you get jealous."

"Just shut up and kiss me."

Without any hesitation, Grayson brought his hand up to the nape of my neck, gently pulling me to him as he lowered his mouth to mine. It is impossible to explain how good it felt to be in his arms again. I was like putty in his hands. His tongue drifted over my bottom lip, and with a slight whimper, I opened my mouth, giving him access to delve deeper. Unconscious of my own movement, I leaned towards him, and in a matter of seconds, we were both lost in the moment. There were no thoughts of our argument the night before or hesitations about the future. I knew I was right where I belonged.

Our hunger for each other escalated, causing the kiss to become wild and heated. My hands wound around his neck, and my fingers raked through his thick, dark hair as I moaned into his mouth. I was becoming completely lost in the moment when

Grayson stepped back and broke our embrace. There was no missing the sexual frustration in his voice. "You're gonna have to stop that shit right now."

"What?"

"Don't play innocent with me, woman." He motioned his head towards the door. "The guys are out there waiting for us, and you're in here trying to take advantage of me."

"Taking advantage of you?" Grayson never seemed to disappoint with his crazy sense of humor. I shook my head and giggled. "I'd never dream of doing something so outlandish."

"Mm-hmm." He gave me a playful wink. "Grab your stuff, babe. We need to get going before Viper blows a gasket."

"Okay, just give me a minute." I rushed into the bathroom and quickly combed through my wet hair, then braided it. Once I was done, I ran back out and said, "All set."

Grayson took my hand and led me out of the room, then down the hall and out the back door. When we reached the parking lot, Viper and Lynch were already there waiting for us, and from the expression on Viper's face, he looked eager to go. "You two ready to roll out?"

"Ready when you are."

Viper gave Grayson a nod, and then he and Lynch got on their motorcycles. Grayson gave me my helmet, and once I had it secured, we got on his Harley and followed Viper and Lynch out of the parking lot. Viper immediately sped ahead, making it clear we weren't out on a leisurely ride, and in what seemed like no time at all, we were pulling into Langford Manor. Grayson quickly parked, and I'd barely gotten off the back of his bike when Viper came over and said, "It's bigger than I thought."

Grayson smiled, and I knew he was itching to say something inappropriate. I gave him a stern look, warning him to keep his thoughts to himself, and then quickly turned to Viper and said, "Well, the entire property is just over eighty acres, but we spend most of our time here focusing on production."

"Okay, let's see it."

Viper wanted to jump right in. I shouldn't have been surprised. He'd been all business from the moment we met, and today was an important step in our partnership. Unfortunately, I was still suffering from my hangover. The Tylenol had done little to help my pounding headache, and my stomach was still doing somersaults. I feared it would get the best of me at times, but I had no choice but to push through and managed to complete the entire tour without actually getting sick. Viper seemed pleased when he came up to me. "I gotta say, you have quite an impressive place here."

"I'm glad you think so." During our tour, Viper had mentioned he and the boys needed to meet with Braylon and his team. Actually, he brought it up on more than one occasion—usually right after he grimaced over something he'd seen or heard. Knowing he was eager to talk to him, I motioned my hand in the direction of the office and smiled. "Braylon is waiting for you inside."

"Good." Before heading inside, he said, "This shouldn't take long. Once I'm done, I'll be heading back."

"Take your time. Country can show Lynch to their living quarters when you're done." I knew I should go to the meeting but just didn't have it in me. I desperately needed to change my clothes and possibly take a nap, so I told him, "I'm going over to my place and freshen up a bit."

"Good deal. You take care, and I'll be in touch soon."

"Sounds good."

Once they headed inside, I walked straight to my place, put on a pot of coffee, and staggered into my room. I changed into a pair of sweats, then dragged myself back into the kitchen for some coffee. As soon as I'd made a cup, I grabbed a box of crackers and carried them back into the bedroom, then put them both on the bedside table and crawled under the covers. I'd barely rested my head on the pillow, and I was out. I woke up later to the sound of someone clanking around in my kitchen. "*Hello?*"

"Hey, babe, it's only me." Grayson peeked his head in the doorway and asked, "How ya feeling?"

"Better." I ran my hand over my face, trying my best to clear the fog. "How long have I been sleeping?"

"About an hour."

"Ugh, that's not long enough." I dropped my head back down on the pillow with a groan. "I think I could sleep for three days."

"That hangover is really kicking your ass, huh?"

"Maybe a little."

"I got something that might help." He headed back to the kitchen, then returned a few minutes later with a sandwich and a bowl of soup. "Grilled cheese and chicken noodle. The best thing for a hangover."

"Oh, really?"

"Mm-hmm. A trick I learned from my grandmother."

"I'm willing to try anything right now." I sat up as he offered me the bowl of soup. I took a small sip, then asked, "So, how did the meeting with Braylon go?"

"Better than I expected." Grayson placed my sandwich on the night table then sat down on the bed next to me. "I think Viper was actually kind of impressed with Braylon and what y'all have done here."

"Well, how about that!"

"Don't get too excited, babe. Nothing's really changed. Viper still wants us to keep watch week to week, and he wants extra cameras put around the perimeter of the property."

"Braylon's been saying the same thing for months." I took another sip of my soup. "I guess I should've listened. I was just being stubborn."

"Who? You? Surely not."

I gave him my best pouty look as I whined, "Hey, *be nice*. I'm suffering enough over here."

"Ah, *bless your heart*," he teased with an exaggerated southern drawl. "Guess you'll be thinking twice before you down a bunch of shots again."

"I most definitely will. With the way I'm feeling, I might never drink again." I lifted my bowl of soup and smiled. "But for now, the soup is helping."

"Glad to hear it." He stood, then leaned over and gave me a quick kiss. "Can I get you anything else?"

"No, I think I'm good."

"Okay, I'll be back when I can."

"You're leaving?"

"I'm gonna give Lynch and Braylon a hand installing those cameras I told you about."

"Oh, do you need me to help?"

"We got it covered. You rest, and I'll stop by when we're done."

I nodded, then watched as he disappeared out of my bedroom. After hearing the door shut, I got out of bed and carried my lunch into the living room. I turned on the TV and found something to watch, then finished the soup and sandwich Grayson had made me. I felt a little guilty lying around while he and the guys were out putting cameras up, but considering my current state, I would've just been in their way.

I decided to use the time to do my rounds and then study for a test I had the following morning. I still felt pretty crummy as I pulled on my sneakers and headed over to the old school. When I walked in, I was pleased to see Mia and Reagan had already taken care of everything. They'd even brought some of the larger plants out to the gym like I'd requested. Since there wasn't anything left for me to do, I headed back to my place to study.

Once I was back at home, I grabbed my laptop and made a spot on the sofa. After tossing a blanket over my legs, I nestled in and started reading through my notes. Unfortunately, even after a nap, I couldn't maintain my focus on studying, and it wasn't long before I gave it up. I closed my laptop and started watching whatever was on the TV.

One movie rolled into the next, and it wasn't long before it was dark outside. Grayson said he would stop back by once they were done with the cameras, so I made a snack and curled up on the sofa again. I had every intention of getting back to my studies, but sadly, that didn't happen. Instead, I fell asleep and didn't wake until I felt myself being lifted from the sofa. I opened my eyes long enough to see Grayson carrying me to bed.

The next morning, I woke up with Grayson sleeping in the bed next to me. As I curled up alongside him, I was thankful that my pounding headache was gone, and I was feeling much better. His eyes were still closed when he muttered, "Morning, babe."

"Good morning."

My fingers started trailing along the lines of his tattoo when they got a mind of their own and slowly drifted down his abdomen. As they reached his boxers, Grayson looked down at me and said, "Careful there, or you might find yourself in trouble."

"I think I could handle a little trouble this morning."

"Is that right?"

"Mm-hmm. Bring it on."

My fingers had barely grazed his thickening erection when he rolled on top of me. He hovered over me, and his eyes met mine with an intensity that sent a wave of heat surging through my body. Without saying a word, his hands dropped down to the hem of my t-shirt and pulled it over my head. His eyes drifted over my bare breasts, and that was all it took. Moments later, our clothes were at our feet, and he was reaching down to remove a condom from his jeans. I immediately shook my head and whispered, "No, Grayson, you don't need it. I'm on the pill."

With a massive smile on his face, he dropped the condom down on the floor, then settled himself between my legs. I gasped when he reached for my thighs and pulled me closer. His hand drifted down between my legs, cupping my heat as his fingers raked across my center. "You're so fucking wet."

Grayson's breath was strained as he looked down at me with hunger in his eyes, and I knew he wanted me just as badly as I wanted him. He brushed his thickness against me, teasing me as he ground his hips against mine until I wrapped my legs around his ass and pulled him deep inside. My entire body was consumed with need and focused on nothing but the touch of his hands on my body, the soft whisper of his kiss, and the tingling sensation that surged through me whenever he shifted deeper within me.

His eyes locked on mine, watching my expression as he started to increase his pace. God, I loved the way Grayson looked at me—as if I was someone precious to him, someone he'd give his life to protect—and I couldn't deny that I felt the same way about him. I knew it was crazy. It was too soon, but I felt it just the same. His dark eyes grew even more intense as he growled, "Need to feel you come undone for me."

His pace continued to increase, faster and harder, setting my entire body on fire. "Yes! Oh God, yes."

He pulled back and crashed into me again and again, driving me wild with every deep thrust. My fingers dug into the comforter, twisting and pulling, as my back arched off the bed. A deep growl vibrated through his chest as my legs tightened around him, and my hips jolted forward, meeting his and taking him even deeper. I inhaled a labored breath while my body trembled and convulsed beneath him as my orgasm took hold. He continued his relentless rhythm, each time more demanding than the last as he came closer to the edge. I was still floating on the high of my own release when I felt his body grow rigid. A deep groan echoed through the room as he buried himself deep inside me, holding still as he found his release.

My body fell limp as my legs dropped to the mattress and let out an exaggerated breath. A sexy little smirk crossed his face as he looked down at me. "Now, that's my kind of wake-up call."

"Mine, too. I'm glad I thought of it."

He chuckled as he lowered himself onto the bed and pulled me to his side. I rested my head on his shoulder and listened to the rapid beat of his heart.

Grayson's arm curled around me, pulling me closer. "You got a big day ahead?"

"Oh, my God." Panic shot through me as I tossed the covers back. "What time is it?"

"Almost eight."

"What! You've gotta be kidding me!" I jumped out of bed and rushed to the bathroom. "I can't believe I forgot!"

"Forgot what?"

Without answering, I turned on the shower and got in without giving the water a chance to warm up. I quickly rinsed my body, then rushed to dry off and get dressed. I was pulling on my jeans when Grayson asked, "Where's the fire?"

"I have class in less than an hour, and I haven't finished studying for my test."

"Need me to do anything?"

"Nothing you can do." I raced back to the bathroom and brushed my teeth. After I pulled up my hair, I darted to the living room, grabbed my bag, and ran out the door as I shouted, "I'll be back in few hours!"

Without waiting for his response, I bolted towards my car and raced to campus. Thankfully, I made it to class before most everyone else and grabbed my usual spot. Once I was settled, I had just enough time to go over my notes and study before the rest of the other students started streaming into the room. Doing my best to ignore their mindless chattering, I continued to cram for my test and was so focused that I never noticed Drake coming into the classroom or that he was sitting right next to me. "*Heyyy*, Kiersten. How's it going?"

"What?" I glanced over to the desk next to me and found him giving me one of his creepy smiles. "Oh, hey, Drake."

"You ready for the big test?"

"Not as ready as I'd hoped to be, but I'll be okay." As much as I wanted to use this last bit of time to study, I didn't have that luxury. I cleared my throat before asking him, "I was told that you were looking for me the other day."

"Yeah, I, uh ... I came out to see if you wanted to grab some pizza and do a little studying together. You know, to get ready for this test and all."

"Oh, well, you could've asked me about that in class."

"I know. I—I," he stammered. "I just didn't get the chance, so I came out to your place to ask you."

"But how did you know where I lived?"

"I kind of followed you out of class." He shifted nervously in his seat. "And then I followed you out to your car. I was trying to catch you before you left, but I didn't get there in time."

"So, you followed me all the way to my house?"

"Yeah, but then I felt stupid about it and left." He shrugged. "I waited a couple of days, and when I finally got the nerve to ask, you weren't even home."

While his story was a little odd, it seemed like a reasonable excuse, especially considering it was Drake. He'd been creepy from day one, and I didn't have any reason not to believe him. But that didn't change the fact that I had an unsettling feeling about the guy. It was time for me to put an end to this thing with him once and for all. "Look, Drake. I don't know any other way to say this, so I'm just going to say it. It's not okay for you to follow me out of class. It's not okay for you to follow me to my car, much less to my house. I need you to hear me when I say I don't want to go out with you or eat pizza and study with you, okay? I'm seeing someone, and I want you to leave me alone."

"Fine. Have it your way." He started gathering his things and stood. "But one day, you're gonna regret not giving me a chance."

I was too relieved watching him move to a different spot in the classroom to even think about his warning—not that I would've ever given it much thought. Drake wasn't like Grayson and his brothers. He was a science nerd and not even remotely intimidating. Once he was seated across the room, I turned my focus back to my notes and studied until the professor started passing out our tests. As soon as I got mine, I immediately started and was pleased to find that I knew all the material covered in the assessment. When I finished, I grabbed my things and stood. I was on my way up to the professor's desk when I noticed Drake had already left. Relieved that I wouldn't have to face him again, I turned in my work and headed out to the parking lot.

Once I got to my car, I pulled out my phone and sent Grayson a message.

ME:

I'm going to be a little later than I planned.

GRAYSON:

Everything okay?

ME:

Yes. I just have a couple of errands to run. How's everything there?

GRAYSON:

Good. Lynch just met Mia.

. . .

ME:

Tell Lynch to behave.

GRAYSON:

Not sure he has it in him to behave, babe.

ME:

It must be a Sinner thing.

GRAYSON:

Maybe.

Get home, and we'll find out if you're right.

ELEVEN

COUNTRY

THERE WAS NOTHING BETTER THAN WAKING UP with Kiersten in the bed next to me. She was so warm and smelled fucking incredible. It was impossible to keep my hands off her. On this particular morning, I woke to find her sprawled across the bed in nothing but a short t-shirt and a pair of lace panties. The minute I laid eyes on her, I had to have her. I felt a little guilty for waking her when she was sleeping so soundly, but I simply couldn't help myself. I eased up on all fours, and her eyes remained closed as I hovered over her for a moment appraising her gorgeous body as her beautiful, full lips curved into a smile.

I immediately slid my hands underneath her and reached for her lace panties, easing them down her long, sexy legs. "Good morning, beautiful."

She kept her eyes closed and mumbled, "Good

morning, handsome."

I lowered my head between her legs, and with my mouth just inches from her, I asked, "Did you sleep well?"

"Mmm-hmmm."

I brushed my tongue across her center and watched with a sense of satisfaction as her back arched off of the bed. "Do you have any idea what you do to me?"

Her eyes barely peeked opened as she looked down at me and shook her head. I eased my fingers deep inside her, massaging the spot that drove her wild. "I can't get you out of my head. With every breath I take, you're right there with me."

A sexy moan vibrated through her chest as I started to move my fingers faster, and her breath quickened as I covered her with my mouth. The sound of her soft whimpers filled the room as I placed my hands on her thighs and held them in place while I continued to work her over with my mouth. Her taste had my cock throbbing with an uncontrollable need to be inside her, and when I couldn't wait any longer, I quickly removed my boxers and settled myself between her legs. I placed my mouth close to her ear and whispered, "You're mine, Kiersten... every inch of you."

Without saying a word, she pressed her lips to mine and kissed me with everything she had. We spent the better part of the morning in bed making love and talking, and we would've stayed longer if I didn't need to get to the office and help out Braylon. After forcing myself out of bed, I took a shower, got dressed, and went on my way.

I had my doubts about spending weeks at a time at Langford Manor. Not only because of my involvement with Kiersten, but because I would be spending so much time away from the club. I quickly realized I had nothing to worry about. We were less than thirty minutes away from the clubhouse, close enough to get back for church and any other gatherings that might arise. And things with Kiersten were good—even better than I thought they could be.

Over the past few days, Kiersten and I had fallen into a bit of a routine. She'd spend her days working on getting her product ready for distribution or doing schoolwork, while Lynch and I worked with Braylon to keep an eye on things. When the day was done, we'd meet up and spend our nights together.

Lynch and I spent most of our mornings walking the perimeter of the Manor, making sure nothing seemed out of sorts. Once we were done, we'd head in to check in with Braylon. Most days, everything ran like clockwork, but on one particular afternoon, Braylon and I noticed one of the cameras on the outer perimeter was flaking out. Braylon pointed to the screen and said, "Looks like it might have a short in it. I'll go check it out."

"I'll do it." Growing tired of being cooped up in the office, I would use just about any excuse to get out of there for a while. "Text me the coordinates, and I'll see what's going on."

"Okay, good idea." He reached into his desk and grabbed a set of keys. As he tossed them over to me, he said, "Take the side-by-side. It's out in the barn."

"Will do."

I took the keys and headed outside. Once I got to the barn, I opened the doors and made my way over to the side-by-side. I was just about to climb inside when I heard Kiersten ask, "You trying to escape?"

"Sorry, babe. You're not getting rid of me that easily."

"I certainly hope not." She started over to me as she asked, "Where ya headed?"

"Going to check on a camera that's on the fritz. You wanna tag along?"

"Sure, I'd love to."

We both climbed in, and I eased out of the barn. After entering the coordinates Braylon had sent me, we were on our way. We hadn't been riding long when Kiersten gave me a little nudge. "Whatcha thinking about over there?"

"Nothing much. Just how this place reminds me a

little of my grandparents' farm." I continued to follow the GPS as I told her, "I spent a lot of time out there when I was a kid. Always loved it."

"Are they still alive?"

"My grandmother is. She's quite a handful. You might've seen her. She lives out at the storage lot with Ada."

Kiersten smiled. "Yeah, I might've watched her and Ada a time or two. They're quite a pair. I had no idea she was your grandmother."

"Well, she is, and you're right, those two *are* quite the pair." I told her all about Gladys and Crockett's, the bar she and my grandfather had bought after they'd gotten married. I told her how Gladys had kept it going long after my grandfather had died but eventually decided it was time to retire and sold the place. I didn't share the fact that Marlowe's crazy sister's boyfriend had bought it as a way to get his revenge on the club, but that Gladys had decided to move in with Ada after the sale and that the two had quickly become friends. "I go over and see them when I can, and they never fail to have dinner waiting for me."

"That's really sweet. It must be nice to have grand-parents like that."

"You don't have grandparents?"

"No. Apparently they died before I was born." She shrugged. "It's always just been my dad and me."

"So, no brothers or sisters?"

"Nope, not even a distant cousin. At least, none that I'm aware of."

"Must've been hard, especially when your mother passed."

"It was. I had my friends from school and my father, but there were times when I wished I had more."

"Yeah, I get that."

When we found the camera's location, I got out and checked to see what was going on with it. Thankfully, it wasn't anything other than a loose wire, which was easily adjusted. Once I was done, I got back inside the side-by-side with Kiersten and said, "Looks like we're all set. You ready to head back?"

"Not yet." She looked over to me with a somber expression. "Would you mind if we ride for a bit?"

"You got it."

I backed up, then followed the edge of the ravine to an open area with a large cattle pond. I eased up to the water's edge and parked. With all the trees and tall grasses, it was quite a sight to see and not surprising why Kiersten liked it there so much. It was getting cool, so I took off my jacket and slipped it around Kiersten's shoulders. As she looked down at the Ruthless Sinners' patch, she said, "You know, you never told me why you joined the Sinners."

"You never asked."

"Well, I'm asking now." She gave me a teasing nudge. "Unless you don't want to tell me."

"Got no problem telling ya, babe, but there's not a lot to say." I leaned back in the seat as I started, "I was helping Gran out at the bar when Viper and several of the brothers came in for the first time. I won't lie, I was pretty fucking terrified. I was just eighteen or so at the time, and they were intimidating as hell."

"Oh, I know the feeling quite well."

"Yeah, I reckon you do." I chuckled. "Well, they kept coming around, more and more, and it wasn't long before my fear turned into something else. I watched them, saw how they interacted, and got sucked in by the sense of brotherhood and power. It practically radiated off of them, and I was drawn to it. So, when Viper invited me to come out and see the clubhouse, I jumped at the chance. As soon as I stepped through those doors, I was hooked. I later discovered that while I was watching Viper and the brothers while I was watching Viper and the brothers, they'd been watching me. They saw something in me, still don't know exactly what, but they asked me to prospect for the club. A year later, I was patched in, and I've been a Sinner ever since."

"Wow, that's some story. You really seem happy with them."

"I am. Along with Gran and my folks, they're my family. Nothing I wouldn't do for them."

"So, you're still close with your folks?"

"Yeah, but I don't get to see them as often I used to. They bought a condo and moved to Florida when my dad retired. They've gotten older now and don't get around to visit as much as they used to."

"So, do you take after your mother or your father?"

"My dad. Definitely my dad."

I pulled out my phone, and once I'd found a picture of them, I turned the screen towards Kiersten. A smile swept across her face as she said, "Your mother's beautiful. You favor her, but you and your dad could be brothers."

"Stacey looks more like my mom." I swiped the screen and pulled up an image of my sister. "She's a few years older than me. Lives in Gatlinburg with her husband and three kids. They have a souvenir shop right in the middle of town."

"That's awesome. I love Gatlinburg."

"I'll have to take you up there sometime for a visit."

"I would love that." Her brows furrowed as she turned to me and said, "I just have one more question."

"Okay, shoot."

"What's with the road name 'Country'?"

"Well, Gran had a lot to do with that. I didn't know the first thing about baling hay or cleaning out stalls until she and Pops taught me, but even then, I found a way to screw things up. Gran got a real kick out of telling the guys what a fuck-up I was at the farm, and one thing led to another."

"I doubt you were a fuck-up, Grayson."

"Nah, I made more than my fair share of mistakes. Even let the hay get wet and almost burned down the fucking barn."

"Oh, well, maybe you were a little bit of a fuck-up, but at least you got a cool road name out of it."

"Yeah, there's always that." We'd spent the better part of our time together talking about me, so I decided to turn the tables on her and asked, "So, what was it like growing up with a man like Billy?"

"A man like Billy?" She cocked her eyebrow. "You mean the kind of man who makes dead bodies disappear?"

"When you put it like that, it makes me wish I hadn't asked."

"No, it's all good. I'm kind of glad you asked." She looked out at the water as she continued, "I can only imagine what you must think of him, but he's a good man. I know that might be hard to believe, especially considering what he does for your club, but he is. He's always loved me and tried his best to take care of me, even more so after Mom died."

"Sounds like he's really tried to be there for you."

"He has. More than you know." Her eyes skirted over to me as she explained, "I guess you could say he's like you and the other Sinners... He's a good man who just happens to do something bad in order to provide for his family."

Tears started to fill her eyes, and I was completely thrown. I had no idea what had upset her. "Hey, are you okay?"

"I've been mad at him for all these years for hiding that part of his life from me, but I haven't judged you or your club like I have him."

"Yeah, but we've never pretended to be something we weren't."

"No, but I have. I'm no better than he is. In fact, I'm just like him."

"No, not even close." I slipped my arm around her waist, and being careful to avoid the steering wheel, I pulled her into my lap. "You're an amazing woman, and you're doing incredible things here. Things you should be proud of. Not sure Billy could ever say the same."

"I just wish I understood. He could've done anything. Why did he decide to do something so insane?"

"I can't answer that one, babe, only Billy can do that. Maybe it's time you talked to him about—"

"No." She shook her head. "I'm just not ready."

"Okay, well, when you are, you just have to be honest with him and demand that he does the same with you."

"You make it sound so simple."

"He's your dad. He would want you to talk to him, even if he isn't happy about what you have to say."

"You're right. I'll talk to him. I just need some time to work up the courage."

"Take all the time you need." I kissed her on the forehead, then said, "We better get back before Braylon sends out a search party."

"You're probably right." She eased out of my lap and over to the passenger seat. I was just about to crank the engine when Kiersten reached over and placed her hand on my arm. "Thank you, Grayson. It means a lot that I can talk to you like this."

"Means a lot to me, too."

I gave her a wink and drove us back to the Manor. We both finished our work for the day, then met up at her place where we spent the entire night tangled in each other's arms—the perfect way to end a long day.

The following few days went by faster than I'd hoped. It seemed like we'd only just gotten there, and it was time to head back to the clubhouse. Since it was our last night, Lynch and I had gathered some wood and made a fire. Kiersten brought us over some drinks, and we sat under the stars talking about this and that.

Lynch had been pretty quiet, so I asked him, "How's it going with Mia?"

"It's not." Lynch tossed another log into the fire. "Don't get me wrong. The chick is smoking, but I'm pretty sure she's into someone else."

"What?" Kiersten seemed baffled. "Who?"

"Braylon." Lynch sat down next to me with a huff. "She's constantly talking about the guy and watches him like a hawk, so either she wants to fuck him or there's something else going on. Either way, I'm out on that shit."

"I had no idea she liked him." Kiersten's eyes danced with mischief as she said, "I wonder if he knows."

"Oh, he knows," I assured her. "It's his job to know, but the question is whether or not he's into her, and if he is, will he do anything about it?"

"Mia is so sweet and thoughtful. *Pretty, too.*" Kiersten was practically beaming as she continued, "I'd love to see Braylon with someone like her. He's such a good guy and deserves a woman who'll be good to him."

"Gee, thanks, Kiersten."

"Oh, come on, Lynch. You can have any girl you want."

"Yeah, any girl but Mia, right?" Lynch scoffed. "Maybe I'll give that Reagan chick a go."

"Well, I'm not sure that's a good idea."

"Oh? And why's that?"

"She's not really into guys."

"What?" Lynch leaned his head back and groaned. "Damn, I need to get laid. I'm ready to get back to the clubhouse."

Unlike Lynch, I wasn't crazy about leaving. I liked being there at the Manor with Kiersten and the others, but we'd already stayed an extra week. I would've volunteered to stay for a third, but we had the run to North Carolina coming up, and Viper wanted us both to be there. I looked over to Lynch. "You'll be back tomorrow, but I doubt you'll have any better luck there than you do here."

"We'll see about that shit. Give me an hour. That's all I'll need," Lynch boasted.

"Mm-hmm. Whatever you say, brother."

While Lynch and I were goofing around, Kiersten found nothing humorous about our conversation, and her smile had completely faded. "So, do you know who will be taking over your shift?"

"Widow and one of our prospects." Widow was one of the older brothers who I had no doubt wasn't thrilled about spending a week away from his ol' lady, Frankie, and her boys, but he'd be here without a single complaint. He'd dedicated his life to the club and never failed when the brothers needed him. I felt his time at the Manor with Kiersten and the others would be no different, and he would see that things continued to run smoothly. "They should be here by noon tomorrow. I've talked to them, and they both know the expectations."

"Oh, okay." She swallowed hard, pushing back her emotion as she told me, "I'm sure they'll do fine."

"They will, and we're only thirty minutes away, so if you need anything—"

"I'll be fine. It's just been really nice having you here."

When Lynch realized Kiersten was upset, he stood up and said, "I think I'm gonna give you two some time to talk and call it a night."

"You don't have to run off."

"Yeah, I kind of do." Lynch took a few steps, then turned back to Kiersten and said, "I did want to ask you about something."

"Okay, what's on your mind?"

"You know how you've done all this research on how marijuana helps people with pain and stuff?"

"Yeah?"

"You ever heard of it helping kids with cerebral palsy?"

"To be honest, the research is pretty limited, but so far, it's been shown to help with pain control and the reduction of spastic movements and seizures. Why?"

"My sister's kid has a hell of a time with it. Reece is just eleven years old. She's very weak, and her muscles are so stiff she can barely walk. There are a lot of kids out there who are in much worse shape. They're in wheelchairs or bedridden, so she's lucky that she's able to get around with a walker"—there was no missing the anguish in Lynch's voice—"but if she just had something to help with the pain ..."

"I'm really sorry she has to deal with that."

"Yeah. Me, too." Lynch ran his fingers through his hair. "These people you donate your stuff to, how does that work?"

"It's usually to someone I know or to a friend of someone—like you and your niece. I'll look over their diagnosis, and if I think I can help, I'll reach out to them. Nine times out of ten, they jump at the chance to get some relief, and so far, everyone I've been working with has shown improvement." I knew Kiersten had been helping others, but I had no idea just how much she'd been doing until now. Kiersten smiled as she asked, "Would you like me to reach out to your sister?"

"Actually, I would."

"Okay, but is she going to be open to the idea? 'Cause, there are *a lot* of people who think negatively about marijuana use."

"At this point, I think she'd be willing to try

anything. They both would." Lynch reached into his pocket and pulled out a card. After he wrote something on it, he offered it to me and said, "My sister's name is Hannah. Here's her number and address. I'll let her know that you'll be getting in touch with her."

"Okay, I'll give her a call tomorrow afternoon."

"Thanks, Kiersten." Lynch turned his attention to me. "Let me know when you're ready to head out tomorrow."

"Will do."

Once Lynch had walked back to the guest quarters, I looked over to Kiersten, and my chest tightened as I watched the light of the fire dance across her beautiful face. It amazed me that she had no idea just how incredible she was. My voice was strained as I told her, "You're awesome."

"No, not so much, but you're sweet to say so." She got up and walked over to me, then sat down in my lap. "Is it bad that I don't want you to leave tomorrow?"

"I'll be back before you know it."

"I know, but I like being able to see you every day."

"You know how vital these first few runs are gonna be. It's important for me to be there; otherwise, I'd stick around for a little longer."

"Does that mean I'll see you when you get back?"

"Absolutely, but I'm not gone yet." I smiled. "We still have tonight."

"Bells and whistles?"

"You can count on it."

I reached up, slipped my hand around the back of her neck, and pulled her close as I pressed my mouth against hers. Her lips were warm and soft, and each swirl of her tongue made the blood rush straight to my cock. Her lips parted in surprise as I fisted her hair in my hand and gave it a soft tug before delving deeper into her mouth. The kiss was urgent, full of need and uncontrollable want, and all her little whimpers and moans spurred me on even more. When I couldn't take it a moment longer, I stood up, lifted her into my arms, and carried her back to her place.

As soon as we'd made it through the door, I lowered her feet to the floor, and when Kiersten looked up at me with those lust-filled eyes, I'd never seen a more beautiful sight. She placed her hands on my chest, lifting up on her tiptoes as she pressed her lips to mine, kissing me with a hunger that matched my own. And just like that, I was completely lost in her—the scent of her hair, the feel of her heart beating against her chest, the taste of her skin. My entire world was centered right there with her in my arms, and I never wanted that feeling to end.

I took her hand and led her into the bedroom where I savored every moment I had left with her.

TWELVE

KIERSTEN

W{.sc HEN IT CAME TIME FOR} G{.sc RAYSON TO LEAVE}, I
tried to remind myself that it wasn't a real goodbye,
that it wasn't the end, but watching him disappear
down my driveway was hard. I'd grown accustomed to
seeing his handsome face every day, and I was going to
miss him. *Really miss him.* In fact, I started missing
him the second he left. I needed something to take my
mind off of things, so I drove over to the campus library
and started researching everything I could about cerebral palsy in children. Before they left, I reached out to
Lynch's sister and asked her to send me over Reece's
medical records. Her uncle was right. She'd had a hell
of a time with her disorder. I wasn't sure I could help
her, but I certainly wanted to try.

I spent hours there—much longer than I'd planned.

I wanted to make sure I'd gone over everything I could find on the benefits and possible disadvantages of marijuana in regard to lessening the symptoms associated with cerebral palsy. I also studied all the information Lynch's sister had sent. I was fairly confident that a small dose could help Reece, but it would ultimately be up to her parents whether she should try it or not. I gathered up all the information I'd found, then sent Hannah a message apologizing for running late, and letting her know I was on my way.

Once she'd replied, I rushed out to my car and started driving towards the city. Half an hour later, I arrived at the address Lynch had given me, and it was a beautiful home—a two-story Colonial with an elegant cobblestone front porch surrounded by gorgeous trees and shrubs. It felt warm and welcoming, and all the fall leaves made it look like a home one might find in a magazine.

I'd barely gotten out of my car when I spotted a stunning brunette walking in my direction. A warm smile crossed her face as she asked, "Kiersten?"

"That's me."

"Great." She extended her hand. "I'm Hannah."

I shook her hand and smiled. "It's so nice to meet you."

"It's great to meet you, too. Conor has told me so

much about you." I'd only heard the guys call Lynch by his road name, so the name Conor threw me for a second but thankfully, I'd figured it out by the time Hannah motioned me to the front door. "Come on in, and I'll introduce you to Reece and Matt."

I nodded, then grabbed my things and followed her up to the house. When we walked inside, the farmhouse theme of her décor made the interior of her home just as picturesque as the exterior. I was still looking around, admiring the beauty of her home, when a young boy came dashing into the living room. "Mom! Mom! Mom!"

"What, *Matt*?"

"Reece broke my controller!"

"What controller?"

"My PlayStation controller." Matt had shaggy, brown hair that hung below his brow, and his freckled nose was crinkled with despair as he looked down at his game controller and shook it. "I was playing, and Reece made me drop it. Now, it's busted."

The words had barely left his mouth when I heard the sounds of a walker and shuffled footsteps coming around the corner. Moments later, Reece appeared. There were braces on both her legs, and while she trembled slightly, she was able to keep herself balanced with the help of her little red walker. She had long, dark hair and dark eyes, just like her mother. Worried about upsetting her brother, she looked up to her mother, and with slightly slurred words, she mumbled, "I'm really swor-ry, Momma."

"It's fine, sweetie. We will get Mathew another one."

"But I don't want another one!" Matt fussed. "I like this one."

"I'm sure you do, but things happen." Hannah brushed her son's hair out of his eyes as she promised, "I'll call your dad and tell him to pick up another one on his way home from work."

"Okay."

Looking utterly defeated, he dropped his head and started back to his room. He hadn't gotten far when Reece muttered, "I'm swor-ry, Maddie."

"Whatever."

"Matt!" Hannah fussed. "There's no reason to be ugly. It was an accident."

"It's always just an accident."

He continued out of the room, and moments later, a door slammed. Hannah immediately turned her attention to me. "I'm so sorry about that."

"It's fine. No need to apologize."

"It seems like there is always something happening around here." Hannah stepped over to Reece and knelt down in front of her. "You okay, sweetheart?"

"Mm-hmm." Her bottom lip quivered as she told her mother, "I... I didn't mean ..."

"It's fine." Hannah gave her a wink. "I'm sure he can survive a few hours without it."

"M-mad."

"Yes, but he'll get over it." Hannah stood, then looked over to me. "This is Kiersten. She's one of Uncle Conor's friends."

"Hi, I'm Reece."

"It's really nice to meet you, Reece. Your uncle has told me so much about you."

"Pret-ty."

"Thank you, Reece. You're pretty, too."

"Hey, sweetie." Hannah placed her hand on Reece's shoulder and said, "Kiersten and I are going to talk for a bit. Let's get you back to your room, and I'll put on one of your shows."

"O-kay."

Hannah looked over to me as she said, "I'll be right back."

"Take your time."

I watched as she helped guide Reece down the hall and back into her bedroom. A few minutes later, she returned to the living room, feigning a smile. "Come have a seat."

"Sure." I followed her over to the sofa, and as soon as we were seated, I said, "Your children are adorable."

"Thank you. They are quite a handful." She let out a deep breath. "Reece wants so much to be like any other kid and tries her best not to let her disabilities slow her down, but there are days like today when they simply get the best of her."

"I'm sure it's difficult for all of you."

"It is, but we've been really blessed that Reece is still able to get around with her walker, and her speech is still holding. So many kids with CP aren't so lucky, but at the same time, the bad days when Reece is in so much pain are unbearable for us all."

"I can only imagine how hard that must be."

"It's overwhelming, and I feel so helpless." Hannah clutched her hands in her lap, twisting them nervously as she spoke, "Conor told me all about you and what you've done to help others who suffer like Reece. Do you think you can help her the way you've helped them?"

"I hope so." I reached into my bag and pulled out all the research I'd brought her. "I looked over the medical records you'd sent, and I spent some time this afternoon going over the pros and cons of marijuana use in regard to children with CP. I'm not a doctor. I can't tell you for certain whether it will help Reece or not."

"But you think it's worth a shot?"

"I think you and your husband need to read over

everything here and then make the decision you think is best for your daughter. You know her better than anyone, including her doctors and especially me." I pulled out a bag of CBD gummies and oil I'd brought and placed them in her hand. "I brought both for you to consider. You don't have to worry about Reece actually 'getting high' off of either of these. They both have a very low concentration of THC and are high in CBD which will help her most with the seizures and muscle spasms. If you decide to try them, start with a small amount and see how she does with it."

"So, she can just eat one of these and not smoke it?"

"Yes. Most folks like the gummies better than the other edibles or a few drops of the oil work great, too, but you're welcome to try whatever you think she will like best."

"And if they work?"

"Let me know, and I'll bring you more."

"That's it?"

"That's it. All I ask is that you keep this between us and away from your son, of course. I'm not suggesting you withhold this from her doctors. In fact, it's something you might want to discuss with them before trying it. Just don't—"

"Mention where we got it."

"Exactly."

"I promise you that I won't mention a word of this to anyone." Hannah reached over and wrapped her arms around me, hugging me tightly. "Thank you so much for doing this."

"It's my pleasure. I hope it will give her some relief."

"Me, too."

"Mom!" Matt called out to his mother.

I immediately stood and said, "I'll get going so you can see to him. If you need anything, just give me a call."

"I definitely will. Thank you again, Kiersten."

I said my final goodbyes, then headed back out to my car. As soon as I turned the key, I noticed that I was running low on gas and groaned. It was almost seven and starting to get dark. I hadn't planned on making another stop, but unfortunately, I didn't have a choice seeing as there wasn't enough gas to make it back home. I drove over to the nearest gas station and filled up my tank, but before leaving, I decided to go inside and grab myself a cold drink and a snack to eat. I'd just made it over to the glass refrigerator case filled with different sodas when I heard a familiar voice say, "Well, hey there, Kiersten."

"Drake?" I quickly turned and found him standing

behind me with a sinister smile. "What are you doing here?"

"Nothing much." He was wearing a black hoodie with the hood pulled over his head and black jogging pants—something I'd never seen him wear before, and the way he was looking at me made the hairs on the back of my neck prickle against my skin. "Just running a few errands and whatnot. What about you?"

"Just taking care of some things." Nashville was a big city. The chances of bumping into Drake off-campus were slim at best, and the whole thing didn't feel right to me. I hoped I was wrong, but I had to ask. "Did you follow me in here?"

"*Wow*. You think a lot of yourself, don't ya?"

"I'm just trying to figure out what you're doing here, Drake."

"I already told you. I'm out running some errands," he answered nonchalantly. "Is there some law that says a man can't come into a gas station to buy a twelve-pack?"

"No, but..." I knew he was up to something. I also knew he wasn't going to admit it, so I shook my head and muttered, "Just forget it."

I nudged my way around him and started towards the front. I hadn't made it far when I felt a hand on my arm and was immediately jerked backward. "Hey, hold on a second."

"Let me go, Drake."

"I'm sorry." He held his hands up in playful surrender. "I was only going to ask if you wanted to grab dinner or something? Drink a few beers. Watch a movie..."

"Are you being serious right now?" I snapped.

"Yeah, actually, I am." Before I could tell him he was off his damn rocker, he added, "I know you aren't interested in dating. You made that point loud and clear, but I don't see why we can't be friends. You know, hang out and get to know each other a little better."

"No, I don't think so."

"You're making this too fucking difficult." His smile faded, and his eyes grew fierce as he growled, "Why can't you just stop being so fucking hard-headed?"

"I've had enough of this, Drake."

I turned and, without looking back, rushed towards the door. Once I was outside, I ran to my car, got inside, and sped off. I checked my rearview mirror several times, making sure Drake wasn't following me as I drove towards the Manor. As soon as I pulled up in the driveway, I parked and hurried inside the office to find Braylon. I was surprised to find Mia was there with him, and from the looks of it, they were in the midst of an in-depth conversation. I had no idea what they were talking about, but they were sitting oddly close, and Mia was blushing. The second they noticed me standing there, Braylon immediately shifted in his seat, creating some distance between them.

"Hey, Kiersten. I didn't hear you pull up." He glanced over at Mia, then cleared his throat. "How did it go with Lynch's sister?"

"Good." To say I felt awkward standing there in front of them was an understatement. It was clear I'd interrupted something. I thought back to what Lynch had said about Mia being interested in Braylon, and looking at them now, I couldn't help but wonder if he was right. I didn't want to ruin their moment with the stupid Drake nonsense, so I said, "I'm gonna head to the house and grab a bite to eat."

"Oh, okay." Braylon seemed relieved. "I'll catch up with you later."

"Mm-hmm."

I quickly skirted out of the room and headed over to my house. As I started across the lot, I had an eerie feeling and stopped to check my surroundings, making sure that no one was around. I didn't see a soul, so I decided it was just my head playing tricks on me. I had no doubt that my encounter with Drake was to blame for my heightened state, which infuriated me. Thinking of all the different ways I'd like to string the guy up, I stormed into my kitchen and grabbed a bottle of wine from my fridge. I poured myself a glass and carried it into the living room. As I sat down on the sofa, I looked around the room, and a sinking feeling washed over me when I realized how empty it felt without Grayson there—which only dampened my mood even more.

I took a few sips of wine, hoping it might ease the knot growing in the pit of my stomach, but it did little to help. There was only one thing that could lift my spirits, so I grabbed my phone and sent Grayson a text message.

ME:

Hey.

GRAYSON:

Hey. How's it going?

ME:

Okay. Would be better if you were here.

. . .

GRAYSON:

Can't disagree with you there.

How'd it go with Lynch's sister?

ME:

Really good.

Hannah was so sweet, and Reece is a trooper.

GRAYSON:

Appreciate you doing that.

ME:

I was more than happy to.

I hope it helps.

GRAYSON:

I'm sure it will.

How was the rest of your day?

I WAS TEMPTED to tell him about my encounter with Drake but decided against it. There was no point in worrying him, especially when he had the run to

North Carolina coming up. Like it or not, I would have to find a way to handle Drake on my own.

ME:

It wasn't too bad.
Yours?

GRAYSON:

Can't complain.
Just been busy getting ready for the run.

ME:

When are you leaving?

GRAYSON:

First thing in the morning.

ME:

I didn't realize you were going so soon.

GRAYSON:

The sooner we go, the sooner we'll get back.

ME:

I'm all for that.

GRAYSON:

Be careful. I might think you actually miss me.

ME:

I might. Just a little.

GRAYSON:

Right back at ya.
I'll be back before you know it.

ME:

I can't wait.
Goodnight, Grayson.

GRAYSON:

Night, babe.

When you dream about me tonight, don't forget to throw in a little hair

pulling and ass slapping.

ME:

Yeah, I think I'll enjoy dreaming of my handprint on that fine ass of yours.

GRAYSON:

Hold up! Not what I had in mind.

ME:

Not your dream, babe.

GRAYSON:

Touché

GIGGLING, I put the phone down on the table and was about to take another drink of my wine when I heard a tap at my door. I usually didn't have visitors after dark, so I was a little hesitant to answer. But I forced myself up off the sofa and went to answer the door. When I opened it, I was surprised to see that it was Mia. "Hey... You got a minute?"

"Sure, come on in." Once she was inside, I closed the door behind her and asked, "Would you like some wine?"

"No, I'm good. Thanks."

As we walked into the living room, I asked, "Is something wrong?"

"No, I just wanted to talk to you about something."

"Okay." I sat back down on the sofa and waited as she sat down next to me. "What's on your mind?"

"It's about Braylon." I could hear the concern in her voice as she continued, "I really like him, Kiersten, but I don't want to step on any toes. I love my job here and don't want to put it in jeopardy."

"You don't have to worry about that, Mia." Mia wasn't only beautiful and sweet, she was a college graduate with a good head on her shoulders, and Braylon was a fantastic guy. He'd dedicated years of his life to the military, and even after he was severely wounded, he never gave up his drive to help others. As far as I could tell, they were perfect for one another. I truly meant it when I told her, "I think it's great that you and Braylon have something going."

"You do?"

"Yes!" I reached over and placed my hand on her arm. "I'm very happy for you both."

"We're not really involved just yet. I've liked Bray for a long time, but I've been afraid to act on it. Partly because I wasn't sure he felt the same, and partly because I wasn't sure how you'd feel about it." She grimaced as she admitted, "I always thought you kind of had a thing for him."

"What?"

"I don't think it anymore. Now that I've seen you with Country, I realize just how wrong I was about that."

"Yeah, Braylon and I are just friends. Good friends, but nothing more."

"So, you're really okay about all this?"

"I'm more than okay. I promise."

"Thank you, Kiersten." Mia reached over and hugged me. "I'm so glad I came and talked to you. I feel a lot better about everything."

"Well, I'm here any time you want to talk."

"And I'm here for you anytime you wanna talk about your oh-so-sexy biker guy."

I giggled. "I'll be sure and keep that in mind."

"Great." Mia stood up and said, "I'll let you get back to your wine, and I'll see you in the morning."

"Sounds good."

Once she'd left, I locked my door and carried my wine into the bedroom, then changed into my pajamas and crawled into bed. The second I curled up with my pillow, I thought about Grayson—his handsome face, his laugh, and the tender touch of his hand. While I missed not having him in bed with me, I found comfort in knowing that I had a man in my life worth missing— and he was someone worth waiting for.

THIRTEEN

COUNTRY

"I went to check in on Jagger yesterday."

Menace had been oddly quiet as we got things loaded up for the run. The second he mentioned Jagger's name, I figured out why. "How's he doing?"

"He's making it." Menace stopped, then looked over his shoulder, ensuring that no one was within earshot before continuing, "He said something that's been bugging me."

"Okay, what exactly did Jagger say?"

"Well, we were talking about Rossi and all the bullshit he put Parker through. I was going on a rant over how he should've never gotten off, and he shouldn't have. The motherfucker killed her entire fucking family and Lynch's grandparents. He should've gotten the fucking chair."

"I can't disagree with you there."

Parker was Menace's ol' lady. They met when she came to the strip club looking for a job. One thing led to another, and Menace discovered she was on the run from Rossi—the Italian mafia asshole who'd killed her folks. In hopes of derailing Rossi, Menace took Parker to Billy's, and Billy gave them both the help they needed. But Rossi was still an issue. The club wasn't in the position to go toe to toe with the mafia, so we left it up to the court system. Unfortunately, that didn't turn out as we'd hoped. Rossi got off, but just as he was making his way down the courthouse steps, he was killed. Everyone, including Viper, thought Menace had a hand in his death, but we were wrong. We still weren't 100 percent sure who was behind it, and we might never know—or so I thought.

I was curious to hear what Jagger had told him, so I pushed, "So, what did he say that's bugging you?"

"Something like, 'I'm glad it all worked out, and the guy got what was coming to him.'"

"Sorry, brother, but I'm not gettin' why that would bug ya. We're all glad the guy got what was coming to him."

"No, brother. It's not what he said. *It's the way he said it.* It's hard to explain, but I got the feeling he had something to do with it."

"Did you ask him about it?"

"Yeah, of course, I asked him, but he blew me off.

Made it sound like the whole idea was crazy, but I just don't know." Menace's brows were furrowed as he asked, "Do you think it's even remotely possible that he could've had a hand in taking down Rossi?"

Menace wasn't one to confide in me or anyone for that matter. He typically sorted shit out on his own, so even though I usually joked around about anything and everything, I didn't want to make light of my brother's concerns, especially over something like this. I closed the SUV's door, then turned to face him. "Honestly, I wouldn't put it past him. There's no telling the kind of connections he's made. He could've struck some kind of deal with another inmate, and the rest is history."

"Yeah, but to go and do something like that without running it by Viper ... or even me. I mean, damn, he's still a Sinner. You don't do that kind of shit without talking to somebody."

"I get what you're saying, but you gotta remember, he's living in a completely different world. They have their own rules inside, their own code, and he's doing what he's gotta do to survive. No matter how many times you go and see him, you've got no idea the hell he goes through in that place. So, if he happened to have something to do with Rossi's death, you can bet your life he did it for you."

"So, what should I do?"

"Not a damn thing. You let this dog lie, brother. It's the only thing you can do."

"And if there's blowback to the club?"

"Jagger wouldn't have done anything that'd cause the club harm. You know that." I motioned my hand to Rafe and Axel as they started walking towards us. "Now, pipe down, Francis and let it be. We've gotta get going."

"You're right." He started walking over to the others and said, "Thanks, brother."

"Don't mention it."

After we made sure everything was loaded and secured, Menace and I got into the SUV with Rafe and Axel. With Axel behind the wheel, we pulled through the main gate and were on our way to Knoxville—the halfway point between our clubhouse and the North Carolina Sinners' chapter. Viper and Dax, the president of the NC chapter, decided it would be easier to meet there once a month to make our exchange. The three-and-a-half-hour ride versus the six-and-a-half suited me just fine. I figured the sooner we got there and back, the sooner I could get back home and over to the Manor to see about Kiersten. While she didn't say anything specific, I got the feeling that something was weighing on her mind, and I wanted to make sure she was okay.

We were about an hour into our drive when Axel turned back to me and asked, "What's up with you?"

"Huh?"

"You sick or something?"

"What the hell are you talking about, brother?"

"You haven't said two words since we got in the truck," Axel explained. "We usually can't get you to shut your trap, so I figure there's gotta be something wrong."

"Ah, he's all right. Just pining over his latest honey hole." Rafe snickered.

I didn't respond. I couldn't. I was too fucking angry with Rafe's referral to Kiersten, so I simply sat there and glared at him. When he realized he'd overstepped, he quickly apologized. "Oh, come on, brother. You know I didn't mean nothin' by it. I was just messin' around."

Again, I didn't respond. If I had, it would've just given the guys fuel for the fire, and I simply wasn't in the mood. I should've expected it. I'd given both Rafe and Menace all kinds of hell when they met their ol' ladies—especially Rafe. Then again, the asshole had it coming. Marlowe worked at Crockett's, and like all men who crossed paths with her, I found her attractive and even asked her out. I hadn't been into her like I was with Kiersten. I was just looking to get laid, and I was pretty sure she knew it. That's why Marlowe made me think she was a lesbian. She had me thinking it for months—right up until the day she and Rafe hooked up. I didn't hold any ill-will towards either of them. Hell, those two were meant for each other. In all the years I'd known Rafe, I'd never seen my brother so happy.

That had me thinking about Kiersten, and once my mind was on her, everything around me turned into a blur. So much so, I hadn't even realized that we'd pulled up to our destination until Rafe gave me a nudge. "Hey, pull your head out of your ass, brother. We're here."

Not believing that I'd been so out of sorts, I glanced out the window and saw the back of the old football stadium where we'd agreed to meet up with our NC chapter. It had been closed down for years and was away from any watchful eyes. I knew the others were waiting, so I ran my hand over my face and tried to clear the fog as I grumbled, "I'll be damned."

"You alright?"

"Yeah, I'm good." I opened my door. "Let's do this."

By the time Rafe and I got out of the truck, Axel and Menace were already out and reacquainting themselves with the brothers from the NC chapter. We'd met them before, but that was at a gathering with some of the other Sinner chapters. Between all the booze and crowds of people, it was often hard to keep track of who was who. I happened to recognize Bates, their club's sergeant-at-arms. At six-four and two hundred and fifty pounds of pure muscle, the man was hard to forget. Bates had jet-black hair and tattoos covering most of his exposed body, including his throat and hands. Even though the guy was a bit menacing, he'd always seemed cool whenever we were together, so I walked over and gave him a bro hug. "Hey, brother. How's it going? It's been a while."

"Yes, it has. It's been going good. You been making it all right?"

"Can't complain. And you?"

"The same." He motioned his hand towards the others. "I'm sure you remember Fallon, our enforcer."

Fallon wasn't as tall as Bates, but he was just as built and had his own fair share of tats. His hair was long like mine and pulled back into a braid. I gave him a side hug as I replied, "I do. It's good to see ya again, brother."

He nodded, then turned to introduce us all to the two younger guys standing beside him. "And this is Hugo and Reed. I'm not sure if you had a chance to meet at the last gathering."

"Not sure if we did. Anyway, it's always good to meet a fellow brother." Menace turned to Bates and said, "We gotta do better about gettin' the clubs together."

"Yeah, we do. It's been too long."

Getting right down to business, Axel motioned his head towards the truck. "We've got the product. Twenty pounds like we discussed."

"This shit really as good as Viper says?"

"Wouldn't be here if it wasn't." Axel was our VP for a reason. He was level-headed and forthright, but at the same time, he didn't take shit from anyone. He told it like it was, and he expected everyone else to do the same. While these were our fellow brothers, we were there to do business, and he treated it as such. "You shouldn't have any trouble moving it, but if you do, let us know, and we'll make some adjustments to the size of the take."

"No worries there. Folks back home are always looking for a good smoke. We shouldn't have any problem unloading it." Bates turned to Hugo and Reed. "Get the goods and load it in the truck."

Rafe and I followed the brothers to the back of the truck, then helped them move the bags over to theirs. Once we had Kiersten's odor-proof bags secured under the rear compartment, they closed the door and I said, "Bring the bags back on the next exchange."

"Will do."

We made our way back to the others, and I heard Fallon ask, "You boys wanna grab something to eat before you head back?"

"Appreciate the offer, brother, but like you, we got a long drive home."

"That we do."

After we all said our goodbyes, Fallon gave Axel a brotherly pat on the bicep as he said, "You boys have a safe trip home."

"You too, brother."

Rafe and I followed Menace and Axel to our truck and got inside. None of us spoke as Axel eased out of the old parking lot and headed back home. We talked a little about how well everything had gone, and I had no doubt that Viper would be pleased. I hoped the same would hold true for Lynch and the other brothers who went to Atlanta to meet up with our South Carolina chapter. They had a farther distance to travel, so we weren't surprised that we made it back to the club-house before them. We met briefly with Viper, then Menace announced, "I'm going to head over to Stilettos and see how things are going there."

"I'll take a ride over there with you." Rafe glanced over at me as he asked, "You coming with?"

I nodded, then followed them both out to the parking lot. Once we were on our bikes, Rafe and I followed Menace out the gate and towards Stilettos. While the two strip clubs did exceptionally well on their own, we made a small fortune by having our girls sell coke to some of our wealthier regulars. The girls were exceptional—not only at stripping but also at moving goods. Marijuana was a hot commodity in Tennessee, so I had no doubt they'd do well with our latest endeavor. As soon as we got to the club, Menace checked to make sure things were running smoothly with the girls while Rafe and I strolled over to the bar next to Locke and Bear. They were talking with Marlowe while she took a break from bartending. As soon as we sat down, she asked, "What are you doing here?"

"Damn, Lowe. Don't gotta sound so disappointed to see us," I teased.

"You know I'm not. I just wasn't expecting you guys to be back so soon." As usual, she was practically beaming as she turned her attention to Rafe. "I'm glad y'all made it back okay. Did everything go the way you hoped?"

"It went fine."

"Good. Glad to hear it." Even though Marlowe worked for the club and was Rafe's ol' lady, she didn't know all the ins and outs of the club. None of the women did. All she knew was what she needed to know—that we had a run and would be gone for the day. "Can I get you guys something to drink?"

"I'm good," Rafe answered.

"Yeah, I'm good, too." I turned to Locke as I asked, "How have things been going here?"

"There haven't been any major blowups since the last rumble with Lynch and those rowdy assholes, so I'd say they've been all right."

"You realize you just jinxed us, right?"

"Suits me fine." A mischievous grin crossed his face. "I don't know about you, but I could use a little excitement around here."

"I'm just fine without it, thanks."

"You know, the girls are moving the new product fast. I wouldn't be surprised if we needed more by the end of the month."

"Seriously?"

"Yeah, I was just as surprised as you are. It looks like going into business with her was the right move."

He hadn't finished his sentence when Menace came up behind us. He seemed more than pleased. "Locke is right. I just checked in with Candy and the others, and they haven't had any problem moving it. In fact, they've had several clients come back for more."

"I'm sure she'll be glad to hear that."

"Viper, too."

The next couple of days seemed to drag by. I tried to keep myself busy with the brothers and taking on extra shifts at the club, but it did little to keep me from thinking about Kiersten. I was tempted to just go and see her, but she was studying for her midterms, and I didn't want to distract her. Besides, I'd be seeing her soon. We'd made plans to get together for the weekend. She'd come down and hang out at the club with me, and then we'd head back to the Manor together. Only that wasn't the way it played out.

After a long shift at Stilettos, I was completely wiped and ready to call it a night. I decided to skip going home and headed over to the clubhouse to crash for the night. I'd barely made it through the front door when Menace came rushing down the hall to meet me. "Have you checked your phone?"

"No. Why?" I pulled it out and looked down at the screen. When I didn't have any messages, I asked, "What's going on?"

"I got an alert on my phone. Looks like there's a fire at the Manor." Per Viper's request, Menace had been given access to all the security at Kiersten's place, so we would also be notified if there were any security breaches. Menace seemed worried when he said, "Riggs called, and they got the same alert but haven't been able to get a hold of Braylon or Kiersten. I haven't either. I tried calling Widow and Jackal and can't seem to get them either."

"Where?" Without waiting for him to answer, I called Kiersten's phone but didn't get an answer. I called a second and third time, but still no answer. Frantic, I looked back at Menace and asked, "Where's the fucking fire, brother?"

"That's just it. We're not sure. On my end, it looks like the whole damn place is up in flames, but when I checked the cameras, I'm not seeing a damn thing. No smoke. No flames. So, maybe it's just a glitch or something."

"Maybe, but I'm not taking any chances." I turned and headed back outside. "I'm heading over there."

"Hold up ... I'm going, too. Need to let Viper know and get Hawk or whoever else is here to tag along. Better to be safe than sorry."

I nodded, then waited as Menace contacted Viper. Once he'd gotten the go-ahead, we rounded up Lynch and Hawk, then gathered whatever artillery we had at the clubhouse and jumped into the SUV. Moments later, we were through the clubhouse gates and speeding towards the Manor. I'd never been what I would consider to be a fearful man. No matter what was going on with the club, I'd always faced whatever came my way without giving it a second thought, but the mere idea of Kiersten being in danger terrified me.

I prayed that there was nothing to be worried about.

But if that wasn't the case, *if Kiersten truly were in danger*, then nothing would stand in my way of protecting her.

Absolutely nothing.

FOURTEEN
KIERSTEN

After spending days cramming for my microbiology and phycology midterms, my brain felt like complete mush. I couldn't even blink without thinking about bacteria, fungi, and single-celled organisms. I wanted to believe that all my studying had paid off, but I wasn't so sure. Usually, it all came pretty naturally to me. I never really had to study all that much, just enough to review the basics, but I'd been so distracted with work and everything in between that I wasn't as focused as usual. So much so, I might've tanked one of the tests, which was something I'd never done before—not even once.

But at least there was one positive. I hadn't seen Drake since the night I ran into him at the gas station. He'd never missed class before, so I was surprised he hadn't shown up to take his exam. I took it as a blessing and left campus without that eerie feeling of someone watching me. A storm was rolling in, so my ride home took a bit longer than I'd hoped. Once I made it back, I checked in with Braylon and Widow. It had been a while since we'd had a bad storm, and I wanted to make sure we were prepared. They were both sitting in the office eating dinner when I walked in looking like a drowned rat. "It's getting pretty nasty out there."

"Yeah, we noticed," Braylon answered. "Did you forget your umbrella?"

"Of course, I did." I giggled. "I didn't remember it until I stepped out of class and saw that it was pouring."

"Sounds about right."

"So, are we good for tonight and this crazy storm?"

"Yeah, we've been watching the weather, and it looks like the worst of it should be past us in an hour or so." Braylon glanced over at Widow and said, "I'll keep watch tonight and make sure the generator kicks on if the power goes out."

"Okay, great. I'm going to do my rounds, then I've got some studying to do. Just let me know if you guys need anything."

"Will do."

I left them both and headed down the hall. I

stopped by each room, checked the timers on the lights, and made sure the daily checklist had been completed. Once I was done, I hurried back to my place. As soon as I'd dried off, I made myself a batch of ramen noodles and a glass of chocolate milk, then carried them into the living room. I spent the next couple of hours watching a scary movie while finishing up an assignment for my genetics class. By the time I was done, the storm had started to let up, so I took a long, hot bath and put on my pj's. I was so looking forward to a good night's sleep as I crawled into bed and snuggled under my covers. Unfortunately, that didn't happen.

I'd barely drifted off when I heard someone pounding on my door. It was well after midnight, so I knew something had to be wrong. I shot out of bed and rushed to the door. When I opened it, I found Mia on my front step, looking absolutely panicked. "What's wrong?"

"I was, umm... I was with Braylon, and he got some warning or something that there was a fire."

"What? Where?"

"Over at the gym. He went to check it out and told me to come and get you."

"Oh shit!"

I pulled on my boots and rushed out of the house, quickly closing the door behind me. The cold night air was damp from the rain and made me shudder, but thankfully the rain itself had let up. It was barely sprinkling as I ran to the gym to find Braylon. I didn't bother to stop and see if Mia was following me. I was too worried about everything I'd worked so hard for going up in flames. I charged through the front doors of the gym as I called out, "Braylon!"

When he didn't answer, I called out again, "Bray! Where are you?"

Still no answer. While I didn't see any flames, I smelled the overwhelming stench of burnt siding. I started searching for the source of the smell when I noticed an orange glow coming from one of the outside windows. I quickly rushed out the back door and over to the side of the building where a small fire was inching across the exterior siding. I was surprised to see that there was a white film covering most of the wall and part of the grass, and then, I spotted the two fire extinguishers. Braylon and Duggar had been there, but I had no idea where they'd gone. I picked up one of the extinguishers and tried to spray it, but it was already empty. I hated there wasn't more I could do, but I knew it was only a matter of time before the gym's sprinkler system went off. I was trying to figure out what I should do next when Mia rushed up behind me and asked, "Where's Bray?"

"I don't know. That's what I'm trying to figure out."

"Well, it looks like he was here."

"Yes, but where is he now?" I looked around, and there was no one in sight. Suddenly, the power went out, and the entire place went black. Even though it was no longer storming, I assumed it had something to do with the crazy weather. Maybe a downed tree or a blown breaker. Regardless, I knew it would be only a short amount of time before the generator kicked on. I had an uneasy feeling as I stood there watching the flames continue to inch their way up the building. Trying my best not to panic, I turned to Mia and asked her, "What about Timms or Widow? Any idea where they might be?"

"I don't know. I haven't seen them."

I didn't know what it was, but something was wrong—very, very wrong.

Unnerved, I rushed to the back doors of the school, but stopped dead in my tracks the second I heard what sounded like gunshots coming from inside. With my heart drumming in my chest, I stood frozen, waiting to see if I heard it again. I turned and searched the grounds for any sign of Braylon or the others. That was when I spotted three figures dressed in all black darting across the back field. I knew then this wasn't just an accidental fire.

On the verge of tears, Mia shrieked, "Were those gunshots?"

"I'm not sure." Trying to remain calm, I told her,

"Go get Reagan. The two of you need to get to your car and go."

"But what about Braylon and—"

"You have to go, Mia. He would want you to be safe."

She nodded, then turned and ran towards Reagan's place. I was considering my next move when I heard another round of shots. I ran up to the back door of the school and tried to peek through the window, but it was too dark to see anything. I had no idea what was going on inside that building. I just knew I had to get to the security button and lock the place down before the other intruders made it inside. Without any further hesitation, I eased the door open and slipped inside. I kicked off my wet boots, then tiptoed down the long, dark hall. I kept my back against the wall and started inching towards the office. I was just about to round the corner when the lights came flickering back on.

Several more shots were fired. Seconds after, there was a loud thud that sounded like a body hitting the ground. The second I heard a man groan, I knew someone had been shot and had fallen. I opened the large wooden door and peeked my head out, and immediately spotted Braylon on the floor. My heart dropped when I saw he had a bullet wound in his thigh and another in his shoulder. Without thinking, I came out of hiding and started racing over to him but stopped when he held up his hand and scowled. More gunfire erupted, drawing my attention to the end of the hall. Relief washed over me when I spotted Timms, Duggar, Widow, and possibly Jackal. Their backs were to me, making it difficult to figure out who was there, but it was evident they were doing what they could to hold off whoever was attacking us.

I didn't move. I just stood there watching them until I heard Braylon whisper, "Kiersten."

I quickly turned to look at him and asked, "What should I do?"

"Lock her down."

He used two fingers to motion over to the security button. I nodded, then crouched down, being careful to stay out of the line of fire and scrambled over to the office wall. I knew what would happen when I pushed that button. The panels would come down, and we would be locked inside with our attackers. Hawk had warned us about the possibility of this very thing happening, and we thought we could handle it. At that moment, I wasn't so sure. Unfortunately, I didn't have a choice. Pushing that button meant I could keep the other intruders from getting inside with us.

I reached into the hidden compartment and pressed the button, and within seconds, the metal panels came down over the windows, sealing us in along with our attackers. The commotion down the hall continued as I leaned back against the wall, trying my best not to be seen. The sound of an object sliding across the floor drew my attention to my feet. I looked down and gasped when I saw it was Braylon's hand-gun. "You gotta get out of here, Kiersten! Go find a place to hide until we come—"

"No!" Knowing our intruders were just around the corner, I cried, "You're hurt, Bray. There's no way in hell I'm leaving you."

"I'm fine. Just a fucking graze." He motioned his hand towards the small handgun at my feet. "Now, take it and go."

"But—"

"Go, Kiersten!"

I did as he ordered, then hurried back down the hall and slipped into one of the classrooms with hydro-ponic feeders. The timer-controlled lights were off, so it was difficult to see as I made my way to the back of the room. I'd always loved being in these rooms. It was always so quiet and serene with all the green plants and warm glow of the lights, and I felt like I'd truly accomplished something when I saw that my plants were growing healthier and hardier than any other on the market. But at that moment, nothing about this room felt comforting or soothing. Instead, all the shadows and strange noises made me feel like I'd stepped into my very own nightmare.

I slipped under one of the tables and drew my knees up to my chest, trembling as the adrenaline rushed through my veins. As I sat there huddled, I could hear gunfire just outside the door, and I was completely terrified. I had no idea who was doing this until I heard a voice come over the school intercom. Bile rose to my throat as I listened to him say, "Kiersten. Oh, Kiersten. I know you're here. I know you can hear me. How does it feel to have your perfect little world shaken to its core? I bet you never thought this day would come, but it did, and it came because of you. You did this, Kiersten. You're the one who was so fucking hard-headed. You're the one who made it difficult."

It was the same words Drake had said to me the other night at the gas station. I thought it was just an odd coincidence until he continued, "All you had to do was give me a chance and hear me out, but no. You were too fucking good for me..."

I had no idea how he'd gotten access to the school's intercom, but I didn't take it as a good sign. To get there meant he'd gotten past not only Braylon and Timms, but Widow and his prospect Jackal as well, and that thought terrified me. I was frozen with fear. All I could do was sit there and listen to Drake's insanity. "That was a mistake that's going to cost you dearly."

As I sat there in the pitch dark, I thought about

everything Drake had just said and was riddled with guilt. I should've known that there was a reason why he'd shown up at the Manor looking for me that day. He was getting a lay of the land, which explained how he knew exactly where to find us. He must've used the fire as a decoy to lure us away just long enough to get inside. I couldn't understand how he'd gotten past all the security cameras. Not that it mattered now. He and his people had infiltrated us, and it was my fault. I'd tried to be careful and watch my back, but clearly, I'd failed miserably, and now everyone at the Manor was paying for my mistake. The thought consumed me with regret as I listened to Drake growl, "It's time to face the music. Come out of hiding, or I'll put a bullet in your buddy's head and finish him off."

"No! Don't!" Braylon shouted. "Stay where you are!"

"Don't be a stupid bitch. Come out or he's as good as dead. It's your choice."

"Kiersten, don't!"

There was a loud burst of static, and then the microphone clicked off, leaving me spiraling with doubt. I knew I couldn't sit there and leave someone I cared about to die—even if it meant putting my own life in jeopardy. I took a deep breath, trying my best to calm my racing heart, then forced myself out of my hiding place. With Braylon's gun in hand, I crept down the dark aisle of the classroom. When I made it to the door, I eased it open and stepped into the hallway. I'd only taken a few steps when I spotted Widow across the hall. His weapon was in his hand, his finger on the trigger, and he had a fierce expression on his face. He saw me but didn't speak. He simply shook his head, warning me not to go any further.

I knew he was trying to protect me, but I couldn't stop. I had to get to Braylon, so I mouthed, "I have to help Braylon."

He shook his head once again—more sternly this time, but I didn't heed his warning. Instead, I continued forward and prayed I could get to Braylon before Drake did something we'd all regret. Cautioning me yet again, Widow hissed, "Goddamn it, Kiersten. Don't take another step."

"I'm sorry, but I have to do something."

"Jackal is headed that way. Just go back and hide like Braylon told you!"

"I'm sorry. I can't. I just can't."

Without giving him a chance to say anything more, I rounded the corner and continued towards the office with Braylon's gun at my side, trying my best to conceal it. When I made it up front, Braylon was no longer lying on the floor. All that remained was a small pool of blood, which only added to my terror. I stepped toward the office door and entered, only to find that the room was empty. I knew they'd just been there. They had to be close, so I opened each of the closets and the private bathroom, but there was no sign of Drake or Braylon.

I stood still, wondering where they might be when Jackal came charging into the room. While he had the same intense expression, he and Widow were polar opposites. Where Widow was older with a beard and a tall, muscular build, Jackal was young and handsome with light golden-blond hair and a slender frame. Without saying a word, he raced toward me and tossed me over his shoulder, then charged out of the room. In a blink, I was face down on the floor, and Jackal was piled on top of me. I had no idea what he was doing until a loud explosion erupted from the office, and debris flew through the air.

I realized then that Jackal was using his own body as a shield, making sure I wasn't harmed in the explosion. I lay there for several moments, thinking he'd move once the dust settled. He didn't. He remained perfectly still even when I whispered, "Jackal ... Jackal?"

He didn't respond, so I shifted his weight to my side, then slipped out from underneath him. As soon as I'd gotten to my knees, I spotted the large shard of glass centered like a large knife in his back. I knelt down and gave him a slight shake as I cried, "Jackal? Jackal, are you okay? Please be okay—"

"Sorry, Kiersten," Drake sneered. "But I don't believe he's gonna answer."

I looked behind me and found Drake standing above me with his gun pressed against Braylon's head. There was another man standing behind them—his weapon was also drawn and pointed directly at me. I looked down the hall, searching frantically for any sign of Widow, Timms, or Duggar. Unfortunately, they were nowhere to be found. I glanced up at Drake and asked, "Why are you doing this?"

"You left me no choice."

"What the hell does that even mean?"

"For a smart girl, you can be really fucking stupid. Seriously, what did you fucking expect me to do? You came into my territory—the one I'd been running for years, and like it was yours for the taking, you started selling your dope." His eyes were full of anger as he glared down at me. "I didn't say a fucking word. I just stood by and let you steal my customers, *my money*, all because I thought we had something—a connection that could lead to something more. Now, I see that isn't going to happen."

I had no idea he was selling marijuana. Nor did I realize that he knew I was selling it. I was completely stunned by the revelation. I was even more stunned when he shook his head and growled, "We could've had it all. We could've joined forces. With my goods and yours, we could've made this *our city*. But you were too fucking stubborn. I'm done trying to be the good guy. I'm taking over. This place of yours is going be mine..."

FIFTEEN

COUNTRY

MY MIND WAS RACING AS WE SPED TOWARDS THE Manor. I desperately wanted to know that Kiersten was okay, so I called her phone over and over again. When she still didn't answer, I tried Braylon, Widow, and Jackal. Again, no answer. I sent them all countless messages, but neither responded. They could've been away from their phones or maybe they'd put out the fire and gone back to bed, but I had a bad feeling that wasn't the case. We'd just made it out of the Nashville city limits when Menace's phone started to ring. Hawk, Lynch, and I watched as he picked it up and looked down at the screen. Dread washed over me the second I saw the expression on his face. I knew right away something was terribly wrong. He looked over at me and said, "It's Riggs."

He brought the phone up to his ear and answered, "This is Menace."

Silence fell over the truck as he paused to listen for a moment, then asked, "Any idea how many there are?"

Another agonizing pause, then Menace asked, "What do we need to do here?"

Menace listened for a few more moments, then replied, "We'll let you know as soon as we get there."

As soon as he hung up, Menace turned his attention to us. "It wasn't just a fire. There are intruders, and the Manor is on lockdown."

"What the fuck?" I roared.

"He just turned on the sprinkler system on at the gym, so the fire shouldn't be much of an issue. I can't say the same for the intruders."

Hawk sounded equally angered when he asked, "Any idea how the hell this happened?"

"Can't say for sure. I'm guessing whoever did this used the storm to their advantage. Hard to see anything with all the wind and rain."

"Fuck! Any idea who it might be?"

"No clue, but it's pretty clear these guys know what they're doing. They set the fire as a decoy. Used it to get them away from the school long enough to get inside."

"Wait, you said the Manor was on lockdown."

"They are."

"So, they're locked inside there with them?"

"It's hard to tell. They've dismantled the camera feed, but Riggs seems to think there are several still outside."

"And Kiersten?"

"Pretty sure she's in there with them."

"Damn it!" I didn't realize just how much I cared about Kiersten until her life was in jeopardy. The mere thought of losing her sent me into a spiraling panic. "We gotta get to her!"

"I know, brother, and we will. Should be there in less than ten minutes," Menace tried to assure me. "She's a smart girl. She can hold on until then."

I ran my hand over my face, trying to slow the thoughts racing through my mind. I couldn't hold back my rage as I growled, "This shit should've never happened. Where the hell were Widow and Jackal?"

"It's after midnight, brother. I'm sure one or both of them were down for the night. Not sure who was on night duty or why they might've been distracted. None of that matters now." Menace's cool demeanor remained intact as he said, "Right now, we need to focus on getting there and doing whatever we gotta do to take these motherfuckers down."

Hawk took out his phone and called Viper and updated him on what was going down. As expected, Viper told Hawk that he would get some of the other brothers together, and they'd come to give us a hand. I was barely keeping it together as I sat there staring out the window when Lynch reached over and placed his hand on my shoulder. "She's going to be okay, brother. We'll make sure of it."

I nodded but couldn't say anything in return. I was too beside myself to speak. I stared out at the road ahead, anxiously counting down the miles as we continued toward the Manor. I was so worked up I felt like I could crawl out of my own skin. I just wanted to get there and make sure Kiersten was okay. When we reached the edge of the property, I noticed two cars—a black BMW and a red Mercedes—parked along the fence row. I'd never seen them before, so I pointed them out to the others. "That's gotta be them. They must've parked here and headed in through the back field."

"Then, we'll do the same."

Menace pulled up behind the red Mercedes, and as soon as the truck stopped, we all got out and began putting on our bulletproof vests. Once I had mine on, I started sprinting towards the tall grass. The night air was cool and damp, and the ground was soft and muddy, making it difficult to run in my boots. I was already getting winded when Lynch, Menace, and Hawk came running up next to me. With all the cloud cover from the previous storms, it was darker than ever, and it felt like we'd been running for a lifetime before we finally came upon the back entrance of the Manor.

Knowing we weren't there alone, we each slowed our pace and pulled out our weapons, being watchful of our surroundings as we continued forward. As we got closer, Menace turned to us and said, "Riggs said for us to go to the back of the school, and he'd get us in."

We nodded, then followed him behind the mid-sized house that Kiersten had renovated into the guest quarters. Hawk led us around back where we could get a better view of the back of the school. I saw movement near the garden and asked, "You seeing that?"

"Yeah," Hawk answered. "I see it. You think that's them, or is that one of Kiersten's crew?"

Before I had a chance to respond, a round of gunfire had us all dropping down for cover. I was eager to find Kiersten and didn't have the patience to deal with some trigger-happy asshole, so I aimed my Glock and fired. Seconds later, the dark figure dropped to the ground and lay there motionless. Lynch chuckled as he whispered, "I guess that settles that."

"Damn right it does."

Hawk remained crouched down as he motioned us forward and led us to the next house and then the next. We were less than fifty feet away from the school when a shot was fired, and Lynch flew back and hit the ground. Menace, Hawk, and I all returned fire, and in a matter of seconds, the shooting stopped, and we all watched with satisfaction as a body collapsed to the muddy, wet ground. Wanting to make sure Lynch was okay, we all turned to our brother and found him clutching his bicep as he cursed, "Mother fucker! Right in the goddamn arm. Fucking pussy shot."

"You alright?" Hawk asked while he reached down and took his hand as I helped Lynch to his feet. "You need to head back to the truck?"

"Fuck, no. I'm fine." Lynch charged over to the body on the ground and fired off another round into the guy's head. "Stupid piece of shit."

"Gotta go, brother," I huffed out as I charged past him. "We don't have time for this bullshit."

With the others following close behind, I rushed up to the school's back door, then waited as Menace reached out to Riggs. As soon as he let him know we were there, he released the security lock on that specific door, then relocked it as soon as we'd made it inside. I'd been in the school many times during my two-week stint at the Manor, so I knew the office was just through the double doors. But I didn't move. None of us did. We each stood there, listening for footsteps, talking, or shooting—any sign that would help us identify the location of our adversaries. At first, there was nothing—just complete and utter silence. Then, I heard it—the faint sound of Kiersten's voice followed by gunshots coming from what sounded like the other side of the school.

"Did you hear that?" I motioned my hands towards the door. "She's here. I heard her."

Menace looked over his shoulder, making sure no one was coming up from behind as Hawk led us to the end of the hall. Before opening the door, Hawk pressed his ear to it, silently listening for a possible opportunity to move forward without making our presence known —at least not yet. After listening for a moment, Hawk turned back to me and asked, "She just called someone by the name Drake. Any idea who that might be?"

"Don't have a clue."

"I think he's got Braylon, too. We need eyes on that fucking security feed."

"I can reach out to Riggs and see."

"There's no time." Hawk inched the door open, then peered through the crack. "The office has been blown to fucking shreds. Jackal is on the floor next to Kiersten's feet, and I'm pretty sure he's dead."

Lynch sounded stunned as he asked, "You sure he isn't just playing possum or something?"

"He's got a two-foot shard of glass in his back, brother. Pretty sure he isn't playing possum."

"Damn it." Lynch sighed. "Poor kid didn't deserve that shit."

Jackal had only been prospecting for a few weeks, but he'd already made an impression on several of the guys, including Lynch. I felt bad for the kid, really bad, but none of us had the luxury of mourning his loss— not until we knew for certain that Kiersten and the others were safe. "What about Kiersten? Is she okay?"

"Yeah, she's holding her own." Hawk kept his voice low, but I could still hear the concern in his voice when he said, "Some asshole is talking to her. Can't make out what he's saying, but he's going on and on about something, and he's got his gun aimed at Braylon's head."

"Damn it. Any others out there with them?"

"Just one other guy, and he has his gun trained on Kiersten." I wanted to barge through those doors and kill the assholes with my bare hands but forced myself to stay put and listen as Hawk told us, "Looks like they're stuck."

"Fuck." Lynch grimaced as he asked, "What about Widow? Where is he?"

"No sign of him or Timms and Duggar." We could hear random gunfire continue across the building, but none of us had a clue as to who was doing the shooting so Hawk suggested, "I know we've all tried reaching him and had no luck, but there's still a chance that Widow has his phone with him. Send him a message and just see if he happens to answer."

Menace nodded, then whipped out his phone. He

punched a few keys, then we all held our breaths as we waited for him to respond. We were all relieved when seconds later, Menace's phone lit up, signaling that he'd gotten a response. Menace read the message, then told us, "He and Duggar are on the opposite end of the building. They're just waiting for their chance to make a move."

Hawk motioned his head towards Menace's phone as he asked, "Is it clear on their end?"

"Not sure." Menace sent Widow another message, then waited for his response. "No. There are two, maybe three more of these guys, and they've got Widow and Duggar cornered. And to make matters worse, both Widow and Duggar are running low on ammo."

"Fuck." I was still trying to piece all the facts together, so I asked, "What about Timms? Where is he?"

"Didn't make it."

"Seriously?"

"Yeah, Widow didn't go into detail about what happened. Just said he was dead."

"Damn." Hawk glanced back at us and asked, "So, how do you wanna play this?"

"I don't see why we wouldn't just bust up in there," I answered. "We can use the element of surprise to our advantage."

Clearly disagreeing with my plan, Hawk shook his head and grumbled, "And what happens when one of them shoots Kiersten or Braylon?"

"We kill them before they get a chance to pull the trigger."

"There are no guarantees we can make that happen."

"Then, what the fuck are we gonna do, 'cause we can't just stand here with our thumbs up our asses and wait for these motherfuckers to kill them."

"We could always go back outside and come in through the hallway door where Widow is." I thought Lynch's idea was absolutely senseless until he continued, "If we can take the heat off of him and Duggar, then maybe they can get to Kiersten and Braylon and end this thing."

"That's not a bad idea, brother."

"No, it's not." Hawk eased the doorway closed. "But we need to move fast. Send him a message and let him know we're coming. Need to know where these motherfuckers are before we go inside."

Menace messaged Widow, letting him know the plan. Once we'd made it around to the other side of the school, Menace sent Riggs a message, letting him know that we'd be needing him to open a second door. By the time we made it outside, Riggs had replied and was waiting to trigger the door. Widow warned us that one of the men was standing close, so Hawk had his weapon drawn as he eased the door open. As soon as he spotted him standing in one of the classroom doorways, he pulled back on the trigger and fired, killing him instantly.

We'd barely made it through the door when the other two men immediately turned their attention away from Widow and Duggar and started shooting at us. I was done dealing with these motherfuckers. I knew we had to get them out of the way if we were ever going to get to Kiersten, so I continued charging forward as I fired off one round after the next. I didn't even stop when a bullet plowed into my chest. Even with the bulletproof vest, it hurt like a motherfucker, but I kept pressing forward until I hit the asshole closest to me. Just as Lynch had done earlier, I shot him again to make sure he was down and stayed down.

Until then, the other shooter had been focused on Menace and Lynch. They were both positioned inside one of the classroom doorways, using it as a protective shield as they tried to take him down. Hawk was behind me, doing everything he could to cover me until the shooter turned his attention to us—forcing us both out of the hall and into one of the old classrooms. The guy either got really fucking brave or just downright stupid and stepped out into the open, giving Widow the opportunity he needed to take a shot.

As soon as the asshole hit the floor, the shooting stopped. Hawk and I immediately came out of the classroom, and with Lynch and Menace following close behind, we rushed over to join Widow and Duggar. Widow gave us a thankful nod as he said, "Don't know who came up with the plan, but we sure appreciate the help back there."

"You can thank Lynch for that," Hawk replied. "It was his idea."

"Well, it worked."

I felt like we were finally making some ground until Widow motioned his head to the office. "We can't do shit. At least not while he has that fucking gun pointed at Kiersten's head."

I looked through the crack in the door, and my chest tightened the second I spotted Kiersten. I knew she had to be terrified, especially with the asshole pointing his goddamn gun at her, but she was putting on a brave front. She wasn't crying or trembling. Instead, she stood tall, trying to talk to him. While I couldn't hear what she was saying, I knew her well enough to know that she was doing everything she could to put an end to this whole fiasco and do it without costing Braylon his life. My only concern was about getting Kiersten away from those men. I looked around, searching for a way to get close enough to help when I noticed that the explosion had created a gaping hole in the office wall. If I was right, we would be able to use that fucking hole as a means to put an end to Drake once and for all. We just had to get into just the right position without drawing his attention outside. It was risky, but it was our only chance.

"I've got it." I turned to face the others as I said, "I know what we've gotta do."

SIXTEEN

KIERSTEN

"You can have it all, Drake. *Everything*. It's yours. I don't care. Please let us go."

"You'd like that, wouldn't you?" A sinister smile crossed his face. "I let you go, and then you and your little buddies get your cop friends to come and take me out. That's not going to happen."

"No, that's crazy. Why would I bring the cops here? I wouldn't want them seeing all this."

"Oh, you should know I'm too smart to fall for that bullshit. With the kind of money you're bringing in here, I'm sure you have the cops in your pocket."

The shooting down the hall suddenly subsided, leaving the entire building enveloped in an eerie silence. I had no idea if that was a good sign or not. I prayed that Duggar, Timms, and Widow were still alive but had no way of knowing for sure. I'd been trying so hard to keep Drake preoccupied, saying anything I could to keep him from pulling that trigger and killing Braylon, but I was afraid my time was about to run out. Out of pure desperation, I tried, "It's not too late. We can still do this. We can go into business together. We can do whatever you want."

"Is that right?"

Drake immediately reached over and grabbed my arm, yanking me over to him. He leaned in and ran his tongue from my lower jaw along the side of my cheek. When he grabbed my face and pulled me in for a kiss, I panicked. I placed my hands on his chest and gave him a hard shove. A sinister chuckle vibrated through his chest as he growled, "I knew you were full of shit."

As soon as the words left his mouth, he lifted his hand and struck me across the face. "I'm done with you and your stupid fucking games."

I brought my hand up to my face, covering it protectively as I watched him start to pace back and forth. He waved his gun in the air as he started ranting to himself. "Stupid fucking cunt. Playing all these fucking games with my head."

Most of what he was saying was incoherent, but it was clear that Drake had gone off the deep end. One minute he was trying to make a play for me, and then he was committed to taking over the Manor and making it his own. Time was running out, and I had no clue what to do. My mind was reeling as I continued to watch him talk to himself. "Enough of the bullshit. I'm going to do what I came here to do. I'm gonna take what's mine, and no one is gonna stop me."

Without warning, he whipped around and aimed his gun at me. Just as he was about to pull the trigger, I pleaded, "Please, Drake. Let's just talk this thing out."

"You had your chance."

"But until tonight, I didn't even know what you wanted from me." There was still no sound coming from the back hall, and I started panicking that they were all dead. I hadn't seen Widow, Timms, or Duggar since the shooting began, and considering they hadn't come to our rescue, it was impossible not to think the worst, and that chilled me to the bone. To make matters worse, Drake's friend still had his gun aimed at my head, and Braylon wasn't looking good at all. His face was pale, and his clothes were soaked in his blood. I tried to buy us both some more time by distracting Drake. "If you'd only been honest with me and told me what was going on, then I would've been more open to the idea of us working together."

"That's bullshit, and you know it," Drake roared. "From day one, you wanted nothing to do with me. You were repulsed by me. I could see it in your eyes whenever we talked... and I can see it in your eyes right now.

You've always thought you were better than me, but I'm here to prove you wrong."

I thought we were alone until I noticed a strange movement out of the corner of my eye by the crumbled section of the office wall, but it was too dark to see much of anything. I wanted to believe it was Widow or one of the others coming to save us but figured the possibility was slim at best and convinced myself it was only my crazy imagination. I turned my attention back to Drake with a defeated sigh. I was losing ground with him, and I didn't have a clue how to turn the tables. I kept my voice low and steady and said, "You've already proven me wrong, Drake. Clearly, there's more to you than I ever knew."

"Damn straight there is! I'm—"

Before he could finish his sentence, there was an unexpected roar of gunshots. I froze as I watched Drake's eyes widen and his head fall back. At first, I couldn't comprehend what was happening, but then I saw the blood and realized he'd been shot—right through his temple. He stood still like a statue with his eyes locked on mine for a split second, and then his body collapsed to the ground—right next to his partner in crime who'd had his gun trained on me for the past half-hour. I was stunned. They'd both been shot at the same time and were lying dead on the floor. It was difficult to make sense of it. One minute

Drake and I were talking, and in the next, he was lying dead on the floor. I didn't move. I simply stood there in utter dismay. I didn't even notice that Widow and Duggar had walked up until Duggar asked, "You two okay?"

Still in a daze, I nodded and said, "Yeah, I'm fine, but Bray's hurt. He needs to get to the hospital."

"I'm okay," Bray argued. "Right now, I'm more concerned about you." He lifted his hand up to my face as he said, "You're bleeding."

"I'm fine, Bray. It's just a few scratches." Noting his seeping wounds, Duggar took off his shirt, then knelt down next to him and quickly wrapped the fabric around Bray's thigh. It was clear I wasn't the only one who thought his wounds needed to be checked. "You, on the other hand, need to get to a doctor and have them check you out."

"Bullet went straight through the shoulder, and the other is just a fucking graze. I'm fine." Sorrow filled his eyes as he looked over to Jackal. "Is he?"

Tears stung my eyes as I watched Widow go over and kneel down next to Jackal. Anguish marked his face as he rolled the prospect onto his side. Widow laid his hand on his brother's chest, then muttered something under his breath. My heart was breaking as I told Bray and Widow, "He died trying to protect me."

"I'm not surprised. He was a good kid ... a damn

good kid." Widow stood, then stepped back over to us. "He did what he came here to do."

"Same for Timms," Duggar announced, causing my heart to drop to my stomach. "He put up a good fight. Even took down one of them with him."

I'd done my best to keep it together, but the second I learned about Timms, the dam broke, and I started to cry. He was like family to me, and I hated that he'd lost his life trying to protect me and the Manor. I was sobbing when the front door swung open, and Grayson and Menace charged inside with Hawk and Lynch following close behind. Grayson's eyes were fixed on mine as he made his way through the others and over to me. He took me in his arms, holding me close in a protective hug. "Tell me you're okay."

"I'm better now." With a sniffle and a quick inhaled breath, I brushed the tears from my cheek. "I can't believe you came."

"Of course, I came. No way in hell I wouldn't."

I'd never been happier to see him and hugged him even tighter. "Thank God you did because I'm not so sure we would've gotten through this thing without you guys."

"Well, it's done now. It's over."

"What about the fire?"

"It's out. You don't have to worry."

"I still can't believe any of this happened." I took a

step back and glanced down at Drake's lifeless body. I had to fight back the tears as I said, "I thought we were prepared for anything, but it all happened so fast. One minute there was a fire, and then there was all the shooting. I had no idea what the hell was going on."

"None of us did."

Grayson walked over to Jackal, and like Widow had done just moments before, he knelt down beside him and placed his hand on his chest. He whispered a few words, then sighed with a shake of his head. After several moments, he stood and made his way back over to me. I looped my arm through his and whispered, "I'm so sorry about Jackal."

"I am, too. He's gonna be missed." Grayson brought his hand up to my cheek. "Are you really okay?"

"I am now." My voice trembled. "But earlier, I was a mess. I don't think I've ever been so terrified in my whole life. There was a point when I honestly didn't think we'd get out of here alive."

Without responding, Grayson reached over and took me in his arms once more. After several moments, he kissed me on the temple, then stepped back as he looked down at Drake. "You got any idea who this Drake guy is?"

"His name is Drake Coburn. We had a few classes together, and he asked me out a couple of times, but I always refused. Other than that, I really didn't know much about him." I shrugged. "I had no idea until tonight that he was a dealer, and I certainly didn't think he was interested in joining forces with me."

"So, this was all about you two joining forces?"

"Yeah, those were his words, not mine." I shook my head. "He'd never mentioned anything about that until he showed up here tonight. I'd always thought the creepy stares and small talk were because he liked me."

"Oh, he was definitely into her," Braylon added. "You could tell just by the way the asshole was looking at her. Besides, he would've just wiped us out and taken things over for himself if he was only interested in the goods. If he'd played it right, he would've gotten the weed and the girl."

"So, this guy really is a whack job?"

"Definitely." Braylon dropped his head in shame as he continued, "But he wouldn't have gotten as far as he did if I hadn't fucked up. I'm so sorry about all this."

"This isn't your fault, Bray," I argued. "There's no way you could've known this was going to happen."

"You're wrong, Kiersten. This was all on me." Anguish marked his face. "It was my job to watch over things tonight and keep this place safe. I dropped the ball, and we lost—"

"No," Widow interrupted. "This shit is on all of us."

"But I was the one in charge of the cameras tonight, and I let myself get distracted with... Mia? Where's Mia?"

"She's okay," I assured him. "I told her to get Regan and leave."

"Thank God. I don't know what I would've done if..."

His voice trailed off when the rumble of motorcycles pulled his attention to the parking lot. Hawk immediately went over and looked out the window, then announced, "Viper's here with Shotgun and Doc. I'll be right back."

As soon as Hawk stepped outside, Widow turned back to Braylon and said, "Now that he's here, we need to get with Doc. He can check your wounds and fix you up."

"What? No. This isn't something for Doc. Bray's been shot and lost a lot of blood," I fussed. "He needs to get to the hospital!"

"Yeah, he does, but what's he gonna say when they ask him what happened? When they ask who shot him?" Widow gave me a scolding look as he helped Bray to his feet. "'Cause they're gonna want to know those things. And they'll want to bring the cops in, and there'll be an investigation—"

"Okay, okay. I get it." I looked back over to Braylon

as I asked Widow, "But will Doc truly be able to help him?"

"This isn't Doc's first rodeo, Kiersten." Widow took hold of his upper arm, being careful not to get too close to his wounded shoulder and led Bray over to the door. Before they walked out, Widow assured me, "Doc will have Lynch and your boy fixed up in no time."

Country leaned over to me as he added, "He's right, babe. Braylon is in good hands with Doc. He's the best."

"I certainly hope you're right."

The words had barely left my mouth when the doors opened and Viper walked inside with Hawk and Shotgun. It was clear by his expression that the Ruthless Sinners' president wasn't pleased as he strode towards us. Without saying a word to anyone, he continued over to Jackal and knelt down beside him. He placed his hand on his back, then whispered something under his breath. After several tender moments with his fallen brother, Viper stood and shook his head as he let out a stream of curses. After inhaling a deep breath, he finally made his way over to Country and me. "Someone gonna tell me what the fuck happened here?"

"We're still trying to figure that out, Prez."

Grayson removed his hand from my waist, and he and Viper walked over to Hawk and Shotgun. I couldn't make out what any of them were saying, but they all kept glancing over in Drake's direction. Even though he'd come there for me and my business, they didn't discuss their club's business with anyone—including their loved ones. I stood there with Duggar, watching silently as Viper's face grew redder and redder with anger. After several long, heated moments, I heard Viper ask, "When will they get here?"

I wasn't sure, but if I had to guess, he was asking about the guys from Satan's Fury MC. With all the security cameras and sensors being tracked by Riggs, I had no doubt that they knew about the attack. I leaned over to Duggar and whispered, "Are you okay?"

"Yes, ma'am. I'm good. Just hate all this shit went down like it did." He ran his hand through his long, shaggy blond hair and sighed. "Timms was a good guy. Didn't deserve to go out like this."

"No, he didn't." I looked around at all the destruction and mayhem Drake had brought to our doorstep, and it was difficult to hold back my emotions. I'd worked so hard to get this place up and running, and things were going so well. It was amazing how quickly it could all change. I was on the brink of crying once again as I told Duggar, "If I'd only known what Drake was up to, then maybe I could've done something to stop it."

"You couldn't have known he'd pull something like

this, Kiersten, and even if you did, there wasn't anything you could've done to prevent it. The guy was off his fucking rocker."

Our conversation ended abruptly as soon as Viper and the others started walking over to us. Viper seemed to have cooled off when he came up to me and said, "We've got a real mess on our hands with this."

"I know, and I'm really sorry about that."

"You and me both." Viper tugged at his beard as he looked over the demolished office and then the dead bodies on the floor. "We're going to have to make some real changes around here, but before we get into all that, we're gonna have to get this mess cleaned up."

"Okay." Even though I dreaded hearing the answer, I asked, "What do we need to do?"

"This is more than we can handle on our own, Kiersten. We're gonna have to call in Billy."

"What?"

"He's the only one I trust to do this and do it right."

My father had always been a meticulous man— from the way he dressed to the way he kept the house. I had no doubt that he was even more so with his work, which was the main reason why Viper and the Sinners used him. It only made sense that he'd want to bring him in now, but the thought of my father coming to the Manor sent me into a tailspin. I was hoping to find a way to tell him about my work on my own, not to find out like this, so I told Viper, "But I didn't want him involved with my work."

"If you feel that strongly about it, then he doesn't have to know you're a part of all this." To my surprise, Viper seemed to understand how upset I was over my father coming here and was willing to do whatever he could to make it easier for me. "You can leave while he's here. We can handle things, and—"

As tempting as it was to hide and carry on with my charade of being the perfect daughter, I couldn't do it anymore. It was time my father knew who I was along with my capabilities. I gathered all the strength I could muster and said, "I truly appreciate the offer, but I can't let you do that."

"You sure?"

"I am." I cleared my throat. "Do you mind if I borrow your phone?"

Viper nodded, then took out his burner from his back pocket. He looked down at the screen, then pressed a few numbers before he offered it to me. "He uses a different line for cleaning calls. It's ready when you are."

My hands were trembling as I took the phone from him and pressed the button. Grayson and the rest of the brothers were watching as I stood there waiting for him to answer. Seconds later, my father's voice came on the line, and he said, "Hey there, Viper.

It's pretty late. I'm guessing that means you've got a job for me."

The words were right there on the tip of my tongue, but I felt like my throat was closing up, and I couldn't speak. I suddenly regretted telling Viper that I would be the one to call my father. I was trying to think of what I should say when I heard my father ask, "Viper, are you there?"

"It's me, Dad."

"Kiersten?"

"Yes." Having everyone's eyes on me was only making it harder to talk, so I stepped away from them and started walking down the hall as I said, "It's me."

"But this is Viper's number. How did you get his phone?" Sounding utterly confused, he asked, "Is he there with you?"

"Yes, but that's not important right now." I glanced over my shoulder, and just as I expected, everyone was still watching my every move. I tried not to think about it as I continued, "Right now, I need you to listen to me. I'm in serious trouble here, and I need your help. I need you and your men to come here *and do what you do*."

"What do you mean by 'do what we do'?"

"I know, Dad. I know all about 'your work.' I've known about it for years, but right now, none of that matters. Right now, I need you. There's been trouble here tonight, and I was hoping you could come and make it go away. Can you do that for me?" I heard my voice tremble, and I feared I might break out into tears again. I didn't want that to happen. Not now. I swallowed hard, pushing back all the emotions that were raging inside of me as I asked him once more, "Can you come and help me?"

"Send me the address, and I'll be there as soon as I can."

"Okay, thank you, Dad."

He didn't respond. He simply hung up the phone and ended the call. In all the years I'd known my father, he'd never once fussed at me or told me I had disappointed him. I'd never really given him a reason to —until tonight. I feared once he'd seen the Manor and all the mayhem that had ensued, he might never look at me the same. Feeling completely lost, I carried the phone back over to Viper and said, "He's on his way."

SEVENTEEN

COUNTRY

As soon as Billy and his crew arrived, he put on his hazmat suit and went straight to work. He didn't speak to anyone—just Viper, and even then, it was all business. *Cut and dry.* He wouldn't even look in Kiersten's direction. I wasn't exactly surprised by his reaction. The guy had to be pissed that his daughter had kept this part of her life a secret from him, but he'd done the same to her. They'd both made a mess of things, but in the end, they loved each other and that trumps a few secrets—or at least I hoped it did, for both of their sakes.

When Riggs showed up with Shadow and Blaze, Kiersten knew we had things to discuss with them, so she went to the kitchen to give Doc a hand with Braylon and Lynch while we met with Fury in the old church. We brought them all up to speed on what had gone down with Drake and all his bullshit and how we'd called Billy in to clean up the mess. After hearing us out, Riggs shook his head and said, "I gotta say, I'm surprised this Drake kid had the means to pull all this off. When I looked into him, he just seemed like your average college kid."

"You looked into him?" Viper asked, sounding just as surprised as I was. "When?"

"He came out to the Manor a few weeks back and was snooping around. When Braylon caught him, Drake said he was there looking for Kiersten." Riggs shrugged. "She thought him coming out to her place was just part of his fixation with her, and I found no reason to believe that wasn't the case."

"And you didn't think to tell us about him coming here?"

"I know it looks bad, Viper, but I assure you that I thought the matter was resolved. Otherwise, I would've come to you with it, or the very least, dug a little deeper and found out more about him."

"Well, you best get to diggin'. You and Menace both need to find everything you can on this guy because I don't want any of this coming back and biting us in the ass."

"You got it."

Menace turned to Riggs as he said, "I'll get my laptop from the truck."

With that, Menace stood and walked out of the church's conference room. Tensions were high as we sat there waiting for him to return. Viper was still reeling from hearing about Drake being at the Manor. I was, too. I found it hard to believe Kiersten had never mentioned him to me. She might've truly thought it wasn't worth it, or she simply didn't think she could trust me with the information. Either way, I intended to find out. Once Menace returned, he and Riggs set to work on finding out everything they could on Drake. They were still going at it when Viper said, "We're going to need to make some changes around here. We can't afford to let anything like this happen again."

"What kind of changes do you have in mind?" Blaze asked.

"Well, there's already been one big change." Viper leaned back in his seat. "Kiersten's girls won't be selling on campus anymore. All distribution will be through us. That should help eliminate unnecessary exposure, but we need more eyes on this place or possibly a few more hands. We'll have to replace Timms and possibly add another."

Everyone's attention was drawn over to the doorway when we noticed Braylon standing in the doorway with Doc. He looked like hell. His arm was bandaged and in a sling, and he had a significant limp from the graze on his thigh. He must've picked up on the fact that he shouldn't have been anywhere near motorcycle clubs when they were in church because he said, "I don't mean to interrupt whatever y'all got going in here."

"You're good." Hawk nodded his head toward Bray's shoulder. "You making it alright?"

"Yeah. I'm good." Braylon glanced over at Doc as he said, "Thanks to him."

"Glad to hear it."

"I wanted to apologize for my fuck up tonight. I let myself get distracted, and it cost us."

"Distracted how?"

"Mia had come into the office." His eyes dropped to the ground, and guilt marked his face as he admitted, "We got to talking, and one thing led to another. Next thing I knew, the fire alarm went off."

"Damn, Bray," Widow fussed. "You're better than that shit."

"I know. When I said this shit was on me, I meant it. I fucked up, and if you want me to call it quits, I will. I have that coming." He cocked his head to the side and sighed, then looked Viper in the eye. "But I want to be here. I owe it to Kiersten and myself to make amends for my mistake. So, if you'll give me a chance and stick it out with me, I'll turn this thing around and do right by all of you."

"No one's showing you to the door, brother. You're

in this with us, and together we'll find a way to make sure this sort of thing never happens again."

Relief washed over Braylon as he said, "I truly appreciate that, and if you are needing a few extra hands, I have a few ex-military guys I could get in touch with. I'm sure they'd be more than willing to come give us a hand."

"We might just do that, but for now, you go get some rest and tend to those wounds. We'll get those names from you when you get back on your feet."

"Okay, thanks. Sounds good."

When he and Doc started to leave, I got up and rushed over to them. "Where's Kiersten?"

"I checked her out and sent her back to her place," Doc answered.

"Okay, I'll go see about her when we get done here."

"Good deal. Hopefully, she'll be out like a light by then. Poor kid was pretty shaken up, so I gave her something to help her sleep."

"Thanks, brother. I appreciate you looking after her."

"No problem at all."

Without saying anything more, Doc took hold of Braylon's arm and helped him over to his place. I walked back to the table and was just sitting down when Menace turned to Viper and said, "There isn't a lot about this guy. Looks like his folks died and left him some property just east of Murfreesboro. Not a big place, but if there's any truth to all the bullshit he was feeding Kiersten, it could be where he's growing his product."

"What are you waiting for? Load up and go check the fucking place out."

"And if we find anything?"

"Take care of it."

Menace didn't have to ask any further questions. He knew Viper's expectations, and Viper trusted us to carry them out. I got up, and with Lynch and Widow close behind, we all followed Menace and the Fury boys out to the parking lot. Since our SUV was still parked out behind the property, we had to track down Duggar and get him to drive us over to it. Once we got to the truck, he headed back to the Manor, and we loaded up and followed Riggs and Blaze to Drake's place. Thankfully, it didn't take long to get there. Daylight was quickly approaching, so we didn't have much time to fuck around. As soon as we were parked, we started up to the front steps. There wasn't much to the place. Just a two-bedroom farmhouse that hadn't been updated in at least twenty years. The yard was overgrown, and there were old tires and tools scattered around the dilapidated garage. The front door was wide open, so we had no trouble getting inside. It had an old, musty smell, and like the outside, the place hadn't been taken care of. There was trash scattered about, and the furniture looked like it had been thoroughly abused. We searched the entire house and didn't find a damn thing, which led me to ask Menace, "Are you sure this is the right place?"

"Yeah, this is it. No doubt about it." He glanced around the rundown kitchen and said, "There's gotta be something we're missing."

We were all gathered in the kitchen when Blaze asked, "Is there a basement?"

"No idea."

We all started looking around, and it wasn't long before Menace discovered a secret hatch door in the bottom of the pantry. As soon as he opened it, the familiar scent of marijuana filled the room, and I knew we'd found what we were looking for. After he turned on the lights, we followed him down the wooden steps and into the small cellar. When we reached the bottom step, I saw that there was a makeshift table in the center of the room that held about twenty small, pitiful marijuana plants—not even a fraction of what Kiersten had out at the Manor. Lynch's brows were furrowed with confusion. "Is this really it?"

"Certainly looks that way."

"But that can't be right," Hawk argued. "The guy

had seven or eight men with him. How the fuck did he manage that when this is all he's got?"

I shook my head with disgust. "Yeah, there's not enough here to wipe my ass. No way this Drake asshole is making any real money off this shit."

"You're right," Hawk agreed. "There's got to be more somewhere."

"I'll go outside and see if there's anything in the barn," Riggs volunteered.

He rushed back up the steps, and we all could hear him stomping through the kitchen as he made his way out of the house. I was looking around to make sure we hadn't missed something when Hawk asked, "What do you guys think we should do with this shit?"

"I figure we got two choices." I looked over to Hawk as I continued, "We can take it back to the Manor or torch the whole place and be done with this shit."

Drake's place was at least ten miles from town without another house anywhere in sight, so burning the place to the ground seemed like the best option until Riggs came back into the house and shouted, "You guys need to come and see this shit."

We all rushed upstairs and out to the barn, where we found a dozen or so crates filled with heavy artillery, each with a variety of handguns, shotguns, and even a couple of semi-automatic rifles and plenty of ammo. Lynch was the first to voice his suspicion. "Holy hell. This guy was in deeper than I thought."

"You think he's moving all this on his own or working with someone?"

"Figure the guy is on his own," Riggs answered. "Otherwise, he wouldn't be so fired up to partner with Kiersten."

"Sure hope you're right about that." Hawk went over and picked up one of the crates. "It'll be daylight soon. Let's get this shit loaded up in the trucks."

"And then what?"

"We're gonna fucking torch the place."

With our plan in place, we carried the crates outside and stacked them in the back of the SUVs. After we got everything loaded, we grabbed a couple of gas cans and spread fuel all over the house and barn. The second we were done, Hawk tossed the match, and the entire place went up in flames. The old wood was dry and rotted, so it wouldn't take long for the entire place to be nothing more than a pile of ash. Once we were certain the fire had taken hold, we loaded up and got the hell out of there.

None of us spoke on the way back to the Manor. The adrenaline had officially worn off, and we were too fucking exhausted to even speak. I leaned my head back on the headrest and closed my eyes, and it wasn't long before I found myself thinking about Kiersten. I could only imagine the hell she'd been through last night, not only with the shootout but the whole fiasco with Billy. I had no doubt it had taken its toll on her, and I was eager to get back and make sure she was okay.

Viper was there waiting for us when we pulled back up to the Manor. Menace and Hawk explained what we'd found and told him how we'd torched the place. He stepped back to the rear of the SUVs and checked out the crates, and like us, he was quite surprised by the number of weapons the guy was holding on to. Viper shook his head. "I gotta admit. I wasn't expecting this shit."

"None of us were."

Viper closed the back hatch of one of them and said, "Somebody is going to be expecting this shipment, and when they don't get it, they're gonna come looking for it."

"Yeah, more than likely. So, what do you want us to do about it?"

"Nothing," Viper replied. "I'll make sure Billy takes care of it. Right now, all we have to worry about is getting someone in here to take care of Kiersten's office. That asshole made a real fucking mess of the place."

"Shouldn't be a problem. When y'all are ready, I'll call Gus and have him send up Guardrail and a few of the brothers. They can have it fixed up in no time," Blaze offered.

"Appreciate it, brother." Viper spotted Billy walking in our direction and ordered, "You boys head over to the guest quarters and get some shut-eye. We'll pick up from here in a couple of hours."

"Sure thing, Prez."

Everyone immediately turned and started walking across the field. We hadn't gotten far when I heard Billy and Viper talking. I struggled to make out what either of them was saying, but it was clear from his tone that Billy was still pissed. If I had to guess, I'd say he was struggling with the fact that the Sinners not only knew about his daughter's secret drug business but that we were also in cahoots with her. Something I was sure he thought he should've been made aware of, but we didn't discuss our business with any outsiders, and like it or not, that included him. I didn't doubt that Viper would set him straight with the club and, hopefully, put this whole thing behind us.

Kiersten, on the other hand, would have a much harder time clearing things up with him, but she had an advantage the Sinners didn't have. She was his daughter, and it was clear by the way he looked at her that he adored her. That in itself would be enough to help them get through this mess—or so I hoped.

On the way over to the guest quarters, I let Hawk

and Lynch know I wouldn't be joining them and that they could find me over at Kiersten's. They were both too tired to give me any shit about it and simply nodded when I turned and started walking over to her place. When I got up to the front door, I wasn't surprised to find it locked. I figured that meant she was sleeping, so I used the key she'd given me and let myself inside. I kicked off my boots and removed my cut and jeans, then laid them across the back of the sofa. After removing my long-sleeved shirt, I made my way into the bedroom and slipped under the covers next to Kiersten.

As I hoped, she was sleeping soundly and hadn't even noticed that I'd gotten in bed with her. I eased up behind and spooned her with her ass by my crotch, then carefully slipped my arm around her waist. I closed my eyes and listened to the soothing sounds of her breath, and in no time, I was out like a fucking light. I have no idea how long I'd been sleeping when I felt Kiersten moving beneath me. Thinking she'd eventually drift back off, I remained perfectly still and didn't say a word. She didn't. Instead, she became even more restless. I pulled her back against my chest and dropped my mouth to her ear as I whispered, "You okay?"

"Yes and no."

"Something you wanna talk about?"

"We lost Timms and Jackal."

"Yeah, we did."

"Braylon and Lynch were shot, my office is destroyed, and I'm pretty sure my father hates me."

"He doesn't hate you, Kiersten."

"Are you sure about that? Because he wouldn't even look at me tonight. I've never seen him so angry before. He was absolutely livid."

"And I'm sure you can understand why." I kissed her lightly on the shoulder. "He just needs a little time to sort things out."

"You know, it's kind of crazy. There was a time when I was so mad at him I couldn't think straight. Back then, I wouldn't care if he was angry or upset with me. I'd just think he had it coming for keeping so much hidden from me, but now, I'm terrified of losing him."

"You aren't going to lose him, Kiersten. Not over something like this."

"Are you sure?"

"I'm more than sure."

"I really hope you're right."

"I am. You'll see." I didn't want to cause her any undue stress, but I had a question that needed to be answered. "Can I ask you something?"

"Of course."

"Why didn't you tell me about Drake?"

"I don't know. At first, I didn't think there was any reason to. I thought he was just interested in dating me or whatever, so I told him straight out that I wasn't interested. The last time I ran into him, you were gone on your run, and I didn't want to worry you with it."

"You wouldn't be bothering me, Kiersten. I'm here for you."

"I know. I just figured I could handle it on my own. Clearly, I was wrong."

"Don't do that. Don't take blame that isn't yours to take."

"But—"

"No buts. This thing with Drake wasn't your fault. Now leave it at that." I gave her another kiss, then laid my head down on the pillow and closed my eyes. "You've had a long night. Go back to sleep."

Without any further protest, she nestled close to me and became perfectly still. After several minutes passed, I thought she'd gone back to sleep, but I quickly realized I was wrong when she inched her hips back, gently pressing her ass against my cock. "What are you doing, babe?"

"I can't sleep," she whispered.

"Is that right?"

"Mm-hmm." She pressed her ass against me again. "I need you to take my mind off of everything ... just for a little while."

"I can do that." I trailed my hand down her stomach and beneath her lace panties as I asked, "You sure this is what you want?"

"Yes, Grayson ... *Please*," she whimpered as my fingers slid between her legs. Her ass nudged back against my growing erection, and I groaned in response. With one simple move, she'd struck a match, lighting a fire that sent a flash of need and want surging through me, burning me to the core. There were no limits to my desire for her. This woman was everything I'd ever wanted, everything I'd ever dreamed of, and she was mine. *All mine.* I guided my fingertips inside her, and the blood rushed to my cock when I found she was already soaked. I'd just begun to stroke her when she moaned, "Oh God, Grayson ..."

The sound of my name from her lips spurred me on, and I couldn't wait a moment longer to be inside her. Before she could protest, I withdrew my fingers and quickly lowered her panties down her legs. Once I'd removed my boxer briefs, I dropped my hands to her hips, pulling her ass against me. Instinctively, her legs spread wide for me, giving me complete access as I positioned myself at her center. A sense of contentment washed over me when her back arched against me as I drove inside her. She was so fucking tight, and just being inside her made me forget about the craziness of the night. Like all the times before, when she was in my arms, there was no one else. *Just her.*

"You drive me crazy, woman. Never wanted anyone like I want you," I growled as my fingers dug into her hips.

I drove into her again and again, fucking her deep and hard. A fevered moan vibrated through her as she started to grind against me, taking me deeper and deeper with every shift of her hips. Knowing what she needed, I slid my hand from her hip down between her legs, and her breath quickened when I reached her clit. Pleasured cries echoed through the room when I began to stroke her with a tormenting rhythm, and it wasn't long before I could feel her muscles contracting all around me as she pleaded, "Don't stop!"

She felt so damn good, so right. Her body started to tremble around me, urging me on as I drove deep inside, over and over, until at last, she let out a groan and clamped down around me. There was no better feeling in the world, and I felt my release building as my muscles in my abdomen and legs grew taut. With one final thrust, I pulled her to me and came deep inside her, growling with complete and utter gratification.

Neither of us moved. We just lay there nestled close together as our breathing started to slow. She reached for my hand, and as she laced her fingers through mine, she tucked my arm under her in a tender embrace. "Grayson?"

"Mm-hmm?"

"I don't want you to leave."

"You want to tell me what you're talking about?"

"I know it's too soon to say this or even think it, but I love you, Grayson. I love you so very much," she replied softly. "I just don't want to lose you."

"Not going to lose me, babe. I'm not going anywhere." I leaned down and kissed her on the forehead. "I'm here for the long haul."

"Really?"

"Mm-hmm. Gonna talk to Viper today about staying on here full time."

Her eyes lit up as she looked up at me and smiled. "But what about the club?"

"Nothing will change there. I'll still fulfill all my duties and spend time at the clubhouse. I'll just be living here."

"Are you sure you want to do that?"

"Why wouldn't I?" Her eyes were locked on mine when I said, "I love you, babe. There's no place I'd rather be than here with you."

"You love me?"

"I thought we already covered that."

"Well, I'm gonna need you to cover it again."

"Yes, Kiersten. I love you." I laid my head back on

the pillow as I teased her. "Not something I planned on happening, but what can I say? You sank those nails in deep. I never stood a chance."

"Grayson!"

"What?" I opened one eye as I kept pestering her. "Don't act like you don't know what I'm talking about. You knew what you were doing."

"Tell me you aren't being serious right now!"

While it was good to see that spark in her eyes had returned, I didn't want to take my teasing too far. I gave her a playful smirk as I admitted, "Yeah, babe. I'm just messing with ya."

She lowered herself back into the crook of my arm with a huff. "That's just wrong."

"I'm sorry. I couldn't help myself."

I leaned down and kissed her briefly, then settled back down on the bed. It wasn't long before she finally drifted back off to sleep. I looked down at her, and my chest swelled in a way it never had before. I had no doubt that I loved her. I felt that same feeling every time I looked at her, thought about her, and even more when I held her in my arms. I knew I didn't deserve a woman as incredible as Kiersten, but she was mine, and I wasn't going to let her go.

Not now. Not ever.

EIGHTEEN

KIERSTEN

It had only been a couple of weeks since the night of Drake's attack, but things were already starting to get back to normal—at least partially so. Guardrail and several of the other Satan's Fury crew came and completely redid my office. They even added a few upgrades that I hadn't expected. The place looked incredible, and it only took them a couple of days. We also had a few new faces on the grounds. Braylon had gotten in contact with some of his old platoon buddies, and just as he'd hoped, they'd agreed to come work with us. Having them there seemed to lift Braylon's spirits, and he was starting to get around a little better. I was concerned he was pushing himself too hard, but he assured me that getting back to work was exactly what he needed.

While I was pleased that things were going so

well, it still seemed strange not having Timms around. I had no doubt that Grayson and his brothers felt the same about Jackal. We'd done our best to give them both a proper burial on the grounds, but I couldn't help but feel like I should've done something more. They'd both died trying to protect me and the others at the Manor, so I got in touch with Menace and had him anonymously wire a large sum of money to their families. I knew it wouldn't replace their loved ones but hoped it might give them a little peace to have a bit of help with some of their financial burdens.

There was one big change that I couldn't have been happier about. Grayson had talked it over with Viper, and like we'd both hoped, the Ruthless Sinners' president gave the okay for Grayson to move to the Manor full-time. I loved having him there with me, I truly did, but there was one small catch. Every morning, just like right now, he'd ask me the exact same question. "Are you going to go talk to your father today?"

Normally, I would come up with some random excuse not to go, but I'd spent most of the night thinking about it and decided it was time to face the music. Grayson was sitting on the edge of the bed, putting on his boots, when I sauntered by him in nothing but my bra and panties. I glanced back over my shoulder and answered nonchalantly, "Actually, I am."

"What?"

"I've decided to go talk to him." I found it endearing that Grayson cared so much about my relationship with my father. I knew he was concerned, not only for me and my well-being but also for my father's. He was an integral piece of the Ruthless Sinners' puzzle, and since I was now in business with them, I needed to be in my father's good graces. But business was the last thing on my mind when I contacted my father. There were times when I was angry with him, but I'd always loved my father. I hated that this estranged distance had settled between us and hoped an honest conversation with him might actually bring us closer. I grabbed my jeans out of my drawer and started to pull them on. "I messaged him while you were in the shower and told him I was coming."

"And he was good with that?"

"I guess so." I pulled on my hoodie and tugged it down around my waist. "He told me he was looking forward to seeing me."

"That's great!" He stood up and walked over to me. As he slipped his arms around my waist, he smiled and said, "I'm really proud of you for doing this. I know it won't be easy, but I think you'll be glad you went to see him."

"I hope so." I inched up on my tiptoes and pressed my lips to his. "I better get going. The sooner I get there, the sooner I can get back and help Braylon finish putting those bookshelves together for the office."

"I'll help him with that. You just go and try to make the best of your visit with your dad."

"Okay." I slipped on my shoes, then started for the door. "I'll let you know when I'm headed back."

I grabbed my keys and purse, then walked out to my car. As soon as I started driving towards my dad's, dread set in, and I was tempted to turn around and put off our talk for another day. Then I remembered the look on Grayson's face when I told him I was finally going to see my father. He'd done so much for me, and I couldn't bear the thought of letting him down. So, I did the only thing I could.

I swallowed my apprehension and pressed forward. I tried not to overthink things as I continued to drive towards Dad's house, but it wasn't easy. Every few miles, my mind would drift back to the night of Drake's attack and the look on my father's face when he saw me standing with the Ruthless Sinners. It was enough to make my heart ache with regret. I wished that I'd talked to him sooner, then maybe all this wouldn't be so hard. Unfortunately, I couldn't go back in time and change things. I had to face the music and try to make things right between us.

When I pulled up at the house, Dad was sitting on the front porch swing waiting for me. I got out and couldn't help but notice that he didn't smile as I made my way up the front steps. Usually, he greeted me with open arms and a big hug, but today, he remained seated and didn't say a word as I walked over and sat down next to him. I feigned a slight smile and mumbled, "Hey."

"Hey."

"Thank you for letting me come today."

"Of course." His brows furrowed. "I'd never turn you away, Kiersten. You're my daughter. My pride and joy. Nothing will ever change that."

"Not even the fact that I've been lying to you?"

"We've both done our fair share of lying." Dad turned and looked at me as he said, "But I never meant to hurt you. I do hope you know that."

"I know that's not what you intended, but you did. The night I found out what you were doing in the basement hurt me in ways I still can't comprehend." I could feel the emotion building inside me as I continued, "I can't tell you how much I wish I'd never gone down there. I wish I'd never seen you burning those bodies in the incinerator. Because seeing you do that stole something from me, and that nearly killed me. I just couldn't bear knowing there was this dark side to you that I never knew existed. It was almost like you reached through time, and you stole my trust in everything I ever thought was real."

"I'm sorry, sweetheart. But you have to know you were never supposed to see that."

"Maybe not, but I did, and I've spent years waiting for you to tell me why."

"I had many reasons for not telling you, Kiersten, but all you need to know is that I did what I did for our family."

"Don't do that. Don't just blow it all off like it was something you had to do," I fussed. "You could've gone back to your job in forensics, but you chose to do this instead. I need you to tell me why."

"I'll tell you, but only because you're in bed with them now."

"In bed with who?"

"*The Sinners.*" His tone was cold and harsh as he said, "You're part of their world now."

"But what do they have to do with—"

"I'm getting there." He took a deep breath and turned to look out towards the pond. It took him several moments, but he eventually said, "Losing your mother nearly destroyed me. My head went to a place it never should've gone. I tried to keep it together for you, but I couldn't let go of the anger. I needed someone to answer for what happened, and other than myself, there was only one other person who came to mind—*her doctor*. I started looking into him and discovered that your mother wasn't the only patient he'd lost under his care."

"But Dad, things happen. Doctors lose patients all the time—"

"Yeah, they do," he interrupted. "But this was different. This was negligence."

"Yes, it was." I was eager to hear the rest of his story, so I asked, "So, what did you do?"

"I went to see him. I wanted to hear him admit what he'd done, and as stupid as it may sound, I needed him to apologize for making such a careless mistake."

"And did he?"

"No, he did not." Dad stood and walked over to the front porch rails. It was clear that reliving this story was hard for him, but that didn't stop him from telling me, "He had no remorse over what had happened to your mother. He blamed her for the mistake and said I had no proof of my claims of his malpractice. I wasn't surprised that he tried to blow me off. This guy had a real God complex, and that only made me angrier. I knew in my heart that he was the reason why your mother was dead, but there was nothing I could do about it."

I hated seeing the dreadful look on Dad's face. It was the same expression he had after Mom had died, and it remained there for years. I always thought it was just the grief of losing her that haunted him, but now I realized it was so much more. After several long moments, he finally continued, "I won't lie. I became a little unhinged about this doctor guy. No matter how hard I tried, I just couldn't let it go. I started following him and even hid cameras in his patient rooms—all in hopes of peeling back all his vicious layers. It was through those cameras that I finally discovered his dirty little secret."

"What secret?"

"He was drugging his female patients. He told them it would help to ease the pain of their migraines or neurological pain, and when they passed out, he raped them."

"Oh, God."

"I couldn't help but wonder if he'd done the same to your mother."

Bile rose to the back of my throat when I thought about the possibility of Mom's doctor taking advantage of her during her most vulnerable moments. The man had to be a complete monster to do something like that. Tears started to fill my eyes as I muttered, "Do you think he did something like that to her?"

"I have no idea. I pray he didn't, but the mere thought of him putting his hands on your mother enraged me. I wanted to kill him. Oh, God, I can't describe how much I wanted to kill him, but I'm no murderer." He came over and sat down next to me. "That's when I decided to go see Viper."

"Viper?" I gasped. "Why would you go see him?"

"I knew all about him and his club. Everyone at the precinct did. There wasn't a cop who didn't want to bring them down for something, but it couldn't be done. Still, that didn't stop them from trying." I couldn't believe what I was hearing. My mind was literally reeling as I listened to him say, "When I first showed up on his doorstep, he thought I was just trying to bullshit him and add to the case the cops were trying to build against the club. And I gotta say, he wasn't an easy man to convince. But then I told him why I was really there."

"So, what happened?"

"I told him about the good doctor and showed him everything I had on him, then I made him a proposition he couldn't refuse."

"What kind of proposition?"

"That's not something I can discuss, not even with you." I'd always wondered how my father got involved with the Sinners, but this was far beyond anything I could've ever imagined. "After he and the brothers dealt with the doctor, I used my skills in forensics to make sure no one would ever suspect that they had anything to do with his death. I was extremely good at it—which opened a door I would have never expected."

"So, this door suddenly opened and what? You started cleaning for the Ruthless Sinners?"

"To start, yes, but with Viper's help, it quickly grew into something more." He reached over to place his hand on my knee. "There's something about all this that you need to understand. The cleaning business is a tough one. I have to do things I never dreamed I'd ever do, but with each job, I'm getting drug lords, cartels, and gang members off the streets. That's something I'd tried to do for years, but even with the evidence I gathered, they still managed to find a loophole and walked free. Now, I have the means to make sure they received the justice they deserved."

"I don't know what to say."

"I know none of what I told you makes this easier for you, but I want you to remember that what I've done was always for you and your mother."

"I will."

He nodded, then removed his hand from my knee and crossed his arms. "Now, I think it's time for us to discuss you and the Manor."

"I'm sorry I never told you about what I was doing. I guess a part of me wanted to keep it a secret from you as some kind of revenge for you keeping so many from me. I know that's not fair, but it's the only explanation I have."

"I understand why you didn't tell me, but what I

don't get is why you started growing marijuana in the first place or even how you got it started."

"Like you, I did it because of Mom." I went on to tell him how I'd learned about the benefits of marijuana use in class and how it had made me think about Mom. I was honest with him. I told him how I'd used my inheritance to build the Manor and how I'd been able to produce a product superior to anyone around. "I don't just sell it for profit. I also have people I donate to. They're either going through cancer treatments or dealing with migraines like Mom, but I'm helping to make their lives a little better."

"Really?"

"Mm-hmm. I just met with a family a few days ago. The daughter has cerebral palsy, and they're hoping this will help with some of the pain she's experiencing."

"I had no idea."

"I wouldn't have been so committed to my business if it didn't involve helping some people."

A smile crossed his face as he said, "Now, that's the daughter I've always known and loved."

"Oh, I don't know about that. I've made plenty of mistakes along the way."

"Like a few weeks back?" He leaned back in the swing. "Was that one of your mistakes?"

"It was, and I paid dearly for it."

"Did you learn something from it?"

"I did. I think we all did."

"Speaking of we ... How did you get involved with Viper and the Sinners?"

"I have you to thank for that." I grimaced. "It started that weekend I came home, and Menace was here."

"Oh, damn. I should've known. Don't tell me anymore. You keep your business dealings to yourself, and I'll do the same."

"Fair enough." I leaned over and placed my hand on his arm as I asked, "So, are we good?"

"Yes, sweetheart. We're good."

"I'm so glad to hear you say that. I was so worried I was going to lose you."

"Not a chance."

"There's one more thing I should tell you."

"If you're going to tell me that you're seeing Country, I already know."

"What?" I gasped. "How?"

"Knew it the second I saw the way he was looking at you. It was the same way I looked at your mother."

"Oh, Dad. That's the sweetest thing I've ever heard."

"I hope he knows I'll have his ass if he ever hurts you."

"I don't think you'll have to worry about that. He's really good to me."

"You love him?"

"Oh, yes. More than I thought possible."

"Then, that's all that matters. I just want you to be happy. That's all I've ever wanted."

I reached over and gave him a big hug as I whispered, "I love you, Daddy."

"I love you, too, sweetheart."

I ended up spending most of the afternoon with Dad. He fixed us some lunch, and we even spent a little time out on the pier fishing. I filled him in on how things were going at school and my plans to go to graduate school. By the time I left, I was feeling better than I thought possible. I hated that I'd waited so long to come and talk to him. I'd wasted so much time worrying over what could possibly go wrong that I hadn't thought about a happy ending. For the first time in years, I finally understood why my father had made the decisions he had, and it helped ease those doubts that had always lingered in the back of my mind. I had my daddy back, and I couldn't be happier.

When I arrived back to the Manor, I went straight to the office to find Grayson. I was eager to tell him how things had gone with Dad, and I also wanted to see how he and Braylon had made out with putting together all the new furniture. I'd hoped they would've been done already, but sadly, that wasn't the case. Instead, I walked in to find Grayson on the floor next to Bray, and there were little piles of wood and screws scattered throughout the room. The second I stepped inside, Grayson held up his hand and ordered, "Hold it right there!"

"What?"

"We've got this under control."

"You sure about that?" I snickered as I said, "'Cause from where I'm standing, it looks like these bookshelves have gotten the best of you."

"It's a workspace, babe."

"A workspace, huh? Well, it looks a bit like a disaster zone to me."

"Are you doubting our abilities here?" Grayson asked, sounding offended.

"I'm just stating the obvious."

"Can't believe you're actually doubting my skills." Grayson gave me a playful scowl. "You should know better than anyone that I'm good with my hands."

"I can't disagree with you there."

"That's right. I was born for this shit. I just need a little time to get organized."

"Mm-hmm. If you say so, *punkin*."

"Don't you punkin me, woman! I'll have your ass for that."

I winked at him. "I certainly hope so."

"Oh, good grief. You two are killin' me!" Braylon whined, then turned to look at me with a scolding expression. "Don't you have some work to do?"

"As a matter of fact, I do." I tiptoed over to Grayson, then leaned down and kissed him. "Thanks for doing all this for me."

"Just doing what I can to make my woman happy."

"Well, I appreciate it." I stood, and as I walked out of the room, I said to them, "I'll let you boys get back to work. Just give me a shout if you need a hand."

"Not gonna happen. We got this covered." I'd barely stepped into the hall when I heard Grayson shout, "You're still gonna pay for the punkin' shit later tonight."

"Looking forward to it!"

NINETEEN

COUNTRY

"How's the new girlfriend?"

"What?"

"Oh, don't play dumb, brother. You know who I'm talking about." I smirked at Jagger. "The hot new shrink that's been coming 'round to see ya."

The second I mentioned her, his eyes grew fierce, and I knew something was up with him and his new therapist. Jagger wasn't one to discuss the women in his life. Hell, it was months later before he told us that he'd broken things off with Sadie—the girl he'd been dating before he got locked up. Even then, he didn't go into much detail, but we all knew why he'd done it. Jagger didn't want her wasting her life away waiting on him to be released. Needless to say, I was intrigued by his reaction to my comment, so when he didn't immediately respond, I goaded him even more, "You two had any conjugal visits yet?"

"Did you really come all this way to give me shit about my new therapist?"

"Oh, come on, brother. Don't be like that." Menace was sitting next to me in the prison's meeting room and smiling at Jagger like the Cheshire Cat. He, too, knew there was something up with him and this chick, but he didn't say a word. Menace just sat there waiting for Jagger to admit he had a thing for her—something we both knew wouldn't happen. I wasn't ready to let it go, so I baited him. "I'm just making sure this counselor chick is fulfilling all your therapeutical needs."

Jagger growled, his tone full of warning. "*Country.*"

"Okay, okay. I'll stop fucking around." It had been several weeks since I'd been able to make it over to the prison, so I was glad to see the fire back in his eyes and figured this new therapist had something to do with it. I knew better than to fuck with him any more than I already had, so I asked, "But in all seriousness, how are things going with her?"

"They're going." Jagger shrugged like it wasn't a big deal. "She's only coming around, so I can get that stupid parole hearing. Nothing more than that."

We left that topic alone and spent the next half hour catching him up to speed on everything that had gone down at the Manor. As soon as we were done,

Jagger cocked his head and sighed. "Damn, I hate to hear about Jackal."

"It was a tough loss."

"I'm sure it was. I hate I wasn't there to help."

"Us, too, brother." Jagger had always been a strong figure in the club. He was very protective of the brotherhood, so his disappointment about not fighting alongside us was understandable. Hell, I would've felt the same damn way if I was in his shoes. "You'll be there next time."

"I sure as hell hope so." A smirk crossed Jagger's face as he leaned closer. "So, you're seriously hooking up with Billy's daughter?"

And just like that, the motherfucker had turned the tables on me. I was tempted to give him a smartass answer like he'd given me regarding his counselor friend but decided against it. "More than just hooking up, but yeah. I'm with her."

"Damn, brother. Billy's not a man to fuck around with." He struggled not to laugh. "I mean, seriously. You gotta have balls of steel to get tied up with her."

"Yeah, I've got some pretty impressive balls, but it ain't like that. Billy's all right. Besides, I have no plans to piss off the guy. Got a good thing with Kiersten, and I intend to keep it that way."

"I certainly hope so 'cause if you fuck up, we'll never find out what he did to ya."

"No doubt about that." Menace glanced over at the clock, and when he noticed the time, he said, "I'm sorry to cut it short, but we've gotta get back for the run this afternoon."

"Leaving kind of late, aren't ya?"

"Just trying to work around the fucking traffic." Menace stood as he told him, "You know how it is coming in and out of Knoxville."

"Yeah, I remember."

Menace and I said our goodbyes to our brother, then turned and headed back through security. Once we'd gathered our things, we made our way out to the parking lot and hopped on our bikes. Before we pulled off, Menace looked over to me. "Jagger seems to be doing all right, don't ya think?"

"Yeah, brother, I think he's doing just fine."

"I'm ready for him to get his ass out of there."

"You and me both."

Without saying anything more, Menace turned the key and started his engine. I followed him out of the prison gate and back to the clubhouse. By the time we got there, Hawk and Axel were already loaded up and waiting for us. Just like the time before, we made the run to meet our NC chapter without a hitch and got back just in time for my shift at Stilettos. On most days, the commute between the clubhouse and the Manor wasn't bad at all, but after driving to Knoxville and back and putting in my hours at the strip club, I knew I'd be wiped. But I didn't care. I was looking forward to getting home and crawling into bed next to my woman. I held on to that thought as I followed Locke into Stilettos.

For a Thursday night, the place was completely slammed. Hell, there wasn't an empty seat in the house. Locke looked around at all the crowded tables and groaned. "Damn, it looks like we're going to be in for a long one."

"Yeah, it's definitely looking that way."

On nights like these, we always made a shit-ton of money, but it came at a cost. I never understood it, but anytime it was packed like this, folks tended to lose their fucking minds and do shit they wouldn't ordinarily do—like throwing a punch at a complete stranger or grabbing some oblivious girl's ass. Trying to mentally prepare for what laid ahead, I made my way over to the front door and stood watch with Lynch. As expected, it wasn't long before a fight broke out next to the main stage. "Fuck. Here we go."

"Hell, yeah. Just what I've been waitin' for."

Lynch being Lynch, he plowed through the drunken crowd and charged over to the three men who were quickly losing control. I followed right behind him and reached Lynch just as he'd slipped his arm around one of the bigger guy's throats. Lynch gave him a hard tug, lifting his feet from the floor as he jerked him away from the others.

As soon as the other two realized what was happening, they decided to turn their aggression towards me, and each took a swing. That was a mistake. I plowed my fist into the smaller one's diaphragm, causing him to topple over as he gasped for breath, then immediately turned my attention to the other. He'd already braced himself and was ready for me to throw a punch, but instead of going directly at him, I waited for him to make the first move. The second he lunged at me, I uppercut him and slammed my fist into his kidneys, then hammered him again with another punch right under his chin. He went flailing back and crashed into one of the tables.

I reached down and grabbed a fistful of his shirt, jerking him up to his feet, then took hold of his arm and grabbed his buddy before storming towards the front door. Lynch had already made it out of the club with the first guy, and I wasn't far behind with the other two. I shoved them both out the front door and growled, "That's it for you boys. Time to call it a night."

"Come on, man. No need to do us like that."

Lynch had enough of their bullshit and roared, "You heard the man. Get the fuck out of here."

Without any further argument, the three men

turned and walked away like a group of dogs with their tails between their legs. Lynch and I watched as they hailed a cab, and once they were gone, Lynch looked at me and chuckled. "Is it bad that I love that shit?"

"Fucking up a bunch of drunks?"

"Abso-fucking-lutely! I love it." He held up his fist and growled, "I can't wait to do it again. It's a fucking rush!"

I laughed as I patted him on the back. "You need help, brother."

"Yeah, you're probably right." Lynch started over to the front door but stopped and turned back to me. "I wanted to tell you I spoke to Hannah earlier today."

"Oh, yeah?" I hadn't heard anything about Lynch's sister or her daughter since the day Kiersten went over to see them. She and I had been curious about whether or not the gummies had helped with Reece's issues, but Kiersten didn't want to seem pushy and was hesitant to reach out to them. "How's she making it?"

"Really good, actually." Lynch seemed relieved. "Reece has been showing some real improvements. Seems Kiersten's gummies have been a real hit over there, so I'm pretty sure Hannah will be calling her soon."

"I'm glad to hear that. I'll be sure and let Kiersten know."

"Please do and tell her how much I appreciate her

doing this for me." He cleared his throat. "I love my sister and hate that she's going through all this, so I'm grateful for all of Kiersten's help."

"She was glad to do it, brother. I know she'll be happy to hear it's working out."

I followed him inside, and together we waited for the possibility of another unraveling. Thankfully, our little display with the first wild crew made an impression on the remainder of the crowd, and we got through the rest of the night without another brawl. I helped the guys get things shut down for the night, and once the doors were locked, I was on my bike, riding back to the Manor. By the time I pulled into the drive, it was well after midnight. I had no doubt that Kiersten was sleeping, so I did my best not to wake her as I unlocked the door and went inside.

Being as quiet as possible, I padded into the bathroom and took a much-needed long, hot shower. I was beyond exhausted and barely able to keep my eyes open as I got out and dried off. I pulled on a fresh pair of boxers, then crawled into bed with Kiersten. On instinct, she immediately nestled up next to me and laid her head on my shoulder. Her eyes were closed as she whispered, "Hey."

"Hey, babe. Sorry I woke you."

"I'm glad you did." Her voice was low and raspy

and sexy-as-fuck as she whispered, "I missed you today."

"Right back at ya." I leaned over and kissed her forehead. "Did you have a good day?"

"It was okay." She did that little hum thing she did when she was worried about something before saying, "I talked to Braylon today."

"About?"

"Mia." She sighed, then continued, "He really likes her, but he's been pushing her away. He still blames himself for what happened with Drake and his men."

"Yeah, I had a feeling that was what was going on. Did you set him straight?"

"I think so, but you never know with Bray. He's so stinking stubborn." She yawned, then hummed once again. "He's a good guy. He deserves to be happy."

"And he will be ... when *he's* ready."

"But if he's never ready?"

"He'll get there." I ran my fingers through her hair. "I know you want to fix it for him, but he's gotta do it on his own. And you gotta trust that he will."

"How did you get so smart?"

"You're the smart one. You're just rubbing off on me a little."

"Is that right?"

"Mm-hmm." I closed my eyes and settled in.

"You're the best thing that could've ever happened to me."

"It's funny you say that 'cause I think the same thing about you."

She eased up and kissed me, then laid her head back down on my shoulder. A few minutes later, she stilled and her breathing slowed, and I knew she'd drifted back off to sleep. I looked down at her and was in complete awe. Kiersten had no idea how incredible she really was, but I knew. I'd known it all along. She was the best of both worlds. She was strong, independent, and beautiful, but at the same time, she was vulnerable with a heart of gold. She made it easy to fall for her. Hell, I was still falling, and as I lay there in bed next to her, I knew I'd never stop.

TWENTY

KIERSTEN

"What the ever-loving fuck?" Lynch roared. "How the hell is she doing that?"

"I don't know, but they're definitely kicking our asses." Shotgun huffed with aggravation.

Lynch pointed over to me with a pout as he complained, "I'm pretty sure she's cheating."

"She isn't cheating," Grayson argued. "She's just better than you."

"She's better than you, too." Lynch pointed to the red solo cup of beer. "Drink up, buttercup."

Grayson looked over to me with a scowl, then lifted the cup and quickly downed it. The guys had gotten together to celebrate Viper's birthday, and they'd all been partying pretty hard when Locke got the bright idea of setting up a beer pong table. At first, the guys seemed a little undecided, but when Locke suggested a match between the brothers and the ol' ladies, suddenly they were all for it. We'd already played several rounds, and the ol' ladies were dominating the guys, which suited me just fine. After the last party, I had no interest in getting smashed again any time soon.

Since I'd made the last shot, I had to go again. I could feel the guys' eyes on me as I prepared to take my next shot. I held the ping pong ball up and aimed it at the next red solo cup, then held my breath as I tossed it in the air. Seconds later, it plopped inside the cup, causing some of the beer to splash out. I threw my arms up in the air and shouted, "Oh, heck yeah! That's what I'm talking about!"

"You've gotta be shittin' me!" Lynch whined. "How in the hell did you just make that?"

"What can I say? I've got skills," I teased him.

"I'll show you skills." Lynch took his ball and tossed it towards our end of the table, and like many before, he missed the cup by a mile. "Damn it!"

I smiled as I pointed to the cup. "Drink up, buttercup."

"Damn it." Lynch grabbed the cup with my ball in it, then quickly drank it. He tossed the empty cup to the ground, then turned to Grayson as he fussed, "You're gonna have to step up your game, brother."

"Me?" Grayson scowled. "You're the one who can't get it in the damn cup. You're worse than a fucking virgin searching for the golden hole."

"Fuck you, brother. You're just taking it easy on 'em 'cause you wanna get laid tonight."

"Damn straight, I do," Grayson grumbled. "Not gonna throw the fucking game and make us lose to do it, though."

"Okay, girls. You're both pretty." Menace snickered as he stepped between Lynch and Grayson, shoving them apart. "Now, quit your whining and play the damn game."

"That was a little intense," Marlowe whispered. "I'm thinking our boys aren't very good at losing."

"No, they aren't, but it's not all that surprising." Delilah glanced over at Hawk. "They rarely lose at anything."

"Ain't that the truth," Frankie laughed. "You think I should take it easy on them?"

"No way." My eyes skirted over to Grayson. Even though he'd already thrown back several shots and drank numerous beers, he still looked completely sober. I was hoping to get him at least a little tipsy, so I told Frankie, "They can take it."

"Alrighty then."

I watched as she eased her hand back and tossed

the ball into the air. When it landed in the cup of beer, all the girls jumped up and cheered. Grayson gave Widow a nudge. "Come on, brother. End this thing once and for all."

"I'm certainly gonna try."

When Widow stepped up to the table, Frankie gave him a wink and smiled. I loved how these beautiful women adored their men just as much as I adored mine. I glanced over at Grayson, and a warmth washed over me when I found him sitting on a stool watching me with the other ol' ladies. He looked at me like I was the only woman in the room. Unfortunately, I wasn't the only one. In fact, the place was filled with hangarounds. They were all eager to get their claws into one of the brothers, so it wasn't a surprise when a pretty little redhead came sauntering over to Grayson and started flirting. I could've gone over and put her in her place, but I knew I could trust Grayson to do the right thing.

My attention was drawn back over to the table when Delilah called out to me, "Hey, Kiersten, it's your turn!"

"Coming!"

The ball was in my hand, and I was preparing to take my shot when I happened to glance over in Grayson's direction and noticed the redhead had wedged herself between his legs just inches from his crotch. Before I had a chance to get angry, Grayson shifted in his seat and said something to the girl that brought a scowl to her pretty face. Seconds later, she stalked away. Smiling, I turned my attention back to the beer pong table and was a little worried when I realized there was only one cup remaining. If I made it, the game would be over, and the ladies would win yet another round. I stepped into position, then tossed the ball. As soon as it fell into the cup, the entire room exploded with a loud roar of cheers and laughter. Delilah and Frankie came over and gave me a high-five. "Way to go, girl! Thanks to you, we smoked them yet again."

"We all did it. Not just me."

"You're just being modest." Frankie winked. "You know you rocked it."

"Well, maybe a little." I laughed, then looked over at Grayson who, like earlier, was watching me again, so I told Frankie, "I think I'll go claim my prize."

"You should definitely do that."

"I'll catch up with you guys later."

"Sure thing. Have fun!"

"Planning on it." I made my way through the others and over to Grayson. As I slipped my arms around his waist, I announced, "We won!"

"I saw that."

"I've come to claim my prize."

"Your prize, huh?"

"Oh, yeah. A win like that totally deserves a prize." I gave him a playful smile as I leaned closer and whispered, "I'm thinking a few bells and whistles might suffice."

"Oh, yeah?"

"Mm-hmm ... But only if you're up for it."

"I'm always up for some bells and whistles, baby. You know that."

Without saying anything more, he took me by the hand and led me out of the bar and down to his room. We knew we'd be drinking and had already planned on staying at the clubhouse. As soon as Grayson closed the door, he kicked off his boots and removed his cut, then he was on me, kissing me in a way that made my knees tremble. Our hands became frantic and possessive as we lost ourselves in the moment. When his hands dropped to my jeans, I looked up at him and said, "There sure are a lot of pretty girls around the club."

"Yeah." His brows furrowed. "And?"

"Lots of temptation."

He slipped his arms around my waist. "You jealous?"

"Just stating a fact."

His gorgeous eyes fell on me, studying me for a

brief moment before he said, "Well, you should know by now that you've got nothing to worry about. You're all I want." I let out a little whimper as his lips trailed along my neck. "You're mine, Kiersten. All mine, and all I'll ever need."

Without saying anything more, his lips crashed down on mine, stealing my breath away. The tips of his fingers trailed along my spine, and I arched towards him, seeking the heat of his touch. As he continued to kiss me, I could feel a fire burning deep inside me, smoldering as it spread through my body. It was a familiar sensation—one I had every time Grayson's hands were on me. It always started with a spark and intensified with every single touch. He reached for the hem of my sweater, then pulled it over my head.

A light hiss slipped through my lips as he brought the tips of his fingers to the straps of my bra and gently brushed them off my shoulders. I shivered with anticipation as I felt the palm of his hand linger over my bare flesh. He looked down at me, sending chills through my body as his eyes roamed over every inch of my exposed skin.

"So fucking beautiful." He ran his rough, calloused finger along the edge of my black satin bra. A rush of heat rolled against my skin as Grayson stood there staring at me, appraising me. Watching his eyes fill with lust made it hard to breathe, hard to think, and only increased my need for him.

I reached out and grasped the hem of his t-shirt, feeling the muscles in his chest quiver as my fingers brushed along his skin. God, I loved how his body responded to my every touch. It made me feel so wanted, so desired. He leaned forward to let me pull the shirt over his head, then I placed my hand on his heart and smiled when I sensed it beating as fast as mine. Just like me, he'd felt every spark, every flicker of heat that surged through our bodies.

"Grayson," I whispered.

"Right here with you, babe," he reassured me. His lips brushed against mine, but not gently like before. Instead, it was hot, demanding, and possessive. I was his, and he wanted to make sure I knew it. I moaned into his mouth, stealing the last of his restraint. He made quick work of my jeans, then lifted me into his arms and carried me over to the bed. Seconds later, I was on my back, and his body was covering mine. His weight pressed me into the bed as his hands, rough and impatient, roamed over my body.

Seconds later, my bra was freed from my body and thrown to the floor, then his mouth closed over my breast, scraping his teeth across my sensitive flesh, knowing just how to drive me wild. My fingers tangled in his hair as he flicked his tongue against my nipple, sending goosebumps prickling across my skin. His hand slid between my legs, and my breath caught as he ran his finger along the edge of my satin panties. His other hand cupped my breast, the rough pad of his thumb stroking across my nipple as he added fuel to the fire burning within me.

Impatient for more, I reached down and tugged at his belt, and he helped me lower his jeans down his hips. I couldn't wait a moment longer. I needed to be taken, to feel him inside of me. I glanced up and was in complete awe of how beautiful Grayson was with his perfectly defined abs and his oh-so-pronounced *V*. When he caught me gawking at him, his eyes danced with mischief. "Like what you see?"

All I could muster was a brief nod and "Mmm-hmm."

His smirk quickly faded as he looked down at me sprawled out on the bed. "You're amazing, Kiersten. Absolutely amazing."

Before I had time to respond, he was back on top of me, centering himself between my legs. He hovered over me, the heat of our breaths mingling between us until the anticipation became too much, and his mouth crashed down around mine. His hand dove into my hair and grasped at the nape of my neck while he delved deeper into my mouth, our tongues twisting and tasting with nothing but passion and desire as his other hand grabbed at my panties and lowered them down my thighs.

Once they were gone, I wrapped my legs around him, engulfing him deep inside me. I placed my hands on his chest and slowly began to move, matching the rhythm of his hips as I rocked mine against him. I'd never felt anything so incredible and wanted to savor the moment and let myself feel every erotic sensation, but Grayson had other plans.

He let out a deep-seated growl as he pulled out and quickly flipped me on my stomach, then lifted me up to take me from behind. With one thrust, he was buried deep inside me. He withdrew for a moment, then slammed into me again, and with each shift of his hips, his rhythm quickly became more powerful and fierce. I was close to the edge, and when he slapped my ass and tugged on my hair, the muscles in my abdomen immediately began to tighten. I reached for the headboard, bracing myself for the next wave of pleasure that crashed through my body. With one last deep thrust, a fire raged inside, consuming every inch of me as my orgasm ripped through my body.

I was left shocked and quivering from the outburst of pleasure, but Grayson wasn't done. Not even close. He drove into me again and again until he found his own release, growling as he lowered his body over my back and we tumbled down onto the bed. I lay there limp beneath him as we both slowly tried to calm our breathing to a relaxed pace. After several long, blissful moments, he eased off of me and rolled over on his side. He reached for me and pulled me to him. As I nestled into the crook of his arm, I giggled and said, "We're going to need to play beer pong more often."

"After the way you played tonight, I doubt the guys will ever be all that eager to play again, at least not anytime soon."

"Well, it was fun, and the winning prize was stellar."

"Stellar, huh?"

"Mm-hmm. You really outdid yourself."

"Just doing what I can to make my woman happy."

"Well, you don't have to worry there." I eased up on my elbow as I looked at him and said, "I've never been happier. I love you very much."

"You better watch it, or you'll earn yourself another go."

"I'd be good with that."

I leaned towards him and pressed my lips to his, and that's all it took. Grayson flipped me over on my back, and we were at it again. I loved making love with him, but more than that, I loved being around him. I didn't have to pretend to be someone I wasn't, just simply be myself. I could have bad days, lose my temper, or stress out over crazy stuff, and he never judged me. He was always there for me. He knew all of me and still loved me, and that meant everything. Grayson was my best friend and the love of my life. He was my present and my future, and I wouldn't have it any other way.

EPILOGUE

FOUR YEARS LATER

"I'M SORRY, BABE, BUT I'M JUST NOT FEELING THIS one."

"But it's so cute, and there's a fireplace in the bedroom."

"There's also an open well in the basement."

"But we could cover it up or something." Kiersten grimaced. "Or maybe that's not a good idea."

"Yeah, probably not."

"Okay, we'll just skip this one and see if the next is any better."

"I don't think it could be much worse."

Kiersten and I both liked living out at the Manor. After we got hitched, we decided to make it our home, so I sold my place and moved in with her permanently. It just made sense. She enjoyed being right there with her work and employees, and I liked that I was close enough to the club and Stilettos to make the trip as often as I needed. There was just one problem. Kiersten was pregnant, and even though we both thought of it as home, her small house simply wasn't big enough to raise a family. We could've built a bigger place at the Manor, but neither of us thought bringing up a kid on a pot farm was a good idea. So, we set out to find a house that was midway between the Manor and the clubhouse, but our search wasn't going as well as I'd hoped.

We'd already been to four houses, and each was worse than the last. I was far from ready to give up, but I was having doubts we'd find a place that fit our needs. As soon as Kiersten told our realtor, Joey, that we weren't interested in the house, we headed back out to the car. While waiting for him to tell us where we'd be going next, Kiersten turned to me and said, "We could always go back and take a second look at that two-story on Maness Street."

"Hell, no." I started the car. "That place was straight out of a horror flick."

"It had a room with a few dolls, Grayson. It wasn't that bad."

"It wasn't a few dolls, babe. It was a room *full of them*, and they were all looking right at me."

"I'm sure the homeowners would take them when they moved out."

"Yeah, but their creepy mojo would still be there."

"Oh, good grief. You are being silly."

I reached over and placed my hand on her pregnant belly as I said, "I'm just looking out for the kid."

"Mm-hmm. You're just scared of old, creepy dollies," Kiersten snickered. "But that's okay. We'll find a house without them."

"It would also be good if we could find a place without a bathroom in the living room."

"Yeah, that was a house I don't think I'll ever forget."

"So, where are we headed now?"

Kiersten looked down at the MLS listings Joey had given us, then said, "I think we're going to check out a place on High Street. Joey seems to think it will be perfect for us."

"He said the same thing about the last two."

"*Grayson.*"

"I'm sure it'll be great."

I waited for Joey to back out of the drive, and then I followed him over to High Street. I was more than a little skeptical that this house would be all that different from the rest, but when we pulled up to the pale-yellow, historical Colonial, I was blown away. The yard was immaculate with freshly mowed grass and a large oak tree that cast just the right amount of shade on the wraparound porch. There were potted ferns and flowers arranged on the front steps and a large, wooden front door with glass panes that seemed to welcome us inside. As soon as she saw it, Kiersten looked over to me. "Oh, my God. It's absolutely perfect!"

"Yeah, it looks pretty incredible, but let's not get too excited until we see inside."

Without saying anything more, Kiersten hopped out of the car and rushed over to Joey. She was practically bursting at the seams as she waited for him to get up the steps and open the front door. As soon as he unlocked it, she darted inside and immediately called out to me, "Grayson! You have to see this."

As I walked past Joey, he smiled and said, "I really do think this is the one."

"I hope you're right."

I headed inside to find Kiersten, and the second I walked through the door, I knew we'd found our new place. It was amazing. The whole house had been renovated with new floors and freshly painted walls, but they'd managed to do it all without taking away from the historical feel of the home. The living room was three times the size of ours, and the sunroom looked out over the fenced-in backyard. It had a pool with a large patio and a small pool house. I could hear Kiersten in the kitchen, so I went to see what she thought of the place. When I walked in, I found her checking out all the fancy appliances in complete awe. "Well? Do you like it?"

"Are you kidding me?" She gasped. "I love it."

"You two should check the upstairs," Joey suggested. "It's really something."

Without a moment's hesitation, Kiersten turned and started for the stairs. She was smiling from ear to ear as she turned back to me and said, "Come on. Let's go see."

"I'm right behind you, babe."

I followed her up the steps, and as we entered the first bedroom, Kiersten gave me a nudge. "No dolls. It's looking promising."

"Yeah, I gotta say, it's pretty great."

"This could be the nursery." Kiersten ran her hand over her tummy as she said, "I think she'll love it."

"She?"

Kiersten wasn't quite three months along, so we hadn't had the ultrasound to find out the baby's sex yet. I thought it was fucking adorable that she assumed we were having a girl. She turned to me and smiled. "He or she will love it."

"I'm sure he or she will think it's great." I motioned my head towards the door. "Why don't we go check out the master?"

"Okay."

I followed her out of the first bedroom and down

the long hall to the master bedroom. When we walked in, I was surprised by how big it was. "Holy cow, it's enormous. You could fit an army in here."

"It's so beautiful." She walked over to the king-sized bed and sighed. "I just love what they've done with the place."

"Yeah, I have to say it's pretty incredible." I stepped into the master bath, and the second I saw the oversized marble shower and whirlpool tub, I said, "Damn, these folks are living large."

"Oh my, that tub is fantastic. I'm soaking in it every single night."

"So, does that mean this is the house you want?"

"Yeah, I think so, but there's one last thing we need to check out."

"And what's that?"

"The master closet." She reached over and took my hand, then led me into the closet. Just like the rest of the house, it was fucking enormous. After I gave her a moment to check it all out, I asked, "Well, does it meet your expectations?"

"Yeah, it'll do." She shut the door, then stepped over to me. As she slipped her arms around my neck, she smiled and said, "I just wanted to make sure there was room in here for this."

She eased up on her tiptoes and pressed her lips against mine. The kiss started soft and slow but quickly became heated, which was no surprise. Even after all this time, I still couldn't get enough of her. We were getting lost in the moment when there was a tap on the closet door. "You two okay in there?"

Kiersten quickly stepped back, breaking our embrace as she answered, "Yep! We're just checking the dimensions."

"Okay, just let me know if you need anything."

When I heard him step away from the door, I looked down at her. "Checking the dimensions? Really?"

"I had to say something, or he would've thought we were up to no good in here."

"I'm pretty sure he already knew that."

"You really think so?"

"I doubt we're the first to get busy in a closet, babe."

"Well, that's just embarrassing." She let out a sigh, then said, "But it is a pretty cool closet."

"Yes, it is. The whole house is pretty great, and it has a pool like you wanted."

"I know! It's just so perfect."

Just seeing the excited look on her face was enough to convince me that we'd finally found the right place. "So, we're buying a house."

"Yeah, we're buying a house, and it's the house of

all houses." She slipped her arm around mine. "I truly love it."

"Then, consider it ours."

"I love you, Grayson."

"And I love you." I placed my hand on her stomach and added, "Both of you."

THE END...

More from the Ruthless Sinners coming soon!
Be sure to check out Jagger's Choice in the Very Naughty MC Christmas Anthology which releases on November 30th.
Short Excerpt of Claiming Menace after Acknowledgments

ACKNOWLEDGMENTS

I am blessed to have so many wonderful people who are willing to give their time and effort to making my books the best they can be. Without them, I wouldn't be able to breathe life into my characters and share their stories with you. To the people I've listed below and so many others, I want to say thank you for taking this journey with me. Your support means the world to me, and I truly mean it when I say I appreciate everything you do. I love you all!

PA: Natalie Weston
Editing/Proofing: Lisa Cullinan-Editor, Marie Peyton-Proofer
Promoting: Amy Jones, Veronica Ines Garcia, Neringa Neringiukas, Whynter M. Raven

BETAS/Early Readers: Amanda Quiles, Tawnya Rae, and Jessey Elliott

Street Team: All the wonderful members of Wilder's Women (You are amazing!)

Best Friend and biggest supporter: My mother (Love you to the moon and back.)

VOLUME ONE

ONE

MENACE

"WHAT THE HELL HAPPENED?"

"It's nothing."

"The fuck it is." I sat there looking at the bruises and cuts on my brother's knuckles and the gash on his cheek, and it was all I could do to keep myself from completely losing it. I knew Jagger could hold his own. Anyone could see that. At six-five and two-hundred and seventy pounds of pure muscle, the guy was a fucking beast. His dark, shaggy hair had grown long, making him look even more vicious, and with his Ruthless Sinners' tattoo sprawled across his massive bicep, it was hard to believe anyone would dare to fuck with him. Enraged by the whole damn thing, I slammed my hand down on the table and growled, "This kind of shit isn't supposed to happen. You're under club protection!"

"And that protection comes at a cost." Jagger remained perfectly calm. "Deluca has put his neck out for me more times than I can count. Last night, it was time for me to return the favor."

"What the fuck happened?"

"I handled it."

"What the hell is that supposed to mean?"

"It means, I'm handling things, so stop worrying about it and let it fucking go." His coal-black eyes grew fierce as he leaned over the table and barked, "And while you're at it, stop with all the fucking visits, brother. You got a life. Don't be wasting it by coming out here. Go live it."

"Not gonna happen, brother. I'm gonna keep on coming here week after week until you get out of this godforsaken place and don't say a fucking word about it 'cause we both know you'd do the same for me."

Jagger didn't argue because he knew I was right. He would've come to see me as often as he could. That was just the kind of man he was. Jagger had no business being behind bars. He was a good guy who'd found himself in an impossible situation. His sister, Stacey, was a known drug addict and all-around troublemaker, but Jagger always stood by her and helped out any way he could, trying his damnedest to make up for the sins of their mother and father.

None of us were surprised when she'd gotten herself tied up with a short-fused, loser boyfriend. One night, the two wound up in a heated argument and things got out of hand. Knowing Jagger would come rushing to her rescue, Stacey called her brother, pleading for his help. By the time he'd arrived at her place, Stacey was hysterical. She was covered in cuts and bruises, her lip was busted, and her wrist was broken. Jagger had lost it. He'd laid into the boyfriend and didn't let up until the guy was no longer breathing. The cops came, and Jagger was arrested for voluntary manslaughter.

The guy was in a difficult position—one any of us could've found ourselves in. Hell, I would've done the same fucking thing if Mallory called to tell me she was in trouble. We'd hoped that considering the circumstance, he'd get off a little easier, but after an agonizing hearing, he was sentenced to six years in prison with the opportunity for parole in four. It could've been worse, much worse, but I couldn't stop myself from feeling guilty for not doing more to keep him out of this fucking hellhole altogether.

Jagger shook his head as he grumbled, "Stubborn ass."

"Damn straight."

Deciding it was time to change the subject, he asked, "How are things going down at the club?"

"Good. Busier than ever. So much so, we've decided to hire a couple more girls to the lineup."

"That's gotta be tough," Jagger mocked. "Having to check out all those hot chicks for the guys."

"It's not all it's cracked up to be."

"You realize you're saying that to a man who hasn't seen an ass or a set of tits in almost *three years*."

"Damn." I grimaced. "Sorry, brother. I wasn't thinking."

"Don't sweat it. I was just fucking with ya."

"Yeah, but I know that shit can't be easy." Since he opened that door, I used the opportunity to ask, "Have you seen or talked to Sadie lately?"

Sadie was Jagger's ol' lady. They'd been together since high school and were good together. Where he was standoffish and often hard-edged, she was sweet and outgoing. She kept him grounded, and he loved her for that. We all thought they'd end up married with kids and the whole nine yards, but after a few months of Jagger behind bars, they'd called it quits. He'd never admit it, but we all knew it wasn't an easy decision for him. He loved her, and they could've had a real future together, but being in prison changed him. The longer Jagger was locked up, the more closed off he became. He tried to convince himself and everyone else that he no longer wanted any part of the outside world. His face was void of expression when he answered, "You know I haven't."

"Because you pushed her away."

"She had no business hanging on to me or to what we had. That shit ended the second I was put behind bars." Anguish marked his face. "We had a good thing, but it's over. Been over for a long time. Seeing or talking to her isn't gonna change that."

Before I could say anything more, the guard called out, signaling our time was up. Jagger quickly stood, then bro-slapped my bicep. "Guess that's my cue. It was good to see ya, brother."

"Good to see you too." When he started to walk away, I called out to him, "Take care of yourself back there, and let us know if you need anything."

"You know I will."

I waited until he was out of view before going back through security. As soon as I made it out to the parking lot, I got on my bike and headed to Stilettos. I had a long day ahead of me, and I wanted to get an early start on the bar inventory. On the way over, I couldn't stop thinking about Jagger. I hated that he was stuck in that fucking place when any one of us would've done the same thing in his situation. It was a no-win predicament, but I wasn't giving up. I'd keep at it until I found some way to get him out of there.

Thoughts of Jagger were still rattling through my

head when I pulled up to the back door of the club. I was so out of sorts I didn't notice Hawk in the parking lot until he called out to me, "Yo, Menace. What are you doing here? I thought you were going out to see Jagger."

"I was, and I did."

"How was he?"

"He's been better." I unlocked the door. "He was involved in some kind of altercation but wouldn't tell me much about it. Just that he had it handled."

"This something Viper needs to be aware of?"

"Jagger would say no, but yeah, he needs to know." Following me inside, I told him, "This thing didn't directly involve Jagger, but he stepped in. So, like it or not, he's in it now."

"Damn." Hawk was the club's sergeant-at-arms. His job was to keep the club and the brothers safe and in order, and to make sure they followed the rules. It was difficult to do that when one of us was behind bars. I could see the concern in his eyes when he said, "I'm about to head back to the clubhouse. I'll talk to him and see how he wants to handle this."

"Sounds good."

We walked into my office, and I sat down at my desk while Hawk remained standing and asked, "So, how many girls you planning on hiring this week?"

"Three or four. Maybe even five. I'm still working on the numbers to figure out just how many we need."

"Well, Country and Lynch have volunteered to help out if you need a hand sorting through any of the applicants."

"Oh, yeah?" I chuckled. "I'll be sure to keep that in mind."

"All right, then. I'll leave you to it." Before he walked out of my office, he joked. "I gotta say, you really got it made, brother."

I wasn't surprised Hawk felt that way. He wasn't the only one. Every one of my brothers envied my role at the strip club, but it wasn't all it was cracked up to be. There was a time when a great pair of tits and the provocative sway of woman's hips would've had my dick roaring to life. I'd hammer one out with one chick, then move to the next. It didn't take long to learn that I wasn't just looking for strippers with great tits and ass. I also had to find chicks who knew how to dance and had a good head on their shoulders. I didn't need them bringing all their fucking troubles knocking at our door. Trust me when I say it wasn't an easy task, but I knew better than to try and convince my brothers of that. I'd just be wasting my breath, so I just did what needed to be done and kept my mouth shut.

As soon as I got settled at my desk, I started working

on the inventory for the bar. I was just starting to make some headway when there was a tap on my office door. I looked up and found Marlowe, who was Rafe's ol' lady and one of the club's new bartenders, standing in front of me with a stack of papers in her hand. "I have a few more applications that you might want to look over."

"Thanks." I took the papers from her hand and dropped them down on my already messy desk. "Give me five minutes; then you can start sending them in."

"You got it."

She walked out, and after I wrapped up the last of the inventory, I cleaned off my desk and prepared for our first applicant. A few minutes later, Marlowe appeared at the doorway and asked, "You ready?"

"Yeah." I reached down and grabbed the first application. After looking at the name, I said, "Go on and send in Jessie."

"You got it."

Shortly afterward, a cute brunette with a radiant smile and just the right amount of curves walked in. She was wearing the typical short skirt and a bright red tank top that clung to her breasts—the same kind of thing every chick wore when they came into my office. I could tell this wasn't her first rodeo when she stepped up to my desk, extended her hand, and said, "Hi, I'm Jessie. I'm here about the night dancer-stripper position."

I nodded, then motioned my hand towards the chair in front of me. "Have a seat and tell me about what experience you have."

"Okay." She sat down and continued, "I've worked at the Pink Pony for almost three years now. I've done really well there, but I think it's time for a change."

"Oh, really? And why's that?"

"Nothing in particular," she lied. "I just think it's time for me to move on."

"Mm-hmm." I should've pushed for more information, but I was eager to get this shit done. "You have any priors I need to be aware of?"

"Nope. I have a clean record. No STDs or psycho boyfriends. I'm in my third semester at Nashville State." She was cool, calm, and collected. It was clear Jessie was confident in her abilities when she said, "I'm good at what I do, and you won't regret hiring me."

"Okay, then. Let's see what ya got."

Without having to clarify, Jessie got up and started to dance around the room as she slipped her tank over her head, revealing her perfectly round, fake breasts. She swayed her hips in a circular motion while easing her miniskirt down her long tan legs. Jessie was right. This girl was good. I could only imagine what she could do with a pole. When she started to remove her thong, I held up my hand and said, "That's good. You can stop there."

"You sure about that?" A lustful spark flashed through her eyes when she added, "I've got other skills you might be interested in."

"You won't be needing those skills here, Jessie. If you get the job, you'll make plenty of money. You don't have to—"

"I know I don't have to." She placed the palms of her hands flat against my desk as she leaned forward and purred. "*I want to.* I think we could have a good time."

It was tempting, very tempting, but I looked down at my groin and there was nothing. Not so much as the slightest twitch. Neither of us were interested in sinking into her or any of the other strippers that came into this office. I'd been in a position like this many times before and had made the mistake of taking various women up on their offers. It was fun, but only for the moment. Things inevitably turned out fucking insane. They'd either think it meant more and become a psycho stalker or they'd expect particular privileges 'cause they sucked my dick. I was too old for that kind of shit, so I shook my head and said, "Not gonna happen. Now get dressed, and I'll call if you make it to the second round."

"Second round?"

"The top four applicants will come back later tonight for a full audition."

"Oh, okay." She quickly got dressed, and on her way out, she said, "Thanks for the opportunity."

I nodded, then looked down at my desk in search of the next application and had just picked it up when Marlowe peeked her head inside the doorway. "How'd it go?"

"Not too bad." I glanced back at the paper and said, "You can send in...Brittney."

"Sure thing."

She hadn't been gone long when Brittney appeared in my doorway. I could tell the moment she stepped into my office she wasn't eighteen—not even close. I quickly sent her on her way and moved to the next. Like Brittney, I could tell the second she walked in she was a no-go. The chick had two left feet and looked completely stoned. I was starting to get impatient when I told Marlowe to send in Brandy. I went through the same spiel with her that I'd gone through with Jessie, and to my surprise, she'd also been working at the Pink Pony. The same held true for the next girl ... and the next. I wasn't a fan of taking business from another club, so when Mazie, yet another girl from the Pink Pony, appeared in front of me, I asked, "What's going on over at the Pink Pony?"

"Nothing," she lied. "It's just time for me to make a change."

"Hmm. Your other buddies said the same thing." I

leaned back in my chair and crossed my arms as I pushed, "I'm not buying, so why don't you tell me what's really going on, or we can end this thing right here and now."

The young redhead let out a defeated sigh, then said, "It's Gary. He's the manager, and I guess you could say he's been abusing his power."

"How's that?"

"He has full control of our schedules, so if we want a good shift or any kind of change to the schedule, we have to provide him with certain services." She sat there in her cropped tank top and barely there skirt, and a look of innocence crossed her face as she admitted, "For some girls, it isn't a big deal, but for me, it's a *really* big deal."

"Sounds like Gary is a fucking tool."

"Gary is a huge fucking tool, but he's my boss. I'm kind of stuck with him unless I can find another job."

"Well, you and your friends won't have to worry about that shit anymore." I placed her application with the other possible candidates, then said, "You can tell the others to be expecting a call back."

"Really?"

"No guarantees, but I'll do my best to find a place for you all. If not here, somewhere that will do you right."

"Thank you so much, Mister—"

"The name's Menace, and no need to thank me. At least, not yet."

"Well, I appreciate you trying to help." She grabbed her purse, then skirted over to the door. "I'll look forward to your call."

I was feeling pretty good about things when she walked out of my office. Between Mazie and her other friends from the Pink Pony, we had the shifts covered and were in good shape. I was about to tell Marlowe we could call it a day when a woman appeared in my doorway, and not just *any woman*. This one wasn't anything like the girls who'd come in before her. She had the deepest blue eyes, soft porcelain skin, and hair so white it made her look like an angel. She was wearing jeans, a white lace top, and sandals—not the kind of thing you'd expect a woman to wear to a stripper interview. *Red flag.*

"Excuse me. The girl out front told me to come see you about the position you have for the...um...the str-dancer position."

She couldn't even say the word stripper. *Red flag.*

"By dancer, I hope you mean *stripper* because this *is* a strip club."

A bright red blush crept over her face the second I said stripper. *Red flag.*

"Oh, yes. Of course." She tried to recover by adding, "That's what I meant."

"Mm-hmm. You got a name?"

"Yes." She smiled bashfully and tucked a strand of her silky hair behind her ear as she answered, "Aubrey. Aubrey...um...Cash."

There was no way in hell that was her real name. *Yet another Red flag.*

I should've sent her packing right then and there, but I didn't. There was something about this chick that had me thinking about Mallory. I'd tried to reach out to my sister many times over the years, but she'd made it clear that she had no interest in reuniting as brother and sister—I simply brought too many memories to the table. Even though she wanted nothing to do with the memories or me, I tried to keep an eye on her. I knew she bounced around from job to job, so I'd put money in her account from time to time. I couldn't help but wonder if she'd ever considered working in a strip club, and if so, had she come face to face with a guy like me. If so, I hoped the guy would give her a chance to see it through. It was that very thought that kept me from sending this Aubrey chick on her way. Doing my best to play along with her charade, I asked, "So, you're here about a job?"

"Yes." She stepped over to my desk and offered me her application. "I was hoping to interview for the opening you posted."

"Do you have any experience?"

"No, but I've been told I'm an okay dancer, and I'm a quick learner."

"Being a quick learner isn't going to get you very far in a place like this."

Her eyes skirted to the floor as she inhaled a deep breath. It was as if she was trying to muster the courage to say whatever was on her mind. After several minutes, she looked up at me and said, "Peter Brant suggested that I come here if I ever needed a job."

"*Peter Brant?*" I didn't know the Brants all that well —just that they were Lynch's grandparents who owned a diner out in Colorado. They'd come down when Lynch was patched in. It was easy to see they were both good people who loved their grandson, which made it that much harder on Lynch when they were murdered during a burglary at their diner. "He and his wife were killed over six months ago."

"Yes, I'm aware. It was awful the way they died, but...I knew them before any of that happened. Look, I really need this job." I heard the urgency in her voice, and I couldn't deny it got to me. I wanted to know why Mr. Brant would suggest that a woman like her should come work in a strip club—a place she clearly didn't belong. "I'm sure there have been lots of women who've applied for the position, and I'm sure they all would do an incredible job, but I give you my word that none of them will work harder than me. I just need a chance to prove it."

Beautiful. Well spoken. Determined. I liked her, but the woman standing in front of me was no stripper. She was all class and could get a job anywhere, which intrigued me. I was curious as to why she was so desperate for a job. I shouldn't have cared. It wasn't my job to care, but I did. I wanted to know just how desperate she really was, so I said, "Okay, let's see what ya got."

"Excuse me?"

"Let's see the moves. *The goods.*"

"You want me to strip? Right here? *Right now?*"

"If you can't handle that, the door's right behind you."

Aubrey turned her head and glanced back at the door, and for a moment, I feared she'd bolt, but she didn't. Instead, she inhaled a deep breath and slipped off her sandals. Her trembling fingers reached for the buttons of her shirt, and she started unfastening them one by one. Her eyes met mine as she slowly slipped the white cotton fabric over her delicate shoulders, letting it slide down her arms. That's when it happened. All my good-guy, brotherly instincts went flying out the window, and my cock, which had been completely flaccid all morning long, stirred to life and started throbbing against my zipper. Fuck.

I wanted to look away, to have a moment to collect myself, but I was completely mesmerized as I watched her top drift down to the floor and pool at her feet. She was trying her damnedest to come off poised and self-assured, but I could see that glimmer of insecurity flickering in her eyes. Aubrey was clearly nervous, but she didn't let that stop her from dropping her hands to her waist and unfastening the button of her jeans. With her baby blues still locked on mine, she lowered the zipper and hooked her thumbs in the waistband. I thought she'd simply stand there and undress, which suited my aching cock just fine, but then she started seductively swaying her hips from side to side, all the while slowly removing her jeans.

Her little show wasn't like anything I'd expect to see on one of our stages, but that didn't mean it wasn't sexy as fuck. *It was.* There wasn't a man on the planet who wouldn't pay a pretty fucking penny to see her on stage, but that shit wasn't going to happen. Hell, the mere thought of anyone else seeing her so exposed, so vulnerable made my stomach twist into an angry knot. When Aubrey reached behind herself and started to unhook her bra, I was done. I couldn't take it a second longer, so I held up my hand and said, "Stop."

"But—"

"*I said stop.*"

TWO

PARKER

I couldn't imagine feeling more mortified as I did standing there in front of the Stilettos' manager in my bra and underwear. I don't know what I was thinking going in there—I blamed the other applicants for my unexpected boost of self-confidence. Before going back for my interview, I'd overheard some of them talking about how they hated where they were working. Apparently, they were all tired of being harassed by their manager and hoped working at Stilettos would be the answer to their troubles. They all sounded so certain that things would be different, that they wouldn't get screwed over working here and would be protected by the brothers. I didn't know what they were talking about until it was my turn to go back to meet with the manager.

I was standing outside his office when I heard